THE
MOURNING BELLS

THE LADY OF ASHES MYSTERIES

Lady of Ashes

Stolen Remains

A Virtuous Death

The Mourning Bells

ALSO BY CHRISTINE TRENT

By the King's Design

A Royal Likeness

The Queen's Dollmaker

Published by Kensington Publishing Corporation

THE
MOURNING BELLS

A Lady of Ashes Mystery

CHRISTINE TRENT

KENSINGTON BOOKS
www.kensingtonbooks.com

KENSINGTON BOOKS are published by

Kensington Publishing Corp.
119 West 40th Street
New York, NY 10018

All Kensington titles, imprints, and distributed lines are available at special quantity discounts for bulk purchases for sales promotion, premiums, fund-raising, educational, or institutional use.

Special book excerpts or customized printings can also be created to fit specific needs. For details, write or phone the office of the Kensington Special Sales Manager: Attn. Special Sales Department. Kensington Publishing Corp., 119 West 40th Street, New York, NY 10018. Phone: 1-800-221-2647.

Kensington and the K logo Reg. U.S. Pat. & TM Off.

eISBN-13: 978-1-61773-644-5
eISBN-10: 1-61773-644-9
First Kensington Electronic Edition: April 2015

ISBN-13: 978-1-61773-643-8
ISBN-10: 1-61773-643-0
First Kensington Trade Paperback Printing: April 2015

10 9 8 7 6 5 4 3 2 1

Printed in the United States of America

To maintain a joyful family requires much from both the parents and the children. Each member of the family has to become, in a special way, the servant of the others.

—Pope John Paul II (May 18, 1920–April 2, 2005)

For James D. and Lois A. Trent,
who so readily took me into their family when I married their son,
and have served me in far greater ways than I have ever served them.

ACKNOWLEDGMENTS

I am the most fortunate of writers to be surrounded by friends and family who help me shepherd my books from plot development to final editing. My thanks to my mother, Georgia Carpenter; my brother, Tony Papadakis; my husband, Jon; my sister-in-law, Marian Wheeler; and friends Diane Townsend and Carolyn McHugh for constantly dropping everything to help me.

Also, I extend a big shout of thanks to Petra Utara, who ensured that I stayed on track for this book, and permitted no whining or complaining on my part to get in the way of the book's deadline.

I am also the most fortunate of writers to have both an editor and agent who genuinely care about my books. I don't deserve Martin Biro at Kensington Books and Helen Breitwieser at Cornerstone Literary, but I am grateful for them every single day as I navigate the crazy world of publishing.

Finally, I am deeply appreciative to the staff at MedStar St. Mary's Hospital's Cancer Care Infusion Services, who have unwittingly done more to help me write than they can possibly realize. From providing me a table and chair each week from which to work while my mother receives treatment, to their unfailing sympathy, grace, and affection in caring for my mother in her hours of need, they ease my mind and make it free to dwell inside Violet's world. Dr. Amir Kahn, Joan Popielski, Mary Abell, Cathy Fenwick, Teresa Gould, Rose Jupiter, Diane Loftus, Rachel Louden, Gloria Nelson, Deborah Pavlik, Patty Svecz, Sherry Wolfe, and Chris Wood—you simply cannot imagine the large space you occupy in my heart.

Sola fide.

CAST OF CHARACTERS

VIOLET HARPER AND HER FAMILY AND FRIENDS

Violet Harper—undertaker
Samuel Harper—Violet's husband
Susanna Tompkins—Violet's newly married daughter
Benjamin Tompkins—Susanna's husband
Mary Cooke—mourning dressmaker and Violet's friend

THE UNDERTAKERS

Harry Blundell—Violet's business partner
Julian Crugg—Violet's nemesis
Birdwell Trumpington—Mr. Crugg's assistant
Augustus Upton—tightly corseted and pompous
James Vernon—bland and uninspiring

THE MEDICAL MEN

Mr. Byron Ambrose—physician and anatomist
Mr. Nathan Blackwell—superintendent of Royal Surrey County Hospital

THE DEPARTED AND ALMOST DEPARTED

Harold Herbert Yates—Where did he go after his body arrived at Brookwood?
Raymond Wesley—Did he follow in Yates's footsteps?
Lord Roger Blount—second son of the Earl of Etchingham
Miss Margery Latham—Blount's fiancée

FRIENDS, ENEMIES, AND BUSYBODIES

Jeffrey Blount, Lord Audley—Roger Blount's elder brother
Uriah Gedding—Brookwood South stationmaster
Cyril Hayes—banker at London East Bank

THE DETECTIVES

Magnus Pompey Hurst—detective chief inspector at Scotland Yard
Langley Pratt—second-class inspector at Scotland Yard

Frère Jacques, Frère Jacques,
Dormez-vous? Dormez-vous?
Sonnez les matines! Sonnez les matines!
Ding dang dong, ding dang dong

Are you sleeping, are you sleeping,
Brother John, Brother John?
Morning bells are ringing! Morning bells are ringing!
Ding dang dong, ding dang dong

—"Frère Jacques,"
French nursery rhyme ca. mid-19th century

All I desire for my own burial is not to be buried alive . . .

—Lord Chesterfield,
in a letter to his daughter-in-law,
March 16, 1769

Prologue

The man tried to grope about, except that it was impossible to do much more than scrabble his fingers along the sides of the coffin, what with the lid being mere inches from his body.

Why is it that everyone always talks of how the passing over from life to death takes a mere painless instant, but neglects to tell anyone about the horror of being confined inside a coffin? the man wondered from his unfortunate vantage point.

Why don't the ministers, during their dignified and dull sermons, warn congregants that the worst part of death isn't the looming specter of hell but the endless journey from dining room table to graveside?

He knew where the lid was only because he had hit his face on it, trying to rise from his confines. It was darker than a crow's wing in here, which only heightened his great fright.

He had shouted several times to whoever might be near him, but to no avail. His body rocked back and forth now, and the increased clattering below him signaled that the funeral train had picked up speed and was making haste for the cemetery.

Surely someone would hear him once they arrived at the cemetery and would unhinge this unholy slab of wood that was like a raised drawbridge, separating a knight pursued by arrows from the safety of the castle.

Dear God, what if I expire again before we get there?

Despite the lack of air and his terrifying situation, this irony was not lost on the man, and he even choked out a guttural laugh that sounded strangely like a sob in his ears. He might die a second time and no one would ever know.

How had this happened? What had he done to deserve this wretched situation? Was there even the remotest possibility that he would be discovered here before he was buried, with spadefuls of dirt ensuring that his shouts and gasps would be silenced forever?

He felt a tear leak from the corner of his right eye. Why, he hadn't cried in more than twenty years, since he was a young boy and his favorite dog had died after being bitten by one of Father's horses. He would offer a thousand of the brainless pups now as a sacrifice to escape this vault of doom.

Someone help me. Please.

1

🌿

August 2, 1869

Until today, undertaker Violet Harper would have sworn that it was impossible for corpses to rise out of their coffins.

Now, she wasn't so sure.

The sun was just breaking over the dome of St. Paul's Cathedral when Violet entered Waterloo station to stand on a dedicated funeral train platform with her undertaking partner, Harry Blundell. They were both watching as six coffins, including one under their own care, were loaded into the long compartments on the railroad hearse van, which contained twelve total slots. Each compartment in the van had a door in the side of it, past which a coffin was pushed so that it lay perpendicular to the train's length. The coffins, stacked in individual compartments, were three high and four wide in the wood carriage. These special carriages were made especially for the London Necropolis Railway and painted chocolate brown, edged in an orange-red vermilion, to match the carriages of the London and South Western Railway, upon whose tracks the LNR ran.

Coffins were placed on large biers with hand cranks by the coffin porters, who wore simple dark-blue uniforms and matching hats with large brims and flat crowns. With one man on the ground cranking the bier up, the second coffin porter rode on the bier and pushed the coffin into its compartment, and was then cranked to the ground for the next coffin.

As the last coffin was pushed into its compartment on the ground level—a little too carelessly, in Violet's opinion—she noticed that it bore a maker's plate from Boyce and Sons Cabinetmakers. It reminded her that she wanted to set up dealings with Putnam Boyce again, now that she was permanently back in her London undertaking business.

But the coffin was hung up on something, and as one of the coffin porters pulled it back out to reposition it, she noticed something disturbing. She held up a hand to stop them.

"What's the matter, Mrs. Harper?" Harry asked in irritation. Harry's wife was expecting, and although she wasn't due for at least a month, he was always impatient to return to the immediate area surrounding their shop.

She waved him off as she moved closer to inspect the coffin. It was one of those confounded "safety" coffins, intended to give loved ones comfort with the idea that if the deceased were not truly dead, he could send an alarm aboveground and be rescued even after burial.

Violet heartily despised these so-called safety contraptions, which took the form of bells, trumpets, and even ladders in vertical coffins, by which someone who awoke to find himself mistakenly buried could literally climb up a ladder and out of his grave.

No matter how often Violet railed against these foolish mechanisms, firmly telling people that only the return of the Lord Christ would cause people to waken in their graves, people still wanted them as a measure of comfort. And as always, unscrupulous undertakers were happy to sell them.

This one had a bell apparatus, with a bell attached to a string following along a folding brass pole that would be unfolded after the coffin went into the ground so that the bell sat above the freshly shoveled dirt.

Violet's insides churned. If she opened the coffin, she would undoubtedly find a string tied to the deceased's fingers and toes, so that with the merest of tugs, he could set the bell jangling.

More frustrating was that this coffin had been made by Putnam

Boyce, a respected cabinetmaker whom Violet had used in the past. Most cabinetmakers made coffins during their slow times, for there was always demand for them in a mortal population. Mr. Boyce's coffins were well crafted, with tightly fitted lids and smooth surfaces. Why, then, was he peddling safety coffins?

Perhaps she would have to rethink her plan to purchase coffins from him.

"Thank you," she said simply to the two coffin porters, who were still looking at her in bewilderment as to why she was halting their work. They pushed the coffin off the bier and into the compartment. With the last coffin now placed inside the hearse van, the train was ready for its journey from Waterloo station to Brookwood station in Woking, Surrey.

Violet climbed into the passenger carriage with Harry. They would accompany Mr. Harland's body to the cemetery, making final arrangements at the chapel until his family arrived later in the day for the funeral.

The LNR had been in operation since 1854, but Violet had only recently become involved with it. Although she had sold Morgan Undertaking to Harry Blundell and his partner, Will Swift, four years ago, Will had recently asked her to buy him back out so that he could join his wife's floral business. During his time with Morgan Undertaking, though, Will had built up a considerable business with wealthy patrons who wanted to start family crypts far outside the stench and overcrowding of London.

Not content with some of London's garden cemeteries, such as Highgate and Kensal Green, they were flocking to Brookwood, which its owners bragged had enough spaces that London need never build another cemetery again. Clearly the gentlemen had no experience with what happened in a cholera or typhoid outbreak, where deaths in the thousands could occur in the space of a few weeks.

However, coffins at the 2,200-acre Brookwood didn't have to be buried in the crowded manner that they did at these other cemeteries, and certainly didn't need to be stacked up to six high as they did inside the ancient and overflowing church graveyards. The owners' idea of creating a cemetery that could accommodate millions of bodies when fully developed—thus alleviating the need to ever build another London cemetery again—was commendable.

The funeral train pulled out of Waterloo with a steamy snort and a jarring lurch as Violet settled into her third-class compartment with Harry. This special train was only comprised of an engine, the hearse vans, and six passenger carriages. The passenger carriages were divided into two sections, conformist and nonconformist, with first-, second-, and third-class carriages within each religious section.

Conformist carriages were for those passengers who belonged to the Church of England, also called the Anglican church. The nonconformist carriages typically conveyed Presbyterians, Methodists, Baptists, Congregationalists, Unitarians, and Quakers, but might be those of other sects, as well. Special care was taken to ensure that people from different social backgrounds and religious leanings didn't have to be distressed by having to mix with others of a different class.

The train ran a single, hour-long route from Waterloo to Woking, southwest of London, so it certainly had no beds or Pullman dining carriages, but it did have comfortable enough seats for the hour's ride, even in third class. The first-class seats included plush cushions, chandeliers, filigreed ornamentation, glass windows instead of bare openings, and doting attendants, but such fripperies were never Violet's concern when there were bodies to be looked after.

The only real inconvenience was having to travel at dawn with the bodies and wait at the cemetery for the train to return to London to pick up mourners at the more civilized hour of eleven thirty in the morning. If the number of mourners for the day justified it, later trains followed.

There were always details to attend to at Brookwood, but it was still earlier in the morning than Violet cared to rise.

The train conductor stepped into their carriage, nodded at Violet, Harry, and the other two undertakers in the car, and passed on through to the next carriage via the open platform between them. The undertakers were always recognized by their severe black dress and tall hats with black crape wrapped around the base of the crown and trailing down their backs. However, the conductor had to dutifully check for any stowaways who might attempt to board the train for a free ride.

Now that they were in relative privacy, seated across from each other, Harry asked, "Do you feel well, Mrs. Harper?"

Violet had had violent experiences with trains in the past, having been involved in a wreck and also having witnessed a train hitting a murderer who had fallen from a platform. She had largely overcome her resulting fear of the hulking, steam-breathing beasts, but always felt an unwelcome twinge as the whistle shrilly blew and the engine started its laborious forward motion.

"Yes, I'm fine," she assured him, even as she swallowed the unpleasant taste in her mouth.

Harry nodded knowingly and then proceeded to change the subject. "What did you notice on the platform?"

"A bit of false hope by loved ones preyed upon by an unscrupulous undertaker. A bell safety coffin."

"Really? How fascinating. I was reading in the latest issue of *Funeral Service Journal* that an American named Vester has developed a new safety coffin that adds a tube connected to a viewing glass inside the coffin." He seemed eager to share both his knowledge and the evidence of his willingness to research the latest in undertaking. "That way, the face of the corpse can be viewed from above. An interesting solution to the inadvertent bell-ringing problem."

Harry referred to the fact that the swelling or position shifting that naturally occurred when the body began to decay would frequently cause the body to ring the bell and send people into a frenzy of grave digging. A viewing tube would enable a mourner or cemetery worker to look down and determine whether the coffin's occupant was still alive.

Not that it mattered, for coffins held very little air, perhaps two hours' worth at most, and so unearthing a coffin in time to rescue someone buried alive was nearly impossible.

Violet was displeased with her own grumpiness but unable to condone even a discussion of the infernal contraptions. She turned dismissively to the window to avoid any further discussion of safety coffins and the deceptive reassurance they gave grieving families. Instead, she contemplated the packed and soot-covered hovels of south London. That dreary cityscape soon opened up to impressive country estates, the rich red-brown coats of Sussex cattle, and the spires of crumbling country churches.

Brookwood station's main platform was deserted except for a few LNR workers, as to be expected so early on this August morning. There were two separate substations serving the cemetery: The North station was located in the center of the nonconformist section, whereas the South station was situated on the east edge of the Anglican cemetery.

The train chugged gently past the main platform and on to the North station, where Violet and Harry remained seated as the nonconformist coffins were unloaded from their hearse van. They then continued on to the South station, where Mr. Harland and the other remaining bodies were unloaded.

Undertakers sometimes neglected to accompany bodies to Brookwood, a failure Violet found shameful and a dereliction of their moral duties. The deceased certainly deserved the respect of an attendant, but many undertakers did not want to rise before the cock's crow to take a third-class ride an hour outside of London.

The nonconformist third-class carriage always carried whatever undertakers were accompanying the train to Surrey so that they were immediately on hand for the coffin unloading. Also, since they rode for free, the LNR wasn't about to provide them with luxury accommodation.

Violet suppressed a yawn. Perhaps the lazy undertakers did have a point about these arduous trips.

Soon, she and Harry stood on the South station platform amid a scattering of coffins, waiting for the LNR's horse-drawn biers to arrive from the company's stables. It was unusual for these conveyances to not be at the ready.

Harry looked particularly irritated. Violet touched his arm to comfort him. "All will be well, you'll see. We cannot return until after the funeral anyway, remember?"

He dropped his scowl. "You're right, Mrs. Harper. I'm just anxious over what the next month will bring. . . ."

"I understand." Violet moved to sit on a backless bench, and Harry followed. The coffin porters were just cranking down the last box from the third level of the hearse van.

Violet watched their work in fascination, almost missing a man in a tall beaver-skin hat poking about one of the coffins as if looking for something. Violet would have thought he was another undertaker except he hadn't been on the train, and his jacket was a light camel color. Perhaps he was a local fellow.

She paid him no more mind, for her attentions were diverted by a distinct sound that at first she unconsciously attributed to a servant's bell. As it penetrated further into her senses, though, the hair stood up on the back of her neck.

Ting. Ting. Ting-a-ling.

Impossible!

Wide-eyed and with only a horrified glance at Harry, who looked as dumbstruck as she was, Violet jumped up from the bench and rushed to the sound.

It was coming from Mr. Boyce's coffin. The bell, dangling down from the tip of the folded brass tubing, danced insistently now. Dropping her reticule to the ground, she knelt down and tugged ineffectively on the coffin lid. It was nailed down in several spots.

Harry was now at her side, and with the burly strength that enabled the man to single-handedly lift empty coffins and move them with effortless ease about the shop, he ripped the lid off as though he were merely opening a tin of biscuits. The two undertakers gasped in unison at the sight of the body inside. Instead of a lifeless corpse there was a man of about thirty years in a rumpled but high-quality frock coat. His coppery beard, mustache, and hair were flecked with early gray and closely cropped, but his bloodshot, pale-blue eyes were wild with panic as he struggled to sit up.

"Havfindabang," the man slurred, weaving where he sat as he squinted in what was now bright morning light, like a mole popping out from its burrow.

Violet stared at him, speechless. She had been undertaking for more than fifteen years and had never, ever come across a body resurrecting itself. Dead bodies sometimes moved on their own, or made noises through the expulsion of gases, but this—this—was inconceivable. This was actually a body sitting up after having been dead for presumably at least a day. She shivered involuntarily, overcome by the implication of what it meant. Surely it was not possible that she herself had ever buried someone who was not truly, irrevocably dead. . . .

She looked over at Harry, who obviously shared her shock in his unblinking eyes and gaping mouth.

"Sir, can you hear me?" Violet said, her voice quavering as she knelt next to the coffin, still in complete disbelief that she was actually witnessing a body arising from a coffin.

He recoiled from the sound of her voice. Harry, shaking his head in complete incredulity, reached in and lifted the man out effortlessly.

"May I be of help?" came an awestruck voice from behind Violet. It was the man in the light coat. She now saw that he was in his forties, and had thick, curly muttonchop whiskers. He, too, must have realized what had happened, for his face was drained of all color. "I am Byron Ambrose. I'm a doctor with offices nearby. I witnessed the, er, disturbing thing that just happened and can hardly believe my eyes. I cannot comprehend how this gentleman could have possibly—" Like Harry, the physician looked incredulous. "If I might have a moment with him to—"

"Misser 'Brose, havfindabang," the man from the coffin repeated senselessly, still tottering and struggling to fully open his eyes.

The physician peered into the man's eyes and pulled open the man's mouth without asking for permission. "Fascinating," he muttered as he looked inside. "Sir, can you understand me?" he asked.

"Yuh," the man said dully, his eyes now darting about wildly. Violet couldn't blame him. How must it feel to wake up in a dark coffin, with no room to move and with no understanding of why you were sequestered into such a tight space?

She shook her head in bewilderment. It was absolutely inconceivable that a dead man could have risen from his coffin. Wasn't it?

The doctor was clearly as baffled as she was. "Sir, if you'll come with me, I'd like to examine you." He turned back to Violet. "I'll help this man recuperate back at my office. His . . . recovery . . . is quite unusual, don't you think? I'll also help him back to his family."

At that moment, the stationmaster arrived to see what the commotion had been. After Violet explained what had happened, the doctor interjected, "I'll help the poor man home, Uriah."

The stationmaster nodded. "That's all right then, Mr. Ambrose."

As the physician offered a supportive arm to the seemingly reincarnated man and the two walked unsteadily away, Violet turned to the stationmaster, who didn't seem particularly surprised by the supernatural event they had just witnessed. "I am Violet Harper, and this is my associate, Harry Blundell."

"Uriah Gedding, at your service, madam." He politely touched the brim of his hat at her and shook Harry's hand. He wore a dark blue uniform with red stripes up the sides of his trousers. His jacket, with brightly polished silver buttons running up both sides and a large red lapel, marked him as the important railway man he was.

"Sir, I presume you have never seen such a—a—such an *extraordinary* occurrence at your station before," Violet said.

Gedding shrugged casually, although whether this was intended to convey that bodies sprang routinely from coffins at Brookwood or that he had no real answer for her, she couldn't be sure.

"May I ask you a few questions, Mr. Gedding?" she asked. Surely the stationmaster would have answers about what had happened.

"Of course, madam." Gedding led Violet and Harry into the one-story station, which was built around a square courtyard filled with pebbled pathways and flowering urns for viewing from anywhere inside.

One side of the square contained the first-class reception room for mourners dropped off by the late-morning train, while the other side housed the ordinary reception room for second- and third-class mourners. Gedding took them through the ordinary room to the offices that lay along the back side of the station. She knew that beyond the offices lay lodgings for certain railroad staff, Gedding included.

Gedding's office was plain, with badly whitewashed walls covered with timetables, maps, and a single drawing obviously made by a child's hand. There was an out-of-place floral tablecloth thrown over the table that served as his desk. A gift from his wife, no doubt.

As Violet and Harry settled into seats across the distracting fabric's profusion of roses, lilies, and hyacinths, Gedding offered them tea. Violet waved a dismissing hand and instead pressed directly to the point. "Mr. Gedding, have you ever experienced what we just saw, a man seemingly rising from the dead out of his coffin?"

Gedding pondered the question only momentarily. "I can't say that I have. I'm just glad there was no one else about for it except you two. Imagine a funeral party witnessing what happened. *The Times* would have flown reporters in on brooms for that news item, and the LNR would have been accused of intentionally shipping live bodies for profit or some such thing." Gedding shuddered, presumably imagining reporters in warlock garb blocking out the sun as they swarmed into his station, laughing menacingly in low-pitched voices.

As if on cue, a sleek tan cat, with chocolate-colored paws, ears, and face, appeared from nowhere and jumped gracefully onto the tablecloth with a plaintive meow. Gedding absentmindedly reached out a hand to pet the animal, which turned to face Violet and Harry. The cat sat down, lazily blinking its sea-green eyes at them.

"Do you keep records about the bodies shipped on your trains?" Violet asked.

"Records?" the stationmaster asked, his face reflecting the confusion in his voice. "What kind of records?"

"The name of the deceased in each coffin, for one. Who the undertaker is, in which part of the cemetery the body will be buried, and so forth."

Gedding scooped up the cat and embraced it to his chest. The cat climbed up and draped itself like a fur stole casually thrown over the shoulder by a wealthy woman. All Violet now saw was a pair of dangling legs and a swishing tail, although the animal's purr resembled an incoming train.

"Mrs. Harper," Gedding began, drawing himself up importantly in his chair. He put up an arm for the cat to prop its back legs on. "We are in the business of moving bodies, not doing an undertaker's job. As you can imagine, anyone who can afford to pay to have a body shipped here is probably not going to abandon that body. We have never had an instance where a coffin went unclaimed."

"But surely you—"

Gedding shifted the animal to his other shoulder, but the cat became irritated by the movement and leaped from its owner's shoulder to the floor, disappearing out of the room in a feline huff. The stationmaster leaned forward and, with his elbows on the tablecloth, brought his hands together in a triangle. "Please understand. The LNR has not had a single complaint yet of a body being mishandled or disappearing. Families and undertakers hire us to put coffins on board, and they always—always—show up to collect them. It is vital that we maintain our sterling reputation, for we are not yet profitable, given our presently limited number of runs each day. Any bad publicity would . . ." Gedding spread out his hands expressively to indicate the disaster that would befall the company.

"I don't think the London Necropolis Railway can be held accountable for what happened," Harry assured the stationmaster.

Gedding immediately seized on this. "Yes, Mr. Blundell, you are absolutely correct. Besides, there has been no crime committed, has there? A man believed dead now lives. Mr. Ambrose is a respectable physician who will see to the man's reunion with his loved ones. His family will rejoice, as will we. I consider the matter resolved, and so should you."

Violet and Harry left Gedding's office. She knew the stationmaster was correct in his assessment, but it bothered her that not only had some undertaker somewhere been careless with a body, but that it was actually possible that those dratted safety coffins might work.

* * *

The horse-drawn biers arrived, with the drivers offering apologies for their tardiness, having been delayed with coffins at the North station. With Mr. Harland now securely resting on the bier, Violet and Harry walked on either side of it to the Anglican chapel, a sweet and peaceful structure surrounded with columns. The driver and his assistant unloaded the coffin into the chapel, with a promise to return later for the ride to the grave.

Violet asked Harry to stay behind to compare final notes with the cemetery director, while she went to inspect the grave site. Ordinarily, she enjoyed such interactions and Harry, who was still young and lacking experience, preferred to take care of the manual aspects of funerals. Today, though, Violet wanted to enjoy the walk under the tree canopies and through the winding pathways on her own, to settle her mind over what had happened back at the station.

The August day was warm but not uncomfortably so. The oak, hawthorn, and elm trees in the cemetery were mostly along the borders of the cemetery, working together in their varying heights to serve as sentinels over the graves, blocking views from outside the cemetery and providing mourners with a sense of peace and steadfastness. Thus far, only around five hundred acres had been excavated and put in order for graves, with only a fraction of those graves occupied. Beyond that, nearly fifteen hundred more acres awaited eventual preparation.

Violet tripped over a tree root but caught herself by grabbing on to the edge of a crypt, this one in the unusual Gothic-inspired shape of a large bed frame. At the head of the "bed" were pointed arches topped with crosses and gargoyles. It was a fantastical crypt, unlike any of the usual oblong boxes with weeping angels resting atop them, or the tall obelisks and crosses marking the occupants beneath them.

She continued along the path to the section containing Mr. Harland's grave site, with only chirping birds for company as she paused to examine the names and dates on some of the graves. Nothing was more than fifteen years old, except for a few ancient graves that had been transferred out of London to alleviate the overcrowding of churchyards there. Most of the sites also lacked the soot and lichen stains that plagued older cemeteries. It was almost as if this cemetery breathed life, not death. For now, anyway.

Violet found Mr. Harland's site, which had been freshly dug. His family already had a crypt, built to resemble a Greek temple, a common style for those who had the money to spend on it. Mr. Harland's grave was dug between two of the columns. She pulled out her measuring tape from her reticule and unrolled it down into the grave. It stopped at the twelve-foot mark. Very good. This was a fresh dig in the Harland family site, so Mr. Harland would rest at the bottom, leaving room for two more family members to be buried on top of him in the future.

She rolled up the tape, satisfied. Several urns of lilies surrounded the temple, and a few chairs were positioned around the grave for the widow and elderly family members, as she had requested. Violet was pleased with Brookwood's efficiency. No wonder Will had started engaging in funerals with them, despite the trip involved.

She strode quickly back to the chapel. She was happy enough with how things were turning out for this funeral, and was ready to forget about the unfortunate, yet fortunate, man who had staggered out of his coffin. Harry was waiting for her outside, and he, too, indicated satisfaction with the proceedings.

They walked back to the station to wait for the family. The reception room was not furnished with gas, but instead relied upon oil lamps for light and a cavernous fireplace on one wall for heat in the winter. Here they would wait another two hours for the mourners to arrive, then accompany them back to the chapel.

Violet paced restlessly inside the reception room, discussing the various details of the funeral with Harry. It wasn't long, though, before their conversation turned back to what had happened on the station platform.

"What do you think?" Harry asked, animated and no longer irritated with his temporary exile from London as he leaned casually against the fireplace mantel and watched her pace. "That seems proof that safety coffins do have some merit. I look forward to posting a newspaper advertisement about it." He became invigorated by his own words. "Imagine the favorable publicity the undertaking profession will receive once people realize that someone has been rescued by a safety coffin. Why, it could erase a hundred years of notoriety. We should order a great sampling of these coffins before the other under—"

"No," Violet interrupted, her voice firm. "Absolutely not." She stopped pacing and whirled on him. "Whatever happened back there was . . . was . . . incomprehensible. Harry, we both know it's not possible for a dead body to come back to life, except for the Resurrection."

Harry straightened to his full height. "Ordinarily I would say yes, you're right. But we saw it occur with our very own eyes. You cannot deny that the man arose, quite terrified and babbling, but also quite alive."

Violet frowned. Yes, it had occurred just as Harry described. But even if—if!—the man had not been truly dead and was saved by a bell coffin, it was a rare circumstance. So despite the excitement it would generate among mourners who imagined they could hold out hope that their loved one might come out of the grave a week or two after death, it would ultimately prove to be a leaden disappointment to all of them. And eventually it would bring shame to the undertaking profession, which was already tarnished by the few charlatans who practiced it.

She softened her tone. "Harry, we must think this through. Whatever medical condition that man experienced was not typical. We have both seen enough bodies in our lives to know when they are dead. The ashy skin, the vacant eyes, the odors. Don't you think it more likely that the undertaker who put him in a coffin was incompetent?"

Harry considered this. "Yes, perhaps, but—"

"If we want to maintain our reputation, we have a responsibility to keep quiet about this until we know for sure who put that man in a coffin before he was ready."

"How would we do that? We have no authority, and no undertaker is under obligation to talk to us."

Violet had encountered more difficult situations than this before, and even uncovered killers in the process. This was no murder, just a simple case of bad undertaking. How challenging could it possibly be to ferret out the inept funeral man in their midst?

"I'll take care of it, Harry. Meanwhile, we have a funeral to perform, to make sure Mr. Harland is sent off well. We must stop such talk, at least until we know for certain what happened."

Harry shrugged. "As you say, Mrs. Harper. I'll keep quiet. But after what we just witnessed, I have to say I'm convinced."

Mr. Harland's funeral went off well enough except for a problem with a relative who availed himself of a little too much gin inside the reception room and almost stumbled into the grave before Mr. Harland himself was laid in it.

It was with tired relief that Violet and Harry made the hour-long train ride back to London in silence. Violet's peaceful walk through Brookwood was now but a distant memory as she was consumed with the bell coffin experience.

The stationmaster had stated that no crime had been committed. Perhaps in the eyes of the law, no. But in Violet's mind, a careless undertaker had perpetrated an inexcusable act on an innocent person.

Whatever undertaker had put that man in his coffin no more deserved to wear his hat and tails than a Newgate Prison inmate did.

2

T hat evening, as she and Sam prepared for dinner with their
daughter, Susanna, and her own husband, Benjamin, Violet
told Sam about the bizarre incident at the train station.

"It baffles me that some undertaker mistakenly took the man to
be dead," Violet declared, sitting before the mirrored dressing
table of their bedchamber and repinning her hair, which had come
loose during the day's events.

Her husband sat on the bed, propped up against Violet's pillows
with his legs stretched out and his ankles crossed, rubbing his chin
in contemplation of what she'd said. Her bedclothes would smell
of him later, which was a pleasant extra to simply having him next
to her. She had nearly lost her Sam twice, once to war and once to
an explosion. Every day she worried about losing him again, although he said the same of her.

"But, as Harry said, you saw it with your own eyes."

Violet brushed furiously at a lock of hair that refused to stay confined and began to jam several more hairpins in it. "I know, I know.
But you've seen a dead body before, Sam. Even the most amateur
undertaker should know whether someone is deceased or not."

"Maybe the family didn't employ an undertaker's services and
simply purchased a coffin on their own."

Violet paused in midmotion, meeting his eyes in the mirror. She
hadn't considered that possibility before. Perhaps Sam was right.
If the man had suffered a long-term illness and the family assumed

he had died, they might have skipped an undertaker's services and arranged with Brookwood themselves. Still . . .

She picked up her final hairpin, which was topped with a carved red rose, and conceded, "That may be true. I think I'll go ahead and look into it anyway, just to be sure," she said, turning away from the mirror to face him.

"At least this will be a placid endeavor, with no additional bodies trailing behind you, as usually seems to be the case," he said, his dark eyes sparkling in amusement.

She threw the hairpin at Sam, and it landed on his chest. Laughing, he picked up the tortoiseshell pin, swung his legs to the floor, and came to Violet. He gently inserted the pronged piece in her hair before leaning down and placing a gentle kiss on her neck.

"Enough of this serious talk. Let's go see our daughter and son-in-law. I have news of my own to share."

They joined Susanna and Benjamin in the sitting room, and then together went to the dining room to await the evening's meal offering from Mrs. Wren, their day cook. The Harpers had quarters above the Morgan Undertaking shop, which Violet now co-owned with Harry. While Harry lived nearby with his wife, Violet and Sam had renovated the modest flat above the shop so that she could be as close to the shop as possible. Their lodgings contained a sitting room, a study, a dining room, a bedroom, a kitchen with a new coal stove, and a washroom with a flushing toilet, a convenience Violet had quickly become accustomed to when they were first gaining popularity in London a few years ago.

The quarters were fine for just Violet and Sam, but with Susanna visiting from Colorado, things had become a bit . . . disarrayed. Susanna and her new husband were making do with sleeping on the settees in the sitting room, but their belongings were piled up everywhere. The fireplace mantel in that room was covered in Susanna's face creams and hair combs, since she used the mantel and the mirror above it as her makeshift dressing table, and the two of them simply used their open traveling trunks as clothespresses. Newspapers, books, teacups, and bedcoverings were scattered across every square inch of available space. On top of all that, Mrs. Softpaws, Susanna's fluffy black-and-white cat, whom Susanna had insisted come along for the visit to London, was unhappy with her strange surroundings. So she had taken to scratching at the furniture when no one was looking—and when they were looking, she was usually atop a walnut-and-glass display cabinet, glaring down at those responsible for her circumstances.

The only bright spots in the room were the two dolls Violet had given Susanna as a wedding gift upon her arrival in London. Made to look like the Prince and Princess of Wales at the time of their wedding, they were exacting in their detail, even down to the princess's trailing, lace-and-flower-embellished veil. The royal couple were posed together on a table, but were near to being buried in an avalanche of belongings.

The condition of the sitting room was such that it made even Violet blanch, and she was hardly a good household chatelaine, usually paying no attention to tarnishing silver or corner cobwebs. At least they had Ruth, their day help, but even poor Ruth couldn't keep up with what resulted from such cramped quarters.

Ruth had come to Violet by way of Mary Cooke, Violet's dearest friend and a dressmaker, who had also seen to the decoration of Violet's new quarters in the latest fabrics from Morris, Marshall, and Faulkner. Ruth was a little dim, but her devotion to the Harpers and to Mary was unquestionable.

Violet could not say the same for the unfortunately named Mrs. Wren, who entered the dining room bearing a steaming tureen of Chantilly soup. Unlike her merry avian namesake, which was tiny, flitting, and chirping, Mrs. Wren mostly resembled a hawk, replete with sharp eyes that missed nothing and a set of thick fingernails that looked as though they could easily rip the flesh completely off an unsuspecting leg of mutton.

Violet had to admit, though, that the woman could have given the much-touted Mrs. Beeton lessons in household cookery.

"Soup," Mrs. Wren said sullenly, placing the tureen on the table for Sam to ladle, while she went back to the kitchen for another dish. Sam began to serve the delectable soup, its bright-green color from the peas accented appetizingly well by the heavenly scent of parsley and onion wafting up from it.

After Sam said grace, they all partook from their bowls, and in between spoonfuls, Violet once more brought up the odd incident at the train station. Susanna, who had served as an assistant undertaker with Violet back in Colorado, shared her mother's reaction.

"These are strange doings, Mother," she mused, putting down her spoon. Susanna already sounded as though she'd been raised in the American West. Was Violet to be the only one in the family who sounded English?

They were interrupted by Mrs. Wren's return, this time with a platter of salmon in caper sauce. "Fish," the woman said as she put the platter in front of Sam again, and critically eyed any soup bowl that was not completely empty as she picked them up from around the table.

Violet adored the briny taste of the capers and anchovies combined with the sweet fleshiness of the salmon. She put a hand to her waist, which had thickened slightly during a recent stay at St. James's Palace, with all of its abundant cuisine. Perhaps she should only take one fillet. She sighed as she dug into her lone piece of fish that perhaps had a bit too much sauce accompanying it.

"Yes, it is odd, and I'm going to look into it, with your help, of course," Violet said.

"How?" her daughter asked, her expression suggesting she was not as fond of the salty tang of this dish as her mother was.

"Tomorrow I plan to visit Mr. Boyce to ask him what undertakers have ordered safety coffins from him. Then, I'd like to split the list with you, and we'll each go interview these undertakers."

"What fun! Yes, of course I'll help you."

Benjamin, who had managed Sam's law practice in Colorado and had taken it over when Sam and Violet had announced their plans to remain in London, raised a good-natured eyebrow. "So you are asking my bride to involve herself in intrigue and investigation? I shall join you. After all, you need protection."

Susanna laughed. "Protection? From what? Sharp mourning brooch pins?"

Benjamin smiled fondly. "Darling, perhaps you've forgotten your mother's penchant for attracting trouble. You'll innocently walk into an undertaker's shop, and all of a sudden have a chandelier fall on your head or a rabid dog crash through the window and bite you."

Sam looked pointedly at Violet. "Perhaps I was wrong in my assessment of this. I hadn't considered loosely hung light fixtures and rabid animals."

Violet rolled her eyes. "This just amounts to a few interviews. I hardly think it will be a Shakespearean tragedy."

Susanna held up a finger. "Ah, speaking of plays, I am reminded that I didn't bring any of my undertaking garb from Colorado, so may I borrow a couple of outfits from you, Mother? I should dress the part."

"Of course," Violet said as Mrs. Wren reentered with a platter of summer salad overflowing with lettuce, mustard and cress, radishes, and cucumbers, and decorated with sliced eggs.

"Salad," Mrs. Wren said in her usual chatty manner, clearing out the salmon plates with her folding talons. Fortunately, Mrs. Wren, like Ruth, was only day help.

"Now it's my turn for news," Sam said as he served the greens to everyone. "You all know that since my consultations with Mr. Nobel, I've decided to buy into a coal mine. Blamed if I didn't end up with a cocked hat over how expensive they are, but I've found one up in Nottinghamshire, so I've been going round to some well-regarded investors to secure financing, and I believe I will have it in hand rather soon."

"Papa, that's wonderful!" Susanna cried.

"Yes, congratulations, old man," Benjamin added in hearty approval. "I guess this means I'll never convince you to move back to Colorado."

Only Violet was reserved. At the sight of excitement and pride playing across Sam's face, she desperately wanted to be happy about his endeavors, but she knew that the coal mine purchase was merely a backdrop to further his interest in Mr. Nobel's dynamite invention. Sam was convinced that dynamite was the future for mine shaft tunneling, and he was determined to make his mark at the leading edge of it.

She finally summoned a smile. "I'm sure one of the investors will be happy to place his confidence in you."

Their final dish arrived. "Pudding," Mrs. Wren said, placing before them a molded sponge cake soaked with lemon rind and brandy. Sam cut slices of the moist dessert and offered them round. Violet sighed once more and refused to take a piece. Mrs. Wren, noticing everything, gave Violet a sharp look of disapproval.

Well, perhaps a tiny slice wouldn't hurt. After all, she would be briskly walking all over London the next few days.

Mrs. Wren nodded in satisfaction when Violet changed her mind and accepted a slice. The brandy-and-lemon-infused confection was exquisite.

If her quest for the truth didn't kill Violet, her new cook might.

Violet started out early the next day, with the intention of returning before any potential customers might visit. Not that Harry couldn't handle things; she just liked to be on hand.

Boyce and Sons Cabinetmakers was located in Curtain Road inside Shoreditch, just north of the old City of London. It was owned by Putnam Boyce, a spry, elderly man who had lost his wife in a cholera epidemic many years ago and today ran the shop with his two sons. His shop's showroom was full of striking samples of his handiwork. A collection of well-crafted clocks, chairs, and musical instruments lined the walls, and the shop was filled with the comforting smell of sawn wood.

Mr. Boyce was moving a little more slowly than the last time Violet had seen him. He held a hand to his hip, as though it bothered him. But he smiled warmly upon seeing Violet and spoke over the clamorous sounds of sawing and scraping issuing from his workshop. "Mrs. Morgan, an honor. I heard you had gone off to the United States to marry an American fellow."

Violet smiled cordially in return. "I did. My name is Harper now, and my husband and I have returned to London to live."

He nodded knowingly. "The lure of the old city was too much to keep you away, eh?"

"The city has indeed beckoned me back, leaving me little choice but to return," she said, reflecting on Queen Victoria's past insistence for her discreet services.

"I must say I am happy to have you back, as well. I've missed your custom, Mrs. Mor—Harper. Your successors went elsewhere for their coffins, although I've picked up other box-building work here and there."

"I would like to engage you again for coffins."

"I'd be delighted." He turned toward the workshop. "Jonathan! Christopher! Come here."

The scraping and sawing ceased, and two men in their early forties emerged from the rear. These must be the sons of Boyce and Sons. Both had their father's sprightliness, although one had a thinning, sandy-brown pate and the other a full head of chestnut hair. Given their father's silvery mane, she wondered which of the men took after his mother.

Boyce introduced the balding one as Christopher and the other as Jonathan.

"This is Mrs. Harper, a local undertaker," Boyce said to his sons. "We'll need to work up some coffins for her."

Violet shook hands with each of them, noticing their rough, calloused hands, no doubt the result of years of toiling with wood.

"What would you like, Mrs. Harper?" Jonathan asked. "Elm burl? Oak? Mahogany?"

"How about one of each, all adult-sized?" she suggested. "I'd also like one in pine, and another painted white in a child's size."

"Anything special?" Jonathan rattled off an obviously memorized list of coffin features. "Vertical boxes? Bells? Feeding tubes? Air tubes? Escape ha—"

Violet held up a hand to stop the flow of words. "No! Nothing like that. Just sturdy, well-varnished coffins that I can add padding and mattresses to."

Jonathan nodded. "We'll have them to you in a few days."

The brothers returned to the workroom. Boyce's pride in them was evident in his gaze that followed their backs.

Violet coughed discreetly, diverting his attention back to her. "Mr. Boyce, I'm here for another reason, as well," she said. "Your son mentioned safety features that could be added to your coffins. Do you make many of such boxes?"

Boyce frowned, and Violet noticed for the first time how dark his eyebrows were compared to his gray hair. "I make them for a fair number of undertakers. Why do you ask?"

"Do you keep a list of which undertakers you make them for?"

"Yes." Now he was looking at her suspiciously.

"I would like a list of them. Particularly the ones for whom you make bell coffins."

"For what reason, Mrs. Harper?" Boyce turned to softly tap the keys on a square piano with ornately carved legs. The immense skill in his fingers for exquisitely shaping wood did not extend to musical talent, for the notes were discordant and an inharmonious counterpoint to the resumed sounds of sawing and sanding emitting from the rear of the shop.

Violet hadn't actually expected him to question her. She was loath to share what had happened, lest Boyce and Sons use it to start promoting safety coffins themselves.

"I . . . I have reason to believe that . . . that . . . they have been renting the coffins for low-cost burials, then reselling them to theaters as brand-new props."

The cabinetmaker abruptly stopped playing. "Well, now, that wouldn't be a proper thing to do."

"No, it wouldn't." Violet warmed up to her lie, hoping she wouldn't be struck dead by the Almighty the moment she left Boyce's shop. "Actors might be climbing into coffins that have actually been occupied by corpses. But I don't want to go to the police without being absolutely sure. I wouldn't want to waste their time on some foolish suspicion."

"Hmm, I guess they wouldn't appreciate being asked to take action on a woman's whim."

"I'm also concerned that such actions would sully the undertaking profession as a whole, and you know that we already suffer some of the greatest blemishes of any merchants in London." At least *that* much was the truth.

"I suppose that's true enough." There was a shadow of uncertainty in Boyce's eyes now.

"I just wish to speak with them, Mr. Boyce," Violet assured him, sensing he was starting to inwardly vacillate. "I have no authority to do anything, nor are they under obligation to tell me anything," Violet added, remembering Harry's words at Brookwood. "I respect the confidentiality of your customer list, and would never reveal the source."

Boyce wavered, clearly searching for a reason not to help her but coming up with nothing. "Very well," he agreed reluctantly. "Let me get my ledger book and some paper. If this were anyone else but you . . ."

The cabinetmaker pulled an iron ring full of keys from a hook on the wall and searched through them. None were marked with words or letters, yet he managed to cull through them all and select the correct one that opened an elegant secretary in his showroom. Behind the secretary's upper doors, which were inlaid with a spectacular ancient Greek temple scene and trimmed in a Greek key border, was a multitude of drawers, large and small. He pulled another key from the ring and opened one of the taller drawers in the secretary. Inside was a leather-bound ledger, similar to what Violet used to manage her own shop's records.

Boyce lowered the writing table portion of the secretary and sat at a chair before it. From another drawer he pulled paper, pen, and ink, then studied his ledger at length. In fact, he took so long that Violet worried he had fallen asleep in front of it, but then he dipped his pen in the inkwell and began writing.

Half an hour later, Violet left with a folded sheet of paper containing a list of undertakers in London who had purchased safety coffins from Boyce and Sons. She didn't open it until she returned to her own shop, and when she did, she was quite disturbed.

One name on the list jumped out at her from among all the others and filled her with more dread than an open crypt on a cloudless night.

Violet finished the rest of her day in the shop without sharing anything with Harry, who didn't seem curious as to when she might begin her investigation into who was responsible for the previous day's bell coffin. Without doubt, worries about his expectant wife were keeping his mind largely occupied. He spent his time in the coffin room, preparing space for the samples that Boyce and Sons would be sending soon, while Violet spent the rest of the day taking inventory of their mourning brooch domes, mourning card samples, jet jewelry, black lace fans and collars, and other accoutrements they always kept on display.

That evening, after supper with her family, served by the ever-cheerful Mrs. Wren, Violet asked Sam and Benjamin to retire to the parlor while she and Susanna looked over the list of twenty-three undertakers Violet had. It was a substantial number of London's hundred or so undertakers serving the city. Mr. Boyce had secured much more than a "fair number" of them.

Taking into account that Mr. Boyce only served a portion of the city's undertakers, Violet was also dismayed at the number of undertakers now trading in safety coffins.

She tore the list in half horizontally, and passed the lower half to Susanna, pointing to the name that had disturbed her so much earlier. "This is Julian Crugg. I know him."

Susanna looked puzzled. "Then why don't you visit him?"

"He doesn't particularly care for me. He once accused me of stealing customers from him."

Susanna's blue eyes widened. "But you would never do that."

"Of course not. When I first returned to London, I was called in by the queen to perform undertaking services for a peer, and I displaced the family undertaker, who happened to be Mr. Crugg."

It was no wonder that Crugg had been angry to lose the Lord Raybourn funeral. The cost of a service for a person of rank or title could vary between five hundred and fifteen hundred pounds. By comparison, the funeral of a gentleman might cost around three hundred pounds, and that of a tradesman of better class might be around sixty pounds. Then there were the members of the laboring class, who, due to their constant financial straits, might only spend around five pounds for a funeral that included a plain pine coffin, no lining or ruffling, no attendants, a flat hearse with no glass walls, and a single horse.

It was certainly in an undertaker's best interests to attract as lofty a clientele as possible. When Julian Crugg lost the funeral to Violet because of the queen's command, he risked losing future funerals for the extended family, representing thousands of pounds.

"He was displeased, to say the least," Violet continued, reviewing her own list. "I think you might have better luck in speaking with him."

"So, what shall we try to discover?" Susanna asked. She was nearly trembling with excitement. Violet wondered if Susanna wasn't just a little bored back in Colorado.

"I think we want to find out, first, how often they have used bell coffins and, second, if they've recently sent a red-haired man in his thirties to Brookwood."

"And what reason would we give for wanting to know this information?"

"Hmm." Violet absently twirled her half of the list around on the table as she conjured up a plausible reason. "Let's say we are writing an article for *The Times* about a rash of red-headed men being saved by safety coffins? People love stories of the supernatural."

"Mother, that's ridiculous."

"Well, how do you think we should go about it?"

Mother and daughter were silent awhile, each contemplating how they might go about interviewing their fellow undertakers.

Finally, Susanna said, "I know. We will just present ourselves as considering the purchase of bell coffins and looking for advice on the best ones."

Violet nodded at her daughter's commonsense approach. "That should work. We can also ask if they use them at Brookwood, and see what sort of interesting information we can glean that way. Be careful, though. This is not the first time I've gone round asking questions of other undertakers. They might think we're attempting to steal trade secrets."

"This will be fun," Susanna exclaimed, clapping her hands together like a little girl. "No wonder you like investigative work."

Violet didn't consider it fun as much as . . . necessary. Necessary for the reputation of undertaking, and necessary to ensure that the dead were properly and respectfully cared for in their time of farewells to the earth.

And to ensure that they were indeed deceased.

Susanna was dressed in a full complement of her mother's undertaking clothing as she and Benjamin headed out the door. It would hopefully lend credibility to her visits with the undertakers on her list. Benjamin, too, wore somber clothing, although he lacked the telltale hat swathed in black crape that ended in two long tails draping down the back.

Her mother had recommended that Benjamin accompany Susanna for protection. Susanna had acquiesced to the idea but was inwardly dispirited about it, for she had wanted to engage in this endeavor on her own. She had only been married a couple of months now, but things weren't quite as . . . exciting . . . as she'd anticipated. Their visit from Colorado to London had been to celebrate their marital happiness with her parents, but Susanna had hoped it would also infuse a bit of stimulation into her marriage.

Susanna's childhood had been traumatic, full of death and a despondent workhouse confinement, until Violet had appeared in her life, bringing stability and love with her. Susanna had largely forgotten the trials of her youth and assumed that marriage, with its resulting routines and patterns, would continue her happiness.

Benjamin was kind and handsome, and Susanna had had high hopes for him. He'd been so doting and took a special interest in ensuring her safety after Mother and Father returned to London. Besides, he was Father's law clerk, and Father thought so much of him. It only seemed natural that she should fall in love with Benjamin Tompkins.

What she wanted was a marriage like her parents', one that was full of life and love and teasing and unabashed kisses. What she seemed to have gotten instead was something much more . . . cloying. Susanna couldn't point to anything in particular that disturbed her about Benjamin. He was steadfast and kind. He adored her and told her so constantly. Susanna was almost ashamed by her feeling that something was defective.

Perhaps she hadn't given it enough time.

Perhaps her expectations were too high.

Or perhaps they would never have what Mother and Father did because they had never experienced all of the crises and tumult that her parents had.

She frowned as she pulled on her black gloves and buttoned them. Was a marriage only truly happy when the participants had endured the worst of what life had to offer? How ironic it would be if that were true.

Well, perhaps today they would experience a little of her parents' tribulations, depending on how things fared with their interviews.

Most of the undertakers whom they visited were friendly but indifferent. One, though, a Mr. Parris, happily showed her his safety coffins. His strangest one involved a tube into which the trapped person would blow, causing a bright yellow flag to shoot out at graveside. Like the others, he insisted that he hadn't sent anyone to Brookwood lately.

By midafternoon, Susanna was bored and nearly starving to death. After a quick meal and tea at a nearby hotel with Benjamin, she suggested that they finish up at Julian Crugg's shop. Rejuvenated from eating, she looked forward to meeting the man about whom her mother seemed so apprehensive. He was located in a side alley off Regent Street, making him convenient to the upper-crust residents of Mayfair.

The shop had large, sparkling windows, with no cracks at all in them. The wood surrounding the glass had been recently painted a deep, shiny black, and the gold lettering announced "Undertaking Services, Julian Crugg, Proprietor." She put her face closer to the glass to peer inside. An undertaker—presumably Mr. Crugg himself—sat on a plush settee facing Susanna's direction. Across from him sat a couple, their backs rigid and unmoving, a sure sign of terrible grief.

Susanna was overwhelmed with the desire to rush in and comfort them. Instead, she turned to Benjamin. "Perhaps we should visit the perfumery we saw back on Regent Street for a few minutes."

A half hour later, with a new bottle of patchouli tucked in her reticule, she and her husband returned to Crugg's shop, where they found him alone.

The door's bell tinkled prettily as they stepped in, and the man looked up from where he was standing behind his counter, flipping through an urn catalog. He immediately stepped out and bowed with both hands held out. Cupped in his palms was a calling card.

"I am Julian Crugg. How may I be of service to you today, sir? Madam?" He looked curiously at Susanna, obviously recognizing her garb. He was middle-aged, thin, and wiry.

Benjamin took the card as Susanna said, "Good afternoon, Mr. Crugg. I am Susanna Tompkins, and this is my husband, Benjamin. We are undertakers in Queen's Road." For the tenth time today, she wished there had been time to create calling cards. How legitimate did she look without one?

The undertaker didn't seem to notice. "May I be of assistance to you on a funeral?"

"Not exactly." Susanna rolled out her speech, perfected after so many visits. "We understand that you are a prominent expert in safety coffins. We haven't used them before, but are considering adding them to our inventory. We hoped you might recommend some models and makers."

The undertaker smiled, then lifted his left hand and snapped his fingers. Almost instantly, another man, with hair hanging so low on his forehead that it nearly covered his eyes, appeared from the back. "Yes, Mr. Crugg?" He inclined his head toward Susanna and Benjamin in greeting, then swiped a hand across his forehead, pushing his hair aside. His pants were too long, and his jacket sleeves too short. Susanna wondered why Mr. Crugg, the owner of an elegant shop, would keep such an unkempt man in his employ.

"Bird, this is Mr. and Mrs. Tompkins, undertakers over in Paddington. They're interested in investing in safety coffins. Bring out our new portable chamber, will you?"

The man went off to do Crugg's bidding.

"Bird?" Susanna asked curiously.

"Birdwell Trumpington, my assistant." Mr. Crugg sniffed contemptuously. "Have you ever heard of such a ridiculous name? His parents must have loathed him, but they died years ago in a shipwreck off the coast of India en route to Calcutta on a holiday, so there's no way to really know. Very tragic. Of course, I never met them, so his story might be an invention, and they may live in Seven Dials right now, for all I know."

Crugg had further insulted his employee with this mention of such a disreputable section of London. How odd. Violet would be interested to know that Crugg employed a man who was both disheveled and such an object of disdain, although Susanna wasn't sure yet if that fact was significant at all.

Mother would also be interested in the seeming plethora of avian-related names in London.

Trumpington rolled out a flat cart, atop which sat what looked like a typical coffin, but with a box fitted over where the deceased's head would lie. The top of this box was fitted with a piece of glass. At the foot of the coffin was a metal crank.

Crugg patted the box portion of the coffin. "We've only just gotten it in and haven't had a chance to set it out for display. This clever device enables the cemetery watchman to keep an eye out on the deceased's body. The body is buried inside the case below. If he begins breathing, naturally the glass will fog up. The watchman can also peer down to see if the eyes are open or the mouth is moving. After several days or a week without any signs of life, or if there is putrefaction emanating from the body, the watchman merely has to crank this lever"—Crugg touched the handle as Trumpington flipped the coffin onto its side, exposing the bottom of it to Susanna and Benjamin—"and the body will drop neatly into the waiting coffin in the grave below." Crugg cranked the handle, and the bottom panel of the artificial coffin opened on hinges.

"How . . . interesting," Susanna murmured.

"What is particularly attractive about this model is that it is reusable. Simply remove it from the grave, drop the real coffin lid over the body, and cover the grave over. The portable chamber is now ready for its next visitor."

Susanna felt faintly queasy at the thought. Mother would definitely be appalled to see this. "What about the effects of decomposition in the chamber?"

Crugg lifted a shoulder, shrugging off her question. "The body is not inside for very long and so the chamber should air out in between funerals. Besides, you will keep a fresh one in your showroom, and your customers need never know the ones in use were used before."

She brought a gloved finger to her mouth and frowned, as if in contemplation of the deceit that he'd just demonstrated. It was time to bring the subject around to where she needed it. "This is fascinating, sir, but what we are particularly interested in are the, ah, entry-level bell coffins."

"Ah, of course." He snapped again at Trumpington, who rolled the portable death chamber to a location across the showroom and began setting it up for display.

Crugg showed Susanna and Benjamin several versions, and Susanna interrupted with questions such as "What classes tend to be most enticed by safety coffins?"

"All classes are enticed. The question is one of affordability. The portable death chamber I showed you earlier can be rented, and so is a better option for the lower classes. More complicated coffins, such as those with escape ladders, can only be purchased by the upper classes. You will quickly learn which ones to suggest to your various customers. Now, may I show you this bell coffin invented by a German named Franz Vester, living in New York? This one has—"

Susanna interrupted his monologue. "Do you do many funerals at Brookwood, Mr. Crugg? What is your experience there?"

Crugg shut the coffin lid he had just lifted. It settled with the clack of wood against wood. "Brookwood? Do you mean the garden cemetery in Surrey? Why, we certainly have a wide range of cemetery affiliations. I undertake for some of the finest families in London, many of whom have tombs on their country estates both north and south of London, as well as in their county church parish graveyards."

Crugg was rambling to distract her, Susanna was sure of it.

"But have you sent anyone to Brookwood recently?" she persisted.

"I—I can't really say without looking at my records."

"So you also wouldn't know if you've put any bell coffins on the Necropolis Railway?"

Crugg's eyes narrowed. "What is it you really want, madam? For I sense that it has nothing to do with bringing safety coffins into your shop."

"Forgive my impertinence," Susanna said, putting a hand on his arm, hoping that she was being successfully flirtatious. She felt Benjamin stiffen next to her, but that couldn't be helped. "I'm really just curious as to whether Brookwood welcomes these coffins, as we have received several requests for funerals there lately."

"Is that so? What's your name again?" he asked with open distrust.

"Susanna Harper." Susanna offered her maiden name without thinking, not quite used to her married name of Tompkins yet. She immediately regretted the lapse.

"I know that name," Crugg said, pouncing on it like Mrs. Softpaws on a spider. "Are you by chance related to Violet Harper?"

"She's my mother, but—" Susanna's protest was cut short.

"Get. Out." Crugg said this through clenched teeth as he pointed to the door. "I want you off my premises immediately."

Mother was certainly right about the man's displeasure about her. She tucked her arm in Benjamin's. "Shall we go?" she asked brightly, pretending the other undertaker's reaction didn't bother her in the least.

"Now see here, Crugg," Benjamin began, and Susanna could feel the tension tightening in her husband's arm muscles. "I'll not have you talk to my wife like that."

"Benjamin, please . . ." Susanna pleaded, trying to diffuse the situation, but she was interrupted by Crugg.

"Very well, sir. If you prefer not to hear it, perhaps she shouldn't darken my doorstep ever again. To think that Mrs. Harper, knowing her sin, stoops to having her daughter do her bidding. I'll not have custom with that viper of a woman ever again, nor with anyone related to her. Good day to you both."

Crugg stalked into the rear of the shop as his assistant gaped at them helplessly.

Susanna, though, was exhilarated. She had left Mr. Crugg in a completely angry, and wary, frame of mind, but he was hiding something, she was sure of it. She couldn't wait to tell Mother.

If Benjamin was trailing somewhere behind her, she hardly noticed in her excitement to return to Morgan Undertaking. Dark clouds gathered overhead, but what Susanna noticed was how bright the world seemed all of a sudden.

Sam left that morning to pursue his banking interests, while Violet visited the undertakers on her own list, some of whom remembered her from her visits while she was investigating the death of Lord Raybourn a couple of months earlier. Most were wary of another visit so soon, but answered her inquisitive questions about bell coffins and Brookwood Cemetery readily and without appearing suspicious.

Shortly after the lunch hour, Violet found herself weary of traipsing about the streets of London. She was beginning to think that maybe she had embarked upon the wildest of goose chases.

And apparently all for naught.

Maybe it was as Sam had suggested yesterday—that the family of the "living dead" hadn't employed an undertaker's services and had purchased the coffin on their own.

And then there was Uriah Gedding, the stationmaster, insisting yesterday morning that no crime had been committed.

Yet there was just something like a guilty conscience that nagged at her. Just a little something about this whole affair that didn't seem quite . . . right.

As she ventured into Chelsea, searching for the shop of one Augustus Upton, Violet could quickly see that this part of London lived up to its reputation as unconventional and bohemian, with the streets and cafes filled with oddly dressed and mannered artists.

She easily found the shop, located in a narrow but elongated building. The jangling of the doorbell announced her entrance. It was unnerving to say the least when a man popped up from a leather chair, strangely placed near the window of his small showroom. It was as if he were curled up like an octopus, waiting for unsuspecting prawns to float by so he could grab them. In fact, his dark hair was parted sharply in the middle, and thick strands hung down around his head like tentacles.

"Good afternoon, dear lady, good afternoon," Upton said, pumping Violet's hand up and down. He was around Violet's age, and was fighting the bulge far harder than she was. In fact, Violet was quite certain she could see the telltale boning of a corset beneath his clothes. "Augustus Upton at your service. My deep sympathies for your loss. Devastating, I'm sure. How may I be of assistance in your time of need?"

"Actually, sir, my name is Violet Harper, and I, too, am an undertaker." She extricated her hand from his sticky grasp. She knew she hadn't met this man before; who could ever forget such pomposity? It was truly befitting to his name.

"You are?" He cocked his head at her in surprise. She half expected him to reach out a tentacle to inspect her. "Why, I guess you *are* in the traditional garb. Can't say as I've met many women in this business. Did you inherit from your husband?"

Women commonly retained businesses that they had worked in with their husbands, and Violet was no exception, having inherited the trade from her first husband, Graham Morgan, now long deceased. It was not a period she preferred to dwell on or even discuss. She nodded briefly. "Yes. I came to see you because I understand you are an expert in safety coffins."

This statement had elicited preening in the other undertakers she'd seen, who were then happy to show off their samples, as well as their knowledge of the contraptions.

Augustus Upton was no different.

"Dear lady, indeed, you have come to the right place. My knowledge of safety devices is unparalleled in London. No, dare I say, unparalleled in all of Great Britain?"

Violet hadn't expected quite this much of a welcome to her questions.

"I am glad to hear that, sir. I am wondering if you—"

"Please, please, you must sit down." Upton strode off as quickly as his corset would allow. He was obviously not used to wearing it. In moments he had returned with a delicate chair whose seat was covered in a deep-blue velvet. He placed it near his leather chair, and they both sat.

Upton templed his fingers together, resting his elbows on the arms of the chair. "Now, what can I answer for you?"

"I would like to know what type of safety coffin you feel is the best." Hopefully he would quickly admit to a preference for bell coffins.

"Ah, there are so many types. I used my first safety coffin—an elaborate affair with multiple tubes and vents—about five years ago. I remember how devastated the family was when their loved one—an ancient woman, really, as delicate as parchment paper and not a likely candidate to survive the burial process—did not awaken and they—"

"Mr. Upton," Violet gently interrupted, "did you find this type of coffin to be the best safety coffin?"

Upton frowned. "Mrs. Harper, if you wish to benefit from my vast experience, you must allow me to instruct you."

Fortunately, he didn't seem to notice Violet clamping her lips together to prevent herself from making a sharp retort.

"Now, where was I? Right, the Pemberton funeral. The family was simply aghast that old Mrs. Pemberton didn't pop up hours later, after they had invested in the safety coffin. Nearly apoplectic, they were. I had to explain that purchasing a safety coffin does not result in an automatic waking of the dead. If it did, I'd be wealthier than the Crown, now wouldn't I?" Upton chuckled at his own joke.

Violet stared past him, hoping that he would reach the end of his rambling anecdote soon. Alas, it was not to be.

"I remember well the Kingsley funeral, too. Every last one of them dead drunk during the proceedings, even the women. Some of them trying to crawl into the coffin to see if they could fit inside with the body. I had quite a time managing that one, I can tell you. Now if there was ever a time that a safety coffin was needed, that was it. You can't imagine . . ."

Upton went on for several more minutes about various times that he had either used a safety coffin or wished he had used one. Finally, Violet couldn't take another moment more and stood while he was in midsentence, stunning him into silence.

"I see, sir, that you have used many safety coffins on many occasions, but appear to be an expert in none of them, so I will take my leave—"

"Dear lady, you misunderstand me. Please, be seated, so I can be of more assistance." He waved her down with his hand, and she reluctantly sat again.

"You have inquired about the best safety coffins. This type of coffin has proved very popular in recent years and comes in many varieties. There are trumpet coffins, escape hatch coffins—what I could tell you about those!—metallic burial cases, bell coffins—"

Violet found her opportunity inside Upton's ongoing autobiography. "Bell coffins. What do you think of bell coffins? Are they effective?"

"I think you would find it valuable for me to instruct you in the world of all safety coffins before you target just one of them."

Violet might be in her dotage before he was finished. She tried another tack. "Have you ever sent bodies via the London Necropolis Railway?"

"I've done some third-class funerals at Brookwood," he said. "As you may know, a third-class funeral is marked by vastly less pomp and plumage than a first-class funeral. In fact—"

"Yes," Violet said, stopping him before he traveled too far down that rail line. "Have you ever conducted any first-class funerals at Brookwood?"

"First-class funerals? Why, I am renowned for my handling of funerals for the upper class. Not all of them want long laying-in periods for the corpse, you know, and I can have them in the ground like that." Upton snapped the fingers of his left hand. "Complete with all of the fancy accoutrements a society family could want. I remember I once—"

"But Brookwood . . ." Violet pressed gently.

Upton smiled in an oily way. "Don't most undertakers service Brookwood at some point, Mrs. Harper?"

Something in his tone had changed, and Violet worried that he might reach a tentacle out at any moment to inject her with his paralyzing saliva before dismembering her.

For all of his braggadocio, Mr. Upton hadn't really answered a single question of Violet's. Why was this? Was he naturally this self-absorbed, or was it a way to avoid her inquiries while still seeming to be cooperative?

It was time to leave.

Outside Upton's shop, a light rain had started and she had no parasol. Violet sighed. Perhaps she should pick up a hansom cab, return home, and leave the remaining three undertakers on her list for tomorrow.

The rain continued overnight, but in the morning was just an irritating mist, intent on loosening hair from beneath pins and hats. Violet stepped out of the cab in Chancery Lane, her damp list in hand, and proceeded to visit the remaining undertakers written on it. All three were in this area of the City of London, which was heavily populated with law offices and tailors to support judicial wardrobes, and Violet hoped to be done soon in order to return to her own shop.

Susanna had wanted to compare notes the previous evening, but Violet put her off, wanting to wait until she had visited these final three shops. Her daughter had pouted in disappointment but had refrained from discussing it.

By noon Violet was finished, but not before having a far more disturbing encounter than the previous day's with Mr. Upton.

James Vernon's undertaking shop was of average size. There was nothing particularly wrong with the shop except that it seemed unloved, as though Mr. Vernon had lost his passion for the profession. Although there were several sample coffins in the shop, there was little else on display. He also didn't have the typical display counters of most undertakers, eschewing them for an ornate walnut desk to one side of the shop, heaped with ledgers and papers.

Where were his catalogs? His mourning jewelry cases? His urn samples? Perhaps he kept them in a back room and brought them out on request, which would be odd, in Violet's opinion, but not wrong by any means.

Like his shop, Mr. Vernon was bland and uninspiring. He was much taller than Violet, reaching at least six feet, with pale hair and matching eyes. Those eyes were disconcerting, for the undertaker blinked constantly, as though he had a piece of grit lodged in each one. He was also considerably older than Violet. She wondered if his age explained why he had seemingly lost the ardor for undertaking. The man himself was polite enough, and more than willing to answer Violet's questions.

"Certainly, I use the LNR quite regularly. When I come across bodies that have been abandoned or are unknown, I send them off to places like King's College and St. Bartholomew's for dissection. They pay well. Quite frankly"—Vernon dropped his voice even though there was no one else in the shop and he had already been speaking in a low monotone—"I find it an easy profit since I don't have to do any preparation, it cleans up London's streets of undesirables, and it helps the medical profession. I'm lucky all undertakers aren't smart enough to do this. I probably shouldn't have even told you about it."

Violet put a hand to her chest. "Sir, are you hiring resurrectionist men?"

Vernon's eyes flew open in a horrified look, his first moment of spirit that Violet had seen. "Of course not! I am respectable. Besides, that trade died out years ago. You should know that."

There were both legal and illegal ways for medical men to obtain bodies for dissection, and the illegal means were horrifying to a religious British public, for they involved the disinterment of recently buried bodies. Night watchmen patrolled cemeteries for just this purpose—to prevent the unlawful snatching of corpses from graves by those called resurrectionists.

Vernon was right, though; the resurrectionist trade had largely died out many years ago. Nevertheless, the specter of grave robbing and intentional desecration of the dead was ever looming in society's mind, along with the fear of being buried alive.

Undertakers could profit greatly on such fears, not only with safety coffins but also with burial devices intended to discourage robbers from breaking into graves. A representative from the Needle Brothers coffin factory once tried to sell Violet a "patent coffin," an iron contraption with concealed springs that prevented its lid from being levered open by a robber. Mr. Vernon didn't seem to have any such devices in his shop.

Violet returned to her questioning. "But the universities you mentioned are in London. How do you use the LNR?"

"The LNR is a convenient way to send bodies to the Royal Surrey County Hospital in Guildford, about seven miles from the Brookwood train station. Before my services, they had a devil of a time obtaining legal corpses for medical training."

"I see." Violet understood the importance of anatomical research, but she cringed at the thought of what the bodies must look like afterward. "Have you ever lost any of these bodies?"

"Lost them? How could something as large as a body be lost?" He looked sincerely confused.

"What I mean is, has a body ever turned out to be alive and therefore lost to death . . . and lost to the hospital?"

Vernon shook his head and admonished her in all seriousness. "Mrs. Harper, dead bodies don't reanimate themselves."

That was what Violet used to think.

The following morning, Sam and Benjamin wanted to visit the British Museum to view an exhibit of medieval law documents. Pleading headaches, gout, tuberculosis, and a number of other illnesses to avoid the tedium of staring at parchment covered in faded Old English, Violet and Susanna remained behind to discuss their findings from the interviews each had conducted. Sam's final bribe upon leaving was that Violet would miss out on the dishes of ice cream he and his son-in-law planned to have on the way home.

That was a sacrifice Violet was willing to make. Susanna, she noticed, was also thoroughly relieved not to accompany the men on their journey.

The two women sat together in the dining room since the sitting room was too messy. Violet told Susanna of all her visits, including those to Mr. Upton and Mr. Vernon, while Susanna spoke only of her interaction with Mr. Crugg. The girl was wound tightly with excitement over it.

"You were right, Mother, he does despise you."

"I think of it more as his having an aversion to me."

Susanna shook her head, her blond hair still loose and unpinned this morning and bouncing along her shoulders. "I'm fairly certain he would be happy to see you burst into flames."

Well, that was certainly disappointing. "What is it you think he's hiding?"

Susanna pondered the question for a moment, then said, "I'm not sure. He didn't want to discuss any specific bodies he'd sent to Brookwood, so I think he's your most likely suspect. And, really, if he's gotten wind elsewhere that one of his bodies ended up alive, is it any wonder he won't discuss it?"

"Hmm, that is true, dear girl. And who are we to force him?" Violet sighed. "I suppose what we are left with, once again, is that no crime has been committed. At least not one that the law recognizes. I guess the matter is over with."

Violet found herself unexpectedly disappointed not to have an investigation at hand. Even more surprising was the fact that Susanna looked crestfallen, as well.

3

Harry was busy with a funeral at Highgate Cemetery in London today, so Violet took charge of accompanying another body on the LNR to Brookwood. Several days had passed since she and Susanna had discussed the undertakers they had visited, but the subject still nagged at Violet.

She had gone back to her daily routine of meeting with the grieving, preparing the dead, and visiting with cemetery directors. Interestingly, Susanna had begun tagging along, offering to help Violet and Harry with their daily duties. Although Violet adored Susanna, and had enjoyed every minute of working together in Colorado, this shop belonged to Violet and Harry. It didn't seem right to have Susanna involved on a daily basis, even if she didn't want any pay for her work.

Violet had the uncomfortable feeling that it might be time for Susanna to go home to Colorado.

She had easily convinced Susanna to take care of the shop today while she and Harry attended to their individual errands. Now, as the early-morning necropolis train pulled out of Waterloo station, with both the conformist and nonconformist funeral vans packed full, Violet willed her usual queasiness away by looking out the window at the thin fog swirling around the carriage like smoke from a recently extinguished fire. Once she felt settled, she took out her copy of Richard Blackmore's latest novel, *Lorna Doone*, from her large reticule, but after only two minutes of attempting to read in the shadowy early-morning light, she felt nauseated again.

It seemed there was nothing else to do but dwell on the man who had seemingly risen from the dead the last time she was at Brookwood. Everything about the situation bothered Violet, from Mr. Upton's long-winded soliloquies that said nothing to Mr. Vernon's side business with anatomists, and especially Julian Crugg's refusal to discuss anything having to do with Brookwood. Susanna thought Crugg was lying, and Violet wished she had been present to see the man's demeanor for herself.

What bothered Violet the most, though, was that maybe she was wrong about safety coffins. Maybe they really were useful. Maybe they could prevent the unintended burial of live persons due to the incompetence of some of those in the funerary business.

Had she ever been responsible for burying someone alive? The thought made her far sicker than the train ride.

Violet stood on the platform at Brookwood North station, surrounded by coffins waiting to be buried in the nonconformist section of the cemetery. At least this time the horse-drawn biers were already present and loading up coffins. To her dismay, she noticed another bell coffin, again with Mr. Boyce's maker's plate on it. Had this coffin been shipped by Crugg, Upton, or Vernon? Or had it perhaps been sent by one of the other undertakers they'd interviewed, someone who hadn't stood out to them?

Again Violet had to remind herself that even though she felt the safety coffin was morally reprehensible and someone happened to have been saved by it last time she was here, *no crime had been committed*.

Realizing that it would be some time before a bier was ready for her own coffin, she ventured over to Mr. Boyce's coffin, knelt down next to it, and stroked the top of it. It was a finely crafted piece made of white oak, with an inlay of dark walnut around the sides and in the top. This man or woman had wealth and was sure to have a first-class funeral.

Well, it didn't look like this bell coffin's occupant was going to be as energetic as the last one she'd seen here. Violet reached her hand up and flicked the bell idly. *Ting-a-ling-a-ling,* the bell sang. *Ting-a-ling-a-ling.*

It was ironic how unlike the peal of a church bell it was, yet both were used to announce life.

She hit the bell a little harder to hear its music once more. *Ting-a-ling-a-ling-a-ling.*

As if in response, there was an immediate knocking from down below. In an instinctive reaction, Violet screeched, loudly and not very much like a demure undertaker at all, falling backward and onto her rump.

She stayed frozen in her awkward position, too frightened by the sound from within the coffin to even breathe. Gathering her wits, she untangled her skirts, went back to the coffin, and began tugging on the lid. To her amazement, she was able to easily remove it; there were no nails holding it in place.

She staggered onto her backside once more when, yet again, a man struggled out of the coffin. He pushed her aside as he crawled out of the coffin, coughing and gasping. He was younger than the first man but just as well attired.

"Sir," Violet said, once again regaining balance and approaching him with concern, "are you quite all right? May I help . . ."

The man had a hunted, feral expression on his face as he rose up, tottering on his feet. "Who are you?" he demanded. Violet smelled the distinct odor of cloves on his breath.

"I'm Violet Harper, sir, and I believe you have been mistakenly—"

"Where am I?"

"Brookwood North train station, sir. You must let me find a doctor for you. You've been—"

The man grunted something unintelligible and began lumbering off.

"Sir!" Violet called, chasing after him and taking his arm when she reached him. "You must let me help you. Surely you need—"

The man pushed Violet away from him, nearly causing her to tumble again. Violet called after him, but he ignored her.

Still bewildered, she took a few steps once more in his direction, but the shock of the experience stopped her in her tracks.

She watched helplessly as he stumbled out of the station and into the nearby woods. What was there to do? She couldn't force him to stay with her. After all, it wasn't a crime to become undead.

But Violet was once again overcome with the idea that there was *something* criminal going on. She just wasn't sure what. How was it possible that two men had popped out of bell coffins, not two weeks apart, before her very eyes? Was this some type of clever huckster's advertisement for safety coffins?

Perhaps she should go to Magnus Pompey Hurst, detective chief inspector at Scotland Yard, with whom she had dealt on other cases. Violet hesitated. He was usually skeptical of her claims. She could only imagine what he would say to this one. No crime had been committed. He'd probably have a good laugh over it at her expense. After all, who could be arrested for a dead person coming back to life?

With the body of Mrs. Elvira Danforth, a senile old woman who had mistaken rat poison for baking soda and accidentally used it in a sponge cake—apparently not trusting her household help to make it for her—now waiting at the chapel for her services, Violet returned to the North station to greet the mourning party.

Given what Violet had seen of Mrs. Danforth's kitchen when she went to visit the body, it was no wonder the woman had made the fatal error. It was difficult to discern the difference among her kitchen, her larder, and her scullery. Of course, if Violet didn't have day help in Mrs. Wren and Ruth, her own small kitchen might be just as catastrophic.

Did that mean if she ever gave up the cook and maid, she ran the risk of doing herself in with rat poison?

She shook her head to clear it of such ridiculous notions. As if she was capable of baking anything edible in the first place!

A distant train whistle alerted her to the imminent arrival of the mourning party. The North station was built on exactly the same plan as the South, intended for Anglican funerals, and Violet posted herself inside the first-class reception room. Railway workers helped people wearing black armbands, hats, gloves, and jewelry off the train and into the reception area, where Violet then greeted them and murmured appropriate words of sympathy. One particularly large woman, who wore the most enormous black ostrich feather in her hat that Violet had ever seen, was fanning herself and mopping her face with a black lace-edged handkerchief, all the while moaning dramatically about "dear Aunt El."

Once everyone was assembled in the reception room—and already several men had purchased multiple cups of ale for themselves—Violet led them on the somber procession to the chapel. The funeral line was made a little less dignified by the drunken men offering incoherent words of comfort to Mrs. Danforth's wailing niece.

Violet was mortified. This was not the behavior she expected from first-class patrons. She discreetly moved within the ranks of the mourners making their way to the chapel and whispered to the niece and her companions about the disrespect they were showing Mrs. Danforth. Those words didn't seem to make a dent in their rude comportment, but a reminder of the special eternal punishments reserved for those who desecrated not just tombs but also funeral processions certainly brought about the desired results.

The niece gaped at her like a strangled flounder, but her tears and howling ceased immediately, and although the men still stumbled along the pathway, they, too, stopped their garrulous talk as the group solemnly walked the remaining hundred feet in reverential silence.

The nonconformist, or dissenters', chapel looked much like the chapel in the Anglican cemetery, with its faux-Tudor timbering and entry doors with rounded arches above them. The group entered the chapel through the tall doors located in the steeple tower, stepping past the waiting horse-drawn bier to do so. A driver sat on a black-velvet-covered box, as still as if he were made of marble. He would remain there until the service was complete.

The interior was as plain as any of hundreds of modest chapels Violet had worked in before. Mrs. Danforth's coffin of mahogany, topped with a veneer of elegantly swirled mahogany burl, sat on a folding bier in the center of the chapel, surrounded by urns of lilies that Violet had arranged earlier. Mourners took their places on the long, simple benches arranged in rows around Mrs. Danforth, while the minister came forward to begin the first-class service.

First-class funerals were for the uppermost strata of society, and so, of course, were the most elegant. Glass hearses, fine hardwood coffins, and magnificently adorned horses and mourners could back up traffic in London for hours as people gathered to watch the distinct personage roll by. Mrs. Danforth's entourage through Brookwood Cemetery was much more sedate than the typical London society funeral procession.

Second-class funerals, intended for wealthy merchants and the like, were toned down a bit, with fewer accoutrements.

Third-class funerals were for the working-class poor, and reflected the status of the deceased, with simple pine coffins, a hearse that was not much more than a black-painted cart, and little embellishment to mark the deceased's journey to the grave.

Violet had coordinated them all, although third-class funerals were infrequent, as her services were generally unaffordable for them. Violet retreated to an alcove in the rear of the chapel, to make herself as inconspicuous as possible. She shivered. It was strange how the interiors of chapels could be cool even on the warmest of burial days, almost as if they instinctively understood the chill associated with mourning and loss and adjusted themselves accordingly.

Some undertakers used this period of the service to spend time elsewhere, perhaps finding their own cup of ale or a slice of sponge cake, or even smoking and gossiping with cemetery workers. Even now, the hearse driver was undoubtedly swiping at the sweat gathered on his brow before reaching into the driver box for a flask.

For Violet, though, it seemed disrespectful, after the departed's long and arduous journey of life, to abandon the body under her care, even for a few moments to satisfy hunger. The thought of food reminded her that she hadn't eaten since before sunrise this morning, an eternity ago, what with all of the tumult that had occurred since. She willed herself to forget about her appetite and to attend to more important things, such as whether it was pure coincidence that another body had sprung out of a coffin today. This was the second such one in ten days that Violet had seen, and she'd never before witnessed such a phenomenon.

They were both men, and both had been laid inside Putnam Boyce's bell coffins. Mr. Boyce's coffins were sold to many undertakers in London, making it difficult to narrow down which undertaker had purchased these two particular coffins.

It suddenly occurred to Violet that the two bodies may have even been cared for by two different undertakers, which would make their individual waking even more bizarre and coincidental.

It had happened at the North station this time, so there was nothing connecting the two bodies by religion. Unfortunately, Violet didn't know whether either man was destined for a first- or second-class funeral. Each man was obviously too well dressed for a third-class funeral. Besides, a safety coffin was an impossible expense for a lower-class family.

Despite all of her intense puzzling over the situation, her mind continued to come back around to the same problem. No actual crime had been committed. In fact, it was more like two joyous miracles had occurred.

The chapel's organ began piping Chopin's haunting funeral march, Violet's signal to return to the service, where she directed the coffin bearers—none of whom had been drinking earlier, fortunately—to lift the coffin for its final procession. They hefted the box and carried it out of the chapel to the hearse. The driver sat rigidly, staring forward, as the box clunked down hollowly onto the hearse, then slid roughly forward into place. Violet would have to return later for the bier, but meanwhile, she had other male mourners pick up the urns and sprays of flowers to carry to the grave site.

As Violet followed the minister and the male entourage out of the chapel, she saw from the corner of her eye that Mrs. Danforth's niece was becoming hysterical once again, and the other women in the party were surrounding her with waving fans and solicitous words. That would keep them occupied here until the men buried Mrs. Danforth, as was customary.

Chopin's protracted dirge emanated from the chapel until Violet and the funeral cortege were well underway, as if it were sympathetically sending them off to their heartbreaking and dismal work. At the grave site, the minister spoke a few more words; then the coffin bearers unloaded Mrs. Danforth and placed her into the harness to be lowered into her grave. This was always a heart-stopping moment for Violet, for even with ropes and pulleys, things could go wrong and a coffin might land badly in the ground.

She breathed an internal sigh of relief when the coffin reached its destination with no fuss. The Presbyterian minister intoned more words from his Book of Common Order as some of the men scooped up spadefuls of dirt and gently tossed them down onto Mrs. Danforth's coffin.

With Mrs. Danforth buried and her grave covered in flowers, the procession followed the empty hearse back to the chapel, where Violet folded the bier and its cover, and the men comforted the women. The undertaker's work was now done for this funeral, except to ensure that a headstone was installed since the woman had not been placed inside a family crypt.

Only first- and second-class funerals were entitled to grave markers. A third-class funeral required a paid upgrade for the privilege of a headstone, and, as with a safety coffin, a marker and the cemetery's fee for it were an unthinkable outlay of money. Rarely did third-class funerals include headstones at Brookwood.

Back at the North station, Violet was handed up into the train while a porter stowed away her bier. Mrs. Danforth's funeral party was in the first-class carriage, while Violet, of course, rode in the third-class carriage next to the hearse vans. There was no one else in her carriage, much to her relief as she wasn't in the mood for conversation now that her insides were once again pestering her for sustenance.

What she wanted even more than food, though, was a word of comfort from Sam. Should she forget about the seemingly resurrected bodies at Brookwood, or was there something to be done about it—a trail to follow, advice to seek, more people to question?

Sam would know what to do.

*   *   *

Sam was preoccupied with his investment meetings as they sat together once again in their bedchamber, the only place they had for privacy with Susanna and Benjamin staying with them. Sam had gone back around to all of the potential investors, but in the end they had all declined. He was too inexperienced in coal mining, said one. Too enthusiastic for that foreign fellow, Nobel, said another. One even told him he was too American, despite Sam's having an English wife.

"What will you do now?" Violet asked as she unpinned her watch from her bodice and removed her jet earrings and necklace.

"I'll go to Threadneedle Street and talk to the Bank of England, of course. After that, I'll visit one or two private banks. I've made a list and plan to start with White, Ludlow, and Company in Haymarket and London East Bank in Cornhill. Among the three I expect one to bubble up with the funds in short order."

Poor Sam, to have endured such rejection. However, his optimism, so typical of the Americans, was infectious, and she was soon convinced that he would indeed soon have his coal mine financing in order. Not that she was altogether convinced about the wisdom of owning a mine. The deplorable conditions, the disease, the accidents . . .

But Sam was convinced that a coal mine that used Mr. Nobel's dynamite would be much safer, and he was determined to prove it so. Violet clamped down on her concerns, equally determined not to be a nagging wife.

Later, at the dinner table, Sam said grace as was his usual habit, then took a bowl of carrot soup, cooked in the liquid from the previous night's beef bones, from Mrs. Wren's talons and served everyone. Violet announced what had happened at Brookwood, that yet another body had come out of his coffin, this time fleeing the scene immediately.

"I'm wondering if I should go see Mr. Hurst at Scotland Yard about it."

Susanna enthusiastically bobbed her head up and down. "Yes, Mother, I think you should. Something very strange is happening. When have we ever seen one body, much less two, arise from coffins? Besides, I still think Mr. Crugg is up to something odious."

Benjamin eagerly agreed with his wife, patting Susanna on the shoulder. Was Violet mistaken, or had a shadow passed over Susanna's face as he did so?

Sam, though, shook his head. "I agree that there is something strange going on, but there is nothing criminal in it. Scotland Yard would chuckle, busy with solving crimes involving poor souls that have died, and suggest you visit one of the scandal sheets to have an article written about it, or that you have a medium accompany you next time and hold a séance over the coffin. I imagine the queen would be enthralled with the idea, and demand that Albert be exhumed immediately in case he might still be able to ring a bell."

"Papa!" Susanna exclaimed, her face a combination of shock and amusement over Sam's pronouncement.

Violet's husband continued. "I could easily defend one of these undertakers in court. I would point to their wisdom in recommending safety coffins for their customers, as they now have been proved to work. And, sweetheart, maybe they *do* work."

Violet winced as though Sam's words caused her physical pain. Her greatest fear was that he was right, and that safety coffins deserved a more prominent place in undertaking.

Susanna, though, was insistent that Violet should pursue the situation on her own, as there was certainly an abnormality to it, and no one else was interested enough to investigate.

Sam shook his head in good-natured resignation. "I won't forbid it, but I sense that somehow this perfectly innocent circumstance will erupt into mayhem as soon as you get involved with tugging on the strings of the truth."

As she readied for bed that night, Violet was conflicted. Sam was right, of course, both in that there was nothing to explore and that she did have a way of ending up in trouble. Yet she couldn't help but think that Susanna was also right. It simply wasn't *normal* for bodies to rise from coffins. Why, no one even knew who either man was. Wouldn't there be relatives and loved ones eager for news?

Sam was already gently snoring as she finished pulling the pins from her hair. Having her body tightly corseted and her tresses firmly pinned each day made the undressing ritual a blissful relief. As she sat before the mirror in her nightdress, firmly ignoring the parts of her that were not quite as trim as they used to be, she gently drew an ivory comb with very fine teeth through her hair, careful not to let it catch in any tangles.

The movement was soothing, and the teeth rubbing against her scalp felt like a rather nice scratching. As Violet combed, she contemplated what to do. Susanna thought the situation deserved attention, but Susanna also seemed enthralled by the excitement of it. If Violet did pursue it, would Susanna want to assist and then never go home to Colorado?

Violet chastised herself for such a disloyal thought. It was joyous to have her daughter with her. Besides, who knew when they might see each other again?

That was no reason to chase phantoms, though. Sam was probably right in his opinion, and she would be wasting precious undertaking time to continue. After all, who chases down a nonmurder? Someone who has lived instead of dying? It was ridiculous.

She put the comb down and stared at the dark liquid in the bowl before her. Susanna had brought several issues of *Godey's Lady's Book*, a popular monthly American magazine, and one issue recommended black tea for ensuring a good head of glossy dark hair.

Violet sighed. She had never cared about such things when she was younger, but now that she was approaching forty, vanity had pushed its way into her life and refused to leave. She'd thought using Castile soap once each week, combined with vigorous nightly brushing to distribute the oils in her hair, was enough, but Mrs. Hale, the magazine's editor, insisted otherwise.

She dipped all ten fingers into the small bowl of tea-infused water, sprinkled the tea from her fingers onto her scalp, then gently rubbed her scalp, going back and dipping her fingers in the tea repeatedly.

That done, Violet picked up her boar's-hair brush that had an ivory handle to match the comb, and used it in long, even strokes from her scalp to the ends of her hair. The sensation was even more relaxing than that of the comb and enabled Violet to think further on the matter that troubled her.

Even if Sam was correct and there was nothing criminal to consider, would it really hurt to investigate a little further? But what should she do next? Whom should she visit? Or revisit?

Undoubtedly, Mr. Crugg was at the top of Susanna's list. But as Violet thought about it, she realized that he didn't fit her opinion that whoever had mishandled the bodies had been incompetent. Crugg might be vile and resentful, but Violet had no reason to think he was unfit for his work.

What about Mr. Upton, the octopus-like man who had so cleverly repulsed her questions about safety coffins and Brookwood? Perhaps another visit to him, with a box of Fry's chocolate blocks, might elicit a few substantial answers.

Furthermore, what about Mr. Vernon, who was disposing of paupers and other undesirables at various hospitals and medical universities? He claimed he performed his work legally—and he behaved forthrightly enough—but there were surely dozens of musty old books and magazine clippings in existence that would teach a man how to skirt the law. And a man working around the law was not an honest man. And a dishonest man was more likely to blunder and bungle his way through things.

The hair should be brushed for at least twenty minutes in the morning, for ten minutes when it is dressed in the middle of the day, and for a like period at night, Mrs. Hale had asserted with authority.

Violet soon realized, though, that this much brushing in one sitting was tiresome for the arms, especially for Violet, whose right arm had once been scalded and scarred in a train collision, and was easily fatigued. She put down the brush and made up her mind.

Of her three suspects, Mr. Vernon was the most likely to have been responsible for the ineptitude she thought had been performed on those two men. When she had time tomorrow, she would pay him another visit.

Violet's hair *did* seem cleaner in the morning, although Sam didn't seem to notice anything when he gave her his daily morning kiss on top of her head. Well, better that he didn't observe anything at all, lest he notice that she had a few gray hairs popping up from some unknown, fertilized bed of them under her scalp. Violet was also glad that Sam hadn't noticed the weight she'd gained since they'd returned to London, although perhaps he was being intentionally oblivious to it.

Violet skipped breakfast to get down to the shop as soon as possible. There were suppliers to be paid, and she hoped to hand her envelopes to the postman on his first pass by the shop today, before she headed out to see Mr. Vernon. With that done, she went over the day's tasks with Harry. There were no funerals scheduled, but Jonathan and Christopher Boyce would be dropping off coffins later in the day, and Harry planned to wait for them, freeing Violet to take as much time as she needed on her mission.

As a precaution, she picked up the box of chocolates she thought Mr. Upton would have liked, thinking Mr. Vernon might, as well. With the chocolate-covered raspberry blocks under her arm, she made her way to Chelsea.

Mr. Vernon blinked in confusion at her arrival, as though trying to place an unfamiliar face. Violet mentioned the London Necropolis Railway, and he said, "Of course, I remember you, Mrs. Harper," but not before Violet noticed a moment of fear reflected in his eyes as he took the box from her and set it aside. Rather ungraciously, in her opinion.

"Pardon my intrusion," she said, trying to carefully formulate her next words. "I thought you might like to know that another man came to life at Brookwood yesterday."

"That is very interesting, indeed. Did you have an opportunity to speak to him?" The undertaker rubbed the hem of both sides of his vest between his thumbs and forefingers.

"I did, in fact. He seemed quite perplexed as to why he was in a coffin."

"How terrible for the man."

Violet tried another approach.

"Do you deny that you shipped a body to Brookwood yesterday?" She tried to sound imposing but didn't think the words sounded particularly formidable in her own ear.

"I had no corpse scheduled yesterday on the LNR," Vernon replied.

No, of course not. "Perhaps you forgot that—"

The shop's bells rang as a customer entered. The customer was an older man, bleary-eyed and grizzled. Completely ignoring Violet's presence, he launched into a diatribe against Vernon. "Where have you been? You were supposed to arrive two hours ago. How long are we supposed to wait for you? Have you no decency?"

Violet stepped away, over to where the undertaker's few sample coffins lay propped open, to give Vernon a bit of privacy to deal with the man. She understood what it was to have irrational customers. The grieving tended to be void of manners and politeness in the aftermath of a death, especially in the face of an unexpected one.

As the customer continued to rail against Vernon, who tried his best to placate the man, Violet wondered if the man had lost a wife, a parent, a child, or someone else. She then realized that although the customer was berating Vernon for dereliction of duty, he had not yet said anything about his loved one. That was curious. Typically, the grieving spoke of nothing else.

Vernon finally managed to calm the man down enough to get him out of the shop, with a promise to see him within the hour. "Don't be late this time," the man growled as the door's bells jangled behind him.

The undertaker came to where Violet now stood among the coffins. He was pale and perspiring, and she noticed his right hand trembling. Had the customer so unnerved him that he was near to breaking down? An experienced undertaker became used to torrential outbursts, threats of violence, and any manner of unusual behavior. What had just happened with his customer wasn't completely abnormal.

"Mr. Vernon, are you quite all right?" Violet asked.

"Yes, yes, of course." He removed a handkerchief from a pocket and mopped his chubby face. "Sometimes clients are very demanding. Well, as you can see, I have my duties to attend to, if you will excuse me."

Vernon was clearly relieved at the thought of getting rid of her.

"Pardon me, sir, was your customer unhappy with his service? Perhaps there is a way I can help you?"

"Ah, no. You know how it is. Sometimes people expect too much of an undertaker. Think it is our job to make them appear lifelike."

Violet frowned. "But that *is* our job."

"Of course, but when we get overwhelmed with too many bodies, certain . . . embellishments . . . have to be put aside to ensure we have everything ready for a backlog of funerals. Some customers are more, ahem, fussy than others and demand perfection."

Violet did not like what she was hearing at all. Vernon was essentially admitting that he was deceptive, if not outright fraudulent, in his work. Undoubtedly he charged the same no matter what he did.

Violet was overcome by a thought and blurted it out without stopping to consider the repercussions of voicing it aloud. "I have a suspicion, Mr. Vernon. I suggest that you are, at a minimum, very lazy in your undertaking practices. You receive bodies and, with little inspection or preparation, toss them into coffins to be delivered to cemeteries, hospitals, or medical schools."

Vernon blanched as his eyes blinked as rapidly as a hummingbird's wings. "I object to your accusation, Mrs. Harper, which you are in no position to make. I am—"

"Sometimes you get confused and aren't sure which body goes where. I also think that in your haste and confusion, you are accepting merely unconscious people and sending them off to their destinations, where they awake in total terror. It has happened twice in my own presence, and who knows how many other times."

Vernon glanced around nervously, as though worried that someone else might enter the shop. He dropped his voice. "Mrs. Harper, I understand you are upset about mysterious doings at Brookwood."

Violet knew that voice; she'd used it many times herself to soothe irate relatives. Did he think she wouldn't know it when she heard it?

"I am by no means upset, Mr. Vernon. I am curious. I am perplexed. And at this moment, I am very suspicious."

Vernon dropped his voice even lower, and this time in a matter of seconds it went from soothing to menacing, a thoroughly incongruent sound from the mousy man. "You are testing me, Mrs. Harper, for no good reason. May I suggest that it would be wise for you to take your leave now?"

What chord had Violet struck so precisely? Was she completely in tune in her assumption of his shoddy practices, or was she missing notes? Or was there something else making Vernon nervous? She couldn't leave yet, not when she might be close to an answer.

With a fluid movement, he took an ominous step closer. She stood her ground, even though she had an overwhelming urge to turn and flee. "Do not attempt to intimidate me, sir. I am merely seeking answers, and if you are a fraud—"

"You dare accuse me?" His voice seemed to throb with suppressed rage as he enunciated his next words slowly. "You stupid, witless woman, you have no idea what you're doing." The hand that was trembling was now clenching and reclenching in a fist, the movement only slightly less rapid as his eyes were spasmodically blinking.

Violet wondered if she'd pushed him too far. It was too late to recant what she'd said, although she stole a glance toward the shop's door. She would have to dodge a couple of coffins to reach it, but she could do so, provided her skirts didn't get caught or tangled up against anything. The shop was fairly sparse, so it shouldn't be too difficult.

She took a breath, exhaled, and dove recklessly back in. "As I said, sir, I am merely an undertaker seeking answers about some bodies that were found—"

To Violet's burgeoning horror, Vernon's right hand snaked out like a striking viper and grabbed her by the throat. She clawed desperately at his hands, scrabbling to remove them, but he was surprisingly more powerful than he looked. His fingers dug in, pressing in to cut off her windpipe. Within seconds, he had lifted her off the ground and her booted feet were reaching uselessly for the ground. She couldn't breathe, the excruciating pain arresting her flailing movements. His grasp was so tight that she was help-less to even utter a noise of protest.

Vernon put his face close to hers, his once pale and timid face suffused with malevolent rage. She could see an unearthly bright-ness in his eyes as he stared intently at her as if in fascination over her suffering.

"You want to discuss corpses? What if we discuss yours?" he growled menacingly. The sound of his voice was starting to fade, as if it came from the far end of a long tunnel.

Just as everything in the room slowly closed into a pinpoint of the pale-gray color of three-day-old dead skin, Violet felt herself lifted even higher. Then she was flying backward, completely weightless until she found herself on her back staring up at the ceiling. She had the completely irrelevant thought that there were rust stains on the ceiling, most likely from rainspouts leaking into the building. The thought evaporated as she began coughing fran-tically, drawing in great, wheezing breaths now that air was finally rushing into her windpipe.

Where was she?

She gasped several times and was only vaguely aware of her limbs being jostled and thrown together. Vernon's face loomed over hers, and he said quietly, "You must learn manners, Mrs. Harper." A large shadow appeared between Vernon and Violet.

"No!" she cried out weakly as she realized what Vernon was doing, but in a moment the world was black and in the darkness she knew that her nose was mere inches from the underside of the cof-fin lid. In fact, she could smell the sickeningly pungent traces of varnish that had probably been applied a couple of weeks ago to this sample coffin.

Taking uncontrollably shallow breaths, her first instinct was to scream, as a crest of pure terror washed over her. *Don't panic*, she thought. *Don't do anything that will take air out of the coffin too quickly.* She knew she had less than two hours of air inside the box. What was she to do? If she begged for mercy and Vernon refused to lis-ten, or had even left the shop, she would use up much of her air. But if she did nothing, she would surely die.

All of a sudden, Violet very much wished she were in a bell coffin.

Wait a minute. Might she be? She clung to that small and improbable hope as she felt around for a cord or metal loop. Nothing. Of course, she was packed in so tightly that it was difficult to do more than stretch her arms just slightly at her sides. No wonder the string had to be attached to the finger before burial. Finding herself needing the very device she despised, Violet was overcome with the strange desire to laugh hysterically.

She took one more deep breath. The air was already getting stale inside the coffin. *Don't panic*, she reminded herself. Then she realized that she hadn't heard the sound of Vernon securing the lid to the coffin. Nor could she hear him moving about outside the coffin. Maybe he was gone, and all she had to do was push the lid off.

Except she couldn't. In the cramped space, it was as if her arms were pinned down to her sides, and she couldn't maneuver them up enough to get leverage under the lid.

That brief flickering of hope was extinguished like a candle stub. She really was going to die inside a coffin in an undertaker's shop. Visions of Susanna giggling over silly things and the way Sam's eyes lit up when Violet entered a room swam in her head. It just wasn't possible that she wouldn't see them again.

But how would anyone find her here? Vernon would just ship her off to Brookwood to be handed over to the Royal Surrey County Hospital.

A bubble of wild laughter erupted from her at the thought, a sign that she had surely lost her sanity during these past few minutes. Or had it been an hour?

Suddenly there was light, nearly overwhelming her in its glorious brightness. Was she dead? Was this the entry to heaven?

It couldn't be because James Vernon loomed over her again, and it had to be impossible that he would be in residence *there*. "Mrs. Harper?" he asked solicitously. Concern and worry etched his face.

Violet realized that she wasn't dead, yet she was still lying in a coffin. Now that she was accustomed to the light, she breathed in deeply and gratefully, welcoming the fresh air that filled her lungs.

Vernon was his previous meek self again. "My goodness, Mrs. Harper, what are you doing in there?" He shook his head, mystification and disbelief in his eyes.

"What do you mean?" Violet said in complete outrage as Vernon offered her an arm and helped her out of the coffin. She hated that she had to accept this odious man's help from the coffin bed. "You pushed me in there, you, you—" Violet was speechless from her ordeal.

He looked at her curiously. "My dear lady, it would be akin to murder to put a live body in a coffin. I would never do such a thing."

Violet blinked. Was Vernon a Bedlamite, or was she? Had she imagined the entire interlude? She put a hand to her neck, now tender to the touch. It affirmed for her that she wasn't the daft one. "You choked me and threatened me just now."

"Mrs. Harper!" He gasped, a look of horror on his face. "You impugn my honor. I am a respectable undertaker, not a marauding villain. I think you may have damaged your senses when you locked yourself in that coffin." His eyelids were in motion again.

What was wrong with the man? One moment he was a wilted flower, the next he transformed into an enraged madman, then the next he was an innocent bystander. Violet wasn't sure whether to shout at the man or cry in frustration. Deciding neither was helpful, she realized the smartest thing to do was to leave the shop before Vernon decided to do something worse, like stuff her in an urn or tie her up in a shroud and dispose of her off Westminster Bridge.

"Pardon me, I must have made a mistake." She spoke through gritted teeth.

He smiled expansively. "We all make mistakes at times, Mrs. Harper. Let not your heart be troubled."

Violet edged her way past the man and out of his shop. By the time she reached the cabstand at the top of the street, she was trembling in delayed reaction to Vernon's abuse. Should she go to the police? Would they even believe her story that an undertaker had pushed a fellow undertaker into a coffin? Violet could almost imagine the ensuing laughter. No, she had had enough humiliation for one day.

A half hour later, as she exited the cab at her own shop, though, her fear had transformed into fury over what had happened—or nearly happened—to her. She headed to the back room to perform some mindless tasks so she could spend time in thought, but Harry greeted her with "Good afternoon, Mrs. Harper. Would you care to take a look at how I've set up the Boyce and Sons coffins?"

Violet stopped, but just for a moment. "Truthfully, Harry, the last thing in the world I wish to see right now is the inside of a coffin."

She left Harry scratching his head in puzzlement.

Roger awoke slowly in the still darkness. He attempted to adjust his eyes to the blackness, but they refused to cooperate. Why couldn't he see anything? He blinked several times. It didn't help. He'd never been in such a black space before, but his mind was as foggy as St. Paul's churchyard on a December morning. He remembered the events of the past few days through a glass darkly, as his grandfather used to say. Everything was just gray, opaque shapes and unintelligible voices.

He rolled to one side. Or attempted to roll to one side. His left shoulder met with an immovable object. What in the name of . . . ?

Roger tried moving the other way and met the same resistance. He also attempted to spread his hands out. They, too, met with resistance. He closed his eyes again, which made no difference to his situation but somehow made it easier to think.

Where am *I? What is happening to me?*

He shook his head, and the gray shapes began to form and lump together, creating coherent—and chillingly frightening—images. Roger now knew exactly where he was and began panting heavily.

It was then that he could feel the thrum of the furious but rhythmic clacking deep below him, and a doleful whistle in the distance. What was that? Was there someone nearby?

"Help me!" he shouted. His words bounced ineffectively around in his confined space.

He flexed his fingers to feel around and realized there was a string tied around his right forefinger. He began tugging frantically on the string.

Ting-a-ling. Ting-a-ling. Ting-a-ling.

Roger waited several moments, but there was no response.

Ting-a-ling-a-ling. Ting-a-ling-a-ling.

Now he pulled incessantly on the bell. Surely someone would answer at any moment.

Yes, at any moment.

He heard a scraping noise. Finally, his rescuers were here. He offered one more gentle *ting-a-ling* to encourage them to hurry. Yet he continued to wait. What had that noise been? It had sounded like . . . like perhaps a tree branch rubbing against the side of metal. What did it mean?

He lay as patiently as his panicked mind would allow for several minutes, then started furiously ringing the bell without stopping. These safety coffins were supposed to prevent anyone from being buried alive.

Why wasn't anyone answering?

4

Three days after her visit with Mr. Vernon, Violet was once again accompanying a body to Brookwood South station. Every trip was a mental struggle with her distaste for trains, but she was determined to ignore her fears and concentrate on her customer. Today it was a very overweight woman by the name of Mrs. Merriman. Violet had had a devil of a time preparing Mrs. Merriman and fitting her into her coffin. Even with Harry's assistance, it had been a miserable couple of hours of redressing her and packing her bloated frame into the box.

Bodies like Mrs. Merriman's were unusual, but perhaps she should talk to Mr. Boyce about creating a larger coffin size for just such situations.

Harry had helped her with getting the body aboard the LNR; then he departed for a meeting with the director of Brompton Cemetery on another matter. Violet and Harry were planning a funeral for an elderly, eccentric man who had wished to be buried with his stuffed parrot. The bird had died years ago, and the man had had its innards removed and stuffed with wool. The thing looked and smelled like stagnant pond water, but if that was what the man wanted . . .

Violet wasn't sure the cemetery director would permit Mr. Mapleton to be interred with his beloved avian friend, but the family had agreed to offer a substantial donation to the cemetery for its acquiescence. Harry's job today was to help satisfy the deceased's—and his family's—wishes.

Violet boarded the third-class carriage and took her usual seat, hoping she could stay awake for the hour-long ride. She had calmed down considerably after visiting James Vernon, although she was positively baffled as to whether the man had a mental disturbance that caused him to act as he did, or if he was attempting to frighten her and cause her to think she was as mad as a March hare in the process.

Nevertheless, she had chosen not to tell her family what had happened, for fear that their response would be an overreaction of such agitation and objection that she wouldn't be able to further pursue her investigations. She would tell Sam later, although she wasn't quite sure when "later" would be.

As the train gave its shrill whistle, indicating that it was ready to depart, another black-clad undertaker jumped aboard and took a seat in the aisle across from Violet. She stole a look at him and almost gasped aloud in surprise.

It was Julian Crugg.

Violet had only met the man twice but would remember him forever. Her first encounter with her fellow undertaker was at the scene of a crime, when Crugg had callously stepped over a dead body that was in his way. The second time was when she'd gone to accuse him of the murder of that same body, and he had retorted that she was slandering him. And, of course, there was the issue of Crugg feeling as though Violet had intentionally pilfered some first-class business, conveniently forgetting that the work had been at the behest of the queen.

The train set off with a lurch and began its musical clacking as it picked up speed along the rails. Just as Violet was about to turn her head to the right to set her thoughts on their outdoor surroundings and away from her queasy stomach, Crugg himself turned toward her. Almost immediately, his face was suffused with rage.

Violet nodded a cool greeting to him, but the man was nearly sputtering. She quickly turned away to view the Tudor-styled Lambeth Palace and Lambeth Field to her right. A group of children was already assembling with cricket bats and balls on part of the expansive lawn, which Archbishop Tait had opened up for sporting events several years ago.

A phlegmy throat-clearing snapped her attention back to the train. Mr. Crugg now sat in the seat across from her, his eyebrows practically knit together in their deep frown.

"Are you here to persecute me further, Mrs. Harper?" he asked without preamble.

Here was another undertaker completely furious with her in the space of a few days. Violet could but hope that he wouldn't attack her physically.

"Do you think I was aware that you would be here today, sir?" she replied stiffly. Today she was in no frame of mind to trifle with the likes of Julian Crugg.

"You've sent your nosy daughter in to see me. Why shouldn't I think that you've been spying on me ever since?" A muscle in Crugg's jaw ticked rapidly. Violet wished there were other undertakers in the carriage with them.

"I assure you, I've had no concern for your whereabouts, Mr. Crugg."

"Yet you will admit that you sent your daughter in to interrogate me over some foolishness. A cowardly act, if I may say so."

Violet shifted uncomfortably in her seat. Perhaps it had been a bit spineless of her. "She and I both have an interest in some strange circumstances surrounding two bodies that were recently sent to Brookwood."

He pinched his lips between two fingers and released them. "What sort of circumstances are these?"

"Susanna didn't tell you? Two bodies shipped in bell coffins turned out to be alive, their occupants springing up from their boxes on the station platform."

Crugg stared at her, and Violet wasn't sure if it was in disbelief or if he was thinking up a lie. "Those are certainly strange circumstances. This happened with two different bodies, you say? Which platform?"

"Actually, it was one at the North station and one at the South station." She watched his expression carefully, but it stayed frozen in place as he considered what Violet had said. As if he'd suddenly reached a decision, Crugg settled back into his seat and unfurrowed his eyebrows.

"That is certainly peculiar. Let's hope that none of my bodies fly out of their coffins when we arrive." He delivered a forced, high-pitched laugh.

"Actually, sir, it is my fervent hope and prayer that I will never see such a thing again," Violet said, probably a little too primly.

Crugg frowned again at having his comment dismissed. "You have a tart tongue, Mrs. Harper."

"My apologies. You wouldn't be the first to inform me of it."

Crugg softened a little at that. They both turned to observe the scenery as they skirted the edges of Wimbledon House and its surrounding parkland in Richmond.

As if the alternating views of Wimbledon's lawns and forest had a calming effect on Crugg, he asked casually, "So, you have funerals in Brookwood today?"

"Just one, at the Anglican cemetery."

"Ah. As for myself, I'm accompanying three bodies."

"You have three funerals to conduct today?" Violet asked. "That is quite a feat."

Crugg shrugged immodestly. "My services are very much in demand."

Perhaps, but how was the man planning to spread himself across three funerals when most of his mourners would arrive on the same train this afternoon? Even if this was a busy day and the LNR decided to add several trains, there still wasn't enough time to do three of them.

Especially for a man as overwrought as Julian Crugg.

They finished their ride in silence, and Violet noted that Crugg never left his spot across from her. As the train whistled and screeched its way into the South station, he said, "Perhaps we might travel back to London together, Mrs. Harper. So you won't be a lady traveling alone in the carriage, of course."

Was this a peace offering, or should she be suspicious? Vivid memories of Mr. Vernon and his solicitousness rose to make her inwardly shudder, but Violet decided to take his offer at face value. "Very well, Mr. Crugg, I shall wait for you on the platform for the two fifteen train."

At least she had resolved her differences with one undertaker, although she couldn't be certain that he didn't wish her as much harm as Mr. Vernon had.

Violet stood on the South station platform with Julian Crugg, waiting as coffins were unloaded. Since they had left London, the sky had grown overcast and the wind had picked up. A warm gust swirled her black skirts around her feet and attempted to lift her hat from her head. She retied the silk sash beneath her chin to anchor the hat down more firmly.

The coffins began accumulating around the two undertakers as they waited for the hearse vans to arrive and haul them to either the Anglican chapel or their respective grave sites. Those who had already had services at churches in London would be driven directly to their plots.

"Is that your body?" Crugg asked, nodding at an ebony coffin near Violet.

"No," she said.

"What of that one?" He pointed to another one.

"No, I don't believe mine has been unloaded."

He nodded and clasped his hands behind him. What was his concern over which was hers?

"I'm still awaiting some of mine, as well," he said. "There seem to be many unaccompanied bodies today."

A young woman in her early twenties wandered out from the first-class reception rooms and stood off to one side. She was fashionably dressed in a gray-and-lavender-checked gown edged along the hem in black, suggesting that she was in the later stages of mourning, particularly since she was meeting the funeral train. Her matching lavender bonnet was decorated with peacock feathers secured by a pin containing the largest pearl Violet had ever seen. Wispy blond curls hung around her heart-shaped face and

Cupid's bow lips. She literally looked like a drawing from the front of a paper-lace-edged Valentine's Day postcard.

The woman began walking down the length of the platform, but seemed to be searching the passenger trains, as if waiting for someone to disembark. Realizing that the carriages were now empty, she approached Violet and Crugg, her hat's feathers waving prettily in the breeze. Apparently the wind had chosen to be kinder to this delicate creature than it was to Violet.

The woman softly said, "How do you do?" to Violet even as she was shifting her attention to the coffins around them. Violet watched as the woman searched among the coffins until she apparently found the one she wanted. It was a darkly stained box made of what Violet immediately recognized as sycamore. It was an expensive wood, typically imported from France or Spain.

After another glance at the woman's stylish dress, Violet decided it had probably spent time in the hands of a French seamstress and had been just as costly as the coffin.

As her eyes idly assessed the coffin, Violet was disturbed to see that it had a bell mechanism attached to it.

The woman knelt down before the coffin, and her skirts flowed around her in a perfect, unjumbled spread. She tugged on the coffin's lid, as if it were a crate of imported silks she wanted to investigate. Crugg's eyes widened in horror, and Violet shouted in alarm, "Miss, don't!" but the woman had the lid thrown off before Violet could reach her.

The woman began speaking softly to the body, sending a chill down Violet's spine and freezing her in place. Violet often spoke to the dead, a measure she employed as a means of respect for the bodies under her care. Susanna, too, was wont to speak soothingly to corpses.

Was this woman an undertaker? If so, why was she dressed like one of couturier Charles Worth's famous models?

All of a sudden, the woman reared back and gasped. "Roger? Roger?" she cried as she moved forward again and touched the shoulder of the coffin's occupant, a young man of about her age with hair only a shade darker than the woman's.

Violet caught no more than this glimpse of him because the woman then threw herself on him, sobbing and moaning. Her fashionable hat went askew and covered the man's face.

To his credit, Crugg immediately stepped in and gently lifted the woman from the corpse. "Madam, please, let me help you," he said.

The woman struggled from Crugg's grasp, still reaching down toward the man, but the undertaker managed to dislodge her attentions. "Madam, are you—"

The woman finally noticed Crugg's attentions and turned on him viciously. "Why is my fiancé dead?" she demanded through her tears. "How did he die? Tell me what happened!"

As the distraught young woman continued railing at Crugg, who did his best to comfort her, Violet knelt down herself to examine the body. At least this one was actually deceased, unlike the others she had lately encountered.

Roger, the woman had called him. He was handsome, even in death, with his hair softly swept back away from his face, and his—

Wait a minute. Taking a covert look back to make sure Crugg and the fiancée were still engrossed in their fuss together and not paying attention to her, Violet reached out a hand and examined Roger's face. It was still . . . pliable. There was no evidence of cosmetics.

In fact, she would almost swear he was still warm from death, although the August heat and his confinement might have contributed to that.

She gently pushed against his lips. His mouth fell open. It hadn't been sewn or propped shut. Frowning, Violet probed his eyelids. They easily rolled back.

Had this man's undertaker not done *anything* to prepare his body? She thought of James Vernon, but this was obviously not some pauper's corpse bound for a medical school or hospital. What in heaven's name . . . ?

"Ahem, Mrs. Harper," Crugg said from behind her. Violet rose quickly and turned, using her body to shield Roger, whose mouth dangled open as if in a silent scream, one eye open with just the white showing. If his fiancée had been hysterical before, the sight of this would send her plunging onto the train track.

The young woman clung to Crugg, weeping against his black coat. With a pained look he said, "I'm going to escort this young lady in for some refreshment and then assist her with finding her fiancé's burial plot. I've managed to pull from her that his family does have a crypt here. I'll see you again for the two fifteen train."

With that, he managed to disengage the woman at least a couple of inches, and walked with her into the station. Violet wanted to tell Crugg about the condition of the body but saw that there was now just one coffin left on the platform, hers, and a hearse driver stood waiting patiently next to it. She needed to turn her attentions to her own funeral.

Mr. Crugg would see Roger for himself soon enough.

As Mrs. Merriman's service concluded in the chapel, Violet once again coordinated the movement of the mourners outside and onto the path toward the family's plot. She had surreptitiously asked two additional men to assist with lifting the woman's coffin, and she didn't think anyone noticed the additional muscle carrying the box.

Outside the chapel, four hearses waited, one for Mrs. Merriman and three others for third-class funerals to be conducted after Mrs. Merriman's. Unlike the private first-class funerals, all third-class funerals for a single day were conducted at one time inside the chapel, so the coffins would be distributed around the room, with the appropriate mourners gathered around each coffin, and the minister would read, pray, and make supplications to the Almighty for all of them at once.

"May your loved ones find peace," Violet said, nodding solemnly at the third-class mourners, all of whom forgot their own grieving for a moment as they craned their necks in curiosity to see what important or famous people might be among the mourners of a first-class funeral.

Once Mrs. Merriman was ensconced in her grave—and not

without grunting and muttered expletives from her pallbearers—Violet murmured condolences to the mourning party and made her way back to the South station to wait for Crugg. A clock on the platform said it was nearly half past one, so she had a wait in front of her. The platform itself was presently deserted except for a young boy in threadbare pants and mismatched shoes sweeping at one end. It gave Violet an idea.

She called him over and handed him a groat. The boy's eyes lit up, and he stared at the coin, openmouthed.

"What is your name?" Violet asked.

"Benjamin. Benny, me mam calls me."

The same name as Violet's son-in-law. "Good afternoon, Benny. How long have you been here?"

The boy wrinkled his nose. "I dunno, m'um. Two hours?" he added, as if hoping that was the right answer.

"Do you remember the crying woman on the platform?"

"The one wot had on them nice clothes?"

"That's the one. Do you remember where she went?"

Benny frowned. "A man in a black hat and suit took her to the reception rooms. First class, I saw. They must be rich, wot?"

"Did you see them leave the reception rooms later?"

He shook his head. "No, m'um. I had me duties to take care of. I hafta go to the stables and muck the stalls, and help polish the hearses, and bring in the wagon of goods for the refreshment stands, and—"

"That's fine, Benny. One more question: Do you remember an open coffin on the platform at the same time that the crying woman was here?"

Confusion reigned in the boy's eyes. "There's lots of coffins here each day, wot?"

"This was a very fine coffin, made of sycamore maple."

Benny shrugged. "They all look the same ta me, m'um."

"That's all right then. You may go." The boy clearly didn't know anything. He scampered off, kissing the coin.

Violet had another idea. She glanced at the platform clock. It was fifteen minutes to the hour. She went inside the station and sought out the stationmaster, Uriah Gedding, in his office. This time, he was crouched over his cat with his back to Violet, cooing at the animal as it attacked a dish of unidentifiable, bloodied meat, gulping it down unchewed as if it were the head of a pride taking the first feed.

Violet shuddered. The animal brought back a terrifying memory of long ago, when she had been accidentally trapped in a lion enclosure at Regent's Park zoo. She brushed away the thought. She wasn't about to be cowed into a corner by a silly housecat.

"Mr. Gedding?" she said.

The stationmaster turned and, recognition dawning in his eyes, gave the cat a final pat—earning him a throaty growl as a reward—and rose to greet Violet. "Attending to another funeral today, Mrs. Harper? I presume you've encountered no more inconveniently living bodies?"

Violet was in no mood to be mocked. "I don't have much time, sir. I was wondering if there are any coffins in the pauper waiting room?" Cellars beneath the station had been converted into reception rooms for coffins not immediately claimed, and were also periodically used for pauper funeral services prior to burial in the poor section of the cemetery.

"You're welcome to check for yourself," Gedding said, taking a burning oil lamp from a hook on the wall. He escorted her back to the platform and to a door at the rear of one side of the station. The wood door was painted a dismal, drab sepia, and did not suggest a kind welcome at all. Gedding handed her the lamp and unlocked the door.

Violet preceded Gedding down a brick staircase, which was damp and mossy, into the cellars. How did porters haul coffins down here without slipping and sending both themselves and their cargo crashing down to the bottom? Her heels sent tapping echoes into the basement area, and she realized that hers were the only heels she heard. She stopped and turned to say something to Gedding, but he was at the top of the stairs, shutting the door behind him with a firm thud, aided by the wind whipping around the building.

Oh. She had thought he was going to inspect the pauper rooms with her. Perhaps he needed to hand-feed his cat some cream.

Like in the upstairs reception rooms, there was no gas or electricity down here, but it stank of sweat and protracted grief. A dim ray of sunlight filtered in through a narrow window at one end of the cavernous space that was actually aboveground. Otherwise, the oil lamp she lifted was her only source of light.

A few scattered oak benches surrounded a minister's lectern in the middle of the space. Filling the long wall behind the lectern were wood niches intended to temporarily store coffins. The cavities were all empty except for one used as lamp and oil storage.

She swung the light around the room again and this time saw that there was a coffin lying unceremoniously on the floor at one end of the room, opposite from the window. If she was not mistaken, the lid was askew. She took a deep breath and tap-tap-tapped her way over to it. She held the lamp over it.

The coffin was empty.

Why would there be an unoccupied coffin carelessly placed in the pauper waiting rooms? There had to have been an occupant at some point—vacant coffins weren't placed on the LNR, or at least they wouldn't be for any reason she could think of. She examined the coffin more closely. It was made of inexpensive white poplar and was definitely not constructed of the same quality as Roger's. She scanned the box further and could find no maker's mark. The interior had no mattress, just a thin muslin lining unevenly nailed in along the sides. It was an altogether stark resting place, but probably more than a poor family could afford.

Violet concluded that this had been a rental coffin, and after the shrouded body had been committed to the ground, the hearse driver had dumped it here to await its next trip to London to pick up another occupant. She heartily disapproved of such careless work, but then, she wasn't in charge of the LNR, nor of Brookwood Cemetery.

She put the lantern on the ground and stood back to think, tapping a forefinger against her lips. Who was this Roger fellow? By the looks of his final home and his fiancée's clothing, he had obviously been wealthy. Why was his fiancée waiting for him at the train station instead of accompanying the entire mourning party later? Violet wished she could have been present when they all arrived so she could have inquired as to what undertaker they'd used. Instead, she was as—

Bang! Something crashed into the narrow window edging the ceiling, nearly sending Violet jumping into the empty coffin on her own.

With her heart fluttering, she turned to the window. She could see nothing this far away, except a shadow of something blocking the window's light. What was it? The thought crept into her mind that someone was trying to frighten her, but who? That thought was replaced by the fear that the object was a human body.

Violet grabbed the oil lamp from the ground and hurried back up the steps to the door. She turned the brass knob, but it spun uselessly in her hand. She rapped on the wood and shouted, "Hello? Hello?" but her voice only echoed behind her downstairs among empty benches and coffin niches.

Had she been intentionally locked into the dank cellar?

She turned the handle once more with the same fruitless result. Then she decided to put more effort into it. With the lamp in her right hand and the knob in her left, she concentrated all of her weight into her left shoulder and threw herself against the door. It gave way immediately and she stumbled back out to the exterior of the building.

How odd. She shut the door and tried to open it again. The knob still didn't work and her tugs were ineffective. She abandoned the door to go around to the back of the building and inspect the window. Violet laughed in relief and exhaled her fright at what she saw there. A limb had blown off a large beech tree behind the building, whose base was so intertwined with overlapping trunks that it looked like tangled locks of hair. It was no wonder one had snapped off and been carried forward against the window.

How silly Violet now felt, realizing she had been fearful of floating debris and a door that had been stuck shut by the wind. *Honestly, Violet Harper, soon you'll be jumping at shadows*, she thought.

For a moment there, she'd thought she'd have to include Uriah Gedding in her list of dubious characters.

Ignoring her hat's tails as they fluttered in the wind like demented birds, she returned to the station platform. The clock showed that it was ten minutes past two. The train would be here shortly. Where was Mr. Crugg? She looked inside both reception rooms but saw no trace of him.

Perhaps she should pay Mr. Gedding another visit. He was still in his office, signing some papers, when Violet entered. The cat was curled up on one corner of the desk, apparently so satisfied and sleepy from its earlier meal that it barely lifted its head to acknowledge her presence.

"Did you find what you wanted, Mrs. Harper?" Mr. Gedding asked, cordially laying down his pen to give her his attention.

"Not exactly. Do you know Julian Crugg, another undertaker who frequents the LNR?"

Gedding spread his hands over the documents. "There are many undertakers who pass through here on a daily basis, Mrs. Harper. I cannot be expected to know each by name."

"He is tall, a bit older than me, and is frequently very . . . agitated."

"Does he have a shop in Mayfair?" Gedding reached over and absentmindedly scratched the cat on the head. The animal raised its head and presented its neck for further attention, and Gedding complied.

"Yes."

"Certainly I know who he is. He was here this morning, comforting a woman in the first-class reception room."

"Have you seen him since?"

"Yes, madam, he returned on the early-afternoon train that went back for mourners."

Had Crugg forgotten about her in all of the commotion with the fiancée? What of his own funerals? How had he handled them if he'd returned home so soon? Violet shook her head. It was difficult not to be skeptical of everyone around her when everyone behaved so suspiciously.

* * *

Samuel Harper was not pleased with what he was hearing. He and Cyril Hayes, who worked for London East Bank, were strolling among the graves inside the churchyard of St. Botolph-without-Bishopsgate, just outside the wall of London. Hayes had insisted on this meeting place, for utmost privacy over what he had to say.

"There is a recently passed law that could spell doom for the banking industry," Hayes had said, raking through his beard with his fingers. The banker had been the most open and welcoming of all of Sam's contacts, not that it had thus far resulted in a loan.

"That doesn't sound very good for either you or me," Sam said, hoping Hayes would get to the point quickly. He didn't enjoy treading over the graves of people who had been buried three centuries ago.

"It isn't. Parliament has passed something so heinous that I cannot imagine what they were thinking. The Debtors Act consolidates all of the country's bankruptcy laws. In doing so, they have not only abolished debtors' prisons; it makes dodging a debt a mere misdemeanor."

"No debtors' prison at all?" Sam asked.

"Only in the cases where money is owed to the Crown, or the debtor actually has the money but refuses to pay the debt."

Sam didn't understand. "That has at least some benefit, doesn't it?"

"Not in the way they did it. They have also decided to eliminate the arrest on mesne process."

Sam had been a lawyer back in the United States and understood this well. "So you have lost your ability to have a man put in custody prior to a judge's order, thus running the risk that he will flee altogether."

"Precisely. We have little recourse against those who would dodge their debts."

"But won't it make banks more cautious in giving out cred— Ah." Now Sam fully comprehended why he wasn't getting a loan. He was an incidental victim of debt dodgers ruining the credit industry.

He would need at least two dishes of ice cream tonight to fully sort this out in his mind and decide what to do next.

That evening, Violet and Sam sat inside his favorite ice cream shop, located just outside Regent's Park. It was run by Carlo Gatti, a Swiss émigré, who, according to rumor, had initially started out with a stall outside Charing Cross station, but his popularity grew, and he soon contracted with the Regent's Canal Company to keep a brick icehouse in the canal and now imported his ice from Norway.

Samuel Harper was probably responsible for half of Gatti's business, and it would be a wonder if Norway didn't completely run out of ice. Violet shook her head with a smile as she watched her husband devour ice cream molded into the shape of a rooster, replete with rose petals added to represent the bird's comb. She gently set aside her own half-eaten ice cream, which was wrapped inside an almond wafer.

Susanna and Benjamin had gone shopping earlier in the day, and their note said they wouldn't return until after the dinner hour, so Violet had dismissed Mrs. Wren's services for the evening, and she and Sam had indulged themselves by substituting supper with ice cream. Violet enjoyed the cold treat, but not nearly so much as Sam did.

While he ate, she told him of what had happened at Brookwood that day, from her nearly harmonious trip with Julian Crugg, to the discovery of the unknown Roger, and ending with her misadventure in the train station's cellar.

Sam licked the last drops from his spoon, set it carefully in his empty dish, and directed his full attention on her. "Before, you were encountering living bodies in coffins and were suspicious of them. Now you say you've discovered a dead body in a coffin, and this, too, is suspicious? Sweetheart, aren't bodies in coffins *supposed* to be dead? That was what made you so upset about the live ones."

Violet shook her head in frustration at the seeming contradiction of her speculation. "I know. It's just the condition in which I found this Roger fellow, whoever he may be. He was so . . . fresh. It was very peculiar."

"I still don't see that you have anything to take to Inspector Hurst." Sam flagged down the shop's hostess.

Violet sighed. "No, I suppose I don't."

The hostess approached. "Yes, sir, can I get you something?"

"I would like to try another, this time something with pistachio ice cream."

As the hostess went off to fulfill Sam's order, Violet looked at him in disbelief. "Another one? Aren't you full?"

"I hate to think there could be untasted flavors going to waste while we sit here."

The hostess returned shortly with Sam's second dish. This time his ice cream had been molded into the shape of a cup of chocolate. Brown-tinted sugar crystals decorated the top to enhance the effect.

Violet smiled indulgently at her husband. "I'll have to ask Mary to let out your trousers soon with all of these sweets you're eating." A ridiculous notion, of course, since Sam hadn't added an ounce of weight anywhere since the day she met him. Violet was the one who needed alterations.

"That reminds me," Sam said. He pulled a small book from his jacket, flipped through it until he reached the page he wanted, then slid it across the table to Violet.

"What is this?" she asked.

"I found it at Hatchards. It's a reprint of Mrs. Mary Eales's recipes. Look at that one." He tapped the left page. "I thought maybe you could try your hand at it."

The recipe was titled "To Make Ice Cream" and contained instructions such as breaking ice up into various-sized pieces, layering salt and ice over cream, and covering everything up with straw to freeze together before adding in fruits for flavoring.

Violet looked up at her husband in disbelief. They'd been married four years and he still didn't realize that her skills as a chatelaine were substandard at best? That although she could easily whip up an embalming fluid brew that would preserve a body into the next century, the simplest pot of coffee was likely to be bitter and half burnt?

"Samuel Harper, you think I would be competent at making this? Besides, there is only a small storage cellar underneath the shop. I'm not sure it's a good place to keep ice."

Sam sighed and held up his hands in defeat. "It was worth a try."

Suddenly Violet felt ashamed of herself. "I'll give it to Mrs. Wren. I'm sure she'll make a treat to rival Mr. Gatti's concoctions."

"I keep forgetting that my wife can only concentrate on burying bodies, not ice. At least you haven't gotten into any trouble with your living bodies that are supposed to be dead. Or is that your dead bodies that are supposed to be alive? I confess I'm getting confused."

Violet bit her lip. She should tell Sam about James Vernon and his erratic behavior that had resulted in her being trapped in a coffin. But if she did that, Sam's protective nature would burst forth like a badger fighting off a pack of dogs.

No, ultimately no harm had been done. It was best to keep it to herself. Mr. Vernon likely needed the confinement of an asylum, not a prison. Which reminded Violet of Mr. Ambrose, the doctor she'd met when the first body had risen from its coffin. Was it for-tuitous—or extremely convenient—that he had been on hand that day? Or was Violet now viewing everyone within ten miles of Brookwood as a suspect?

Nevertheless, it might be of interest to interview the doctor to see what he had to say.

Violet felt even guiltier about concealing information from Sam when arranging to have coffee with her friend Mary Cooke with the express intent of telling her everything, including how she ended up briefly trapped in a coffin.

The two met at an elegant coffeehouse in Mayfair, across from Hyde Park, where the two friends had once discovered a dead body together while boating in the park's Serpentine lake. They made no mention of that shocking day, instead musing on Violet's present situation.

Mary was older than Violet by twenty years. Despite the fact that Mary was old enough to be Violet's mother, the two shared a love of funereal things, Mary with her mourning dressmaking and Violet with her undertaking. They had also both been married twice. Mary had lost her beloved first husband, Matthew Overfelt, to a malignant brain growth. She'd made an unfortunate second marriage with George Cooke, a ne'er-do-well who eventually ran off to Switzerland and became entangled with another woman there, who unceremoniously coshed him in the head when she discovered that he had a wife back in London.

Mary had been in mourning now for a couple of months. The dark circles were gone from under her eyes, but she looked as fragile as a china cup, ready to crack at the slightest pressure. She wore a gown of the deepest ebony silk bombazine, accompanied by the requisite jet necklace, earrings, and bracelet. Her gray hair, normally worn in an impossibly large cloud on her head, was completely concealed under a bonnet trimmed in more black silk. Mary had sewn her own mourning wear, which Violet had no doubt was a difficult thing to do. It was one thing to assist and console the grieving; it was a different thing entirely to be the one in mourning.

They sat at a table next to the window. On the other side of the glass, hardy souls braved the traffic noise and manure smells while Violet and Mary made themselves comfortable inside.

Violet described the events of the past two weeks, with two bodies arising from coffins and a third wept over hysterically by a fiancée, in addition to her visits with other undertakers.

"Do you know who all of the people in the coffins were?" Mary asked.

"Not a single one of them. I only know that the dead man's name was Roger."

"Well, it doesn't seem as though anything unseemly occurred with these bodies."

That was what everyone said, so why was Violet the only one who thought otherwise?

They were served cups of chocolate, with assurance that their pastries would be out presently. Their drinks were thick and delectable.

"The only suspicious thing was Mr. Vernon pushing you into a coffin. But he might have just had a spell of madness." Mary put down her cup and tapped the side of her head. "People get them all the time, dear. I'm sure he is quite mortified over it."

"Not as mortified as I am."

Mary laughed unexpectedly, a rare reaction from her these days. It brought color into her wan face. "Oh my, I suppose it *was* quite an indignity for you." She turned serious again. "A woman's indignities should not be treated lightly."

Violet knew Mary was once again thinking of her wayward husband and how humiliated she had been over his romantic liaison conducted openly in Lausanne. Violet and Sam had never been impressed with George Cooke, but Mary had loved him, so they had begrudgingly accepted him. Violet grieved for her friend's loss.

As if she knew Violet was also dwelling on the subject, Mary said, "Do you know, I think I am mortified, too? As time goes on, I am less bereaved by George's loss and more embarrassed by my poor decision in agreeing to become his wife. Do you think ill of me for it, Violet?"

"Of course not! How could you think such a thing? Your love for him was innocent and pure. I've made plenty of my own decisions—while assuming that others were acting in good faith—that turned out poorly and sometimes nearly fatally. We don't always know what sort of evil lurks in the hearts of others, my friend."

Mary's eyes welled up, and she took another sip from her cup in order to close her eyes and blink back the tears. "Thank you," she whispered, as the cup clattered back down on its saucer.

Violet sought for something, anything, to cheer Mary up. A thought occurred to her. "Remember when you were planning to go to Switzerland and I said we would visit Madame Tussauds upon your return to celebrate your happiness? Well, why don't we go anyway, to, to . . . celebrate our friendship? I understand they are preparing a Suez Canal exhibit in anticipation of November's opening ceremonies."

"Didn't the queen invite you and Sam to attend?"

"Yes. We are deeply honored." Violet just hoped Queen Victoria wouldn't require her services during the trip to Egypt. She'd had quite enough royal duty over the past few months.

For now, though, Violet had something else to discuss.

"I've been thinking about Morgan Undertaking," she said. "Now that I'm staying, I'd like to make some improvements. Poor Will and Harry, they did an admirable job in growing the business, but I think the shop's interior could use some updating. Would you consider making some new draperies for the windows and to separate off the back rooms? I know that I'm once again imposing on you."

Although Mary's true expertise was in fashionable mourning clothing, she also had decorating talent. Mary had redecorated her own quarters above her dressmaking shop, then helped Violet with décor for her rooms above the undertaking shop.

"Of course I will help you," Mary said, her eyes glowing with anticipation. "What fun. We'll go back to Morris, Marshall, and Faulkner this instant to find you some nice fabrics, and then make some measurements in your shop. I'm sure I can have it done for you in the next two weeks."

"Shall we agree to go to Madame Tussauds as soon as the draperies are installed?"

They sealed their plan by raising their cups of chocolate to one another.

Changing subjects, Mary asked, "How goes your visit with Susanna?"

This was an uncomfortable topic because of Violet's conflicted feelings on it. Fortunately, their sweets arrived just then, giving Violet an opportunity to choose her words carefully. "Sam and Benjamin spend a lot of time together, and Susanna has volunteered to work in the shop with me. She has been a big help."

"That doesn't sound like much of a honeymoon for the two of them."

There was that feeling of discomfort again, poking at her innards. "No, but Susanna has always been a natural undertaker. She probably misses the shop back in Colorado already."

"Hmm," Mary said. "Haven't they been here a few weeks already? How long are they planning to visit?"

"I don't know. Susanna seems reluctant to leave. I like to think it's because she missed us so much, but maybe she missed London?"

Mary raised a pale-brown eyebrow. "Weren't most of her memories of London those of living in a workhouse and watching her birth family die? I'm sure it's because she misses you, dear."

"I've missed her, too, but our flat has become a bit overwhelmed. Mrs. Softpaws glares at me every time she sees me, and although I appreciate that she is keeping the place free of spiders and mice, I'm not particularly happy to find her day's catch on my pillow. Ruth is a sweet girl and says nothing about the extra cleaning work, but Mrs. Wren is grumpy."

"More so than usual?" Mary asked, cutting into her toasted tea cakes. Butter oozed out from between the layers.

"Hard to believe, isn't it? You know, I love having my girl with me, but perhaps she and Benjamin need their own quarters if they plan to stay much lon—" Violet stopped abruptly, staring out the window in surprise. A shiver of apprehension crawled up her spine.

A man stared back in at her.

"Violet? What's wrong, dear?" Mary asked.

Without answering, Violet jumped up from the table and dashed outside, running in the direction that she guessed the man was going. The streets were as crowded as they always were, and within moments she realized she couldn't make any progress in the throng of people. She was also too short to see much of what was ahead of her. Deflated, she returned to the coffeehouse, where Mary still sat over her tea cakes with an expression of confusion.

"What's wrong?" Violet's friend asked.

"I thought I saw Mr. Crugg looking in on us."

With a fork, Mary swiped her last morsel of cake through the butter drippings on her plate. "The undertaker who doesn't like you? Why would he be seeking you out? It's probably just a coincidence. He happened by and noticed you here."

"Perhaps." Violet was thoroughly unconvinced but could think of no reason why the undertaker might be clandestinely looking for her, so she let the matter drop.

The rest of the afternoon was spent fingering chintzes, brocades, and velvets, then deciding how to use them in the shop. With Mary's advice, Violet selected a color palette of mossy green, crimson, gold, and pale cream, inspired by an imaginative wallpaper inside Mr. Morris's shop that drifted artfully with swirled acanthus leaves and bright flowers. By the time she left his shop, Violet had ordered enough fabric and wallpaper to redo an entire block of shops, not just her own.

It had been pleasurable to bury herself in the colors and textures, leaving behind the disquiet of Brookwood, but the unnerving sensation that something sinister was going on persisted.

5

"A bit to the right, please, Mrs. Harper." The photographer pointed to the corpse's face.

Violet positioned the woman's head farther to the right so that her high cheekbones would be better displayed. A bit of cotton inside the late Mrs. Goring's cheeks and some Blushing Rose on the outside had helped re-create the look of a middle-aged woman who, her family said, was known for her love of clever jokes and pranks. Once her head was positioned so that the left side of her face faced the camera, Violet held it while she moved the chair Mrs. Goring was seated in, to follow the head's positioning.

Violet let Mrs. Goring's head gently rest against the floral-papered wall of the woman's bedchamber. Her body was already roped to the chair at the shoulders, and the roping was covered over with an elegant shawl. Through the camera lens, it would look as though Mrs. Goring were sitting up on her own.

Hmm. Something wasn't right.

"Wait," Violet said to Mr. Robinson, who was ready to begin taking the postmortem daguerreotypes the family had ordered. He was positioned behind a portable table neatly set with all of the tools of his trade, including his square camera box, and didn't look happy with her interference.

Violet had used Henry Peach Robinson for postmortem photography once before, and they'd had a rocky start together, with Robinson accusing Violet of not being a good businesswoman, and

Violet snapping right back that he was cheating his clients. However, she had to admit the man had talent, and although she still preferred Mr. Laroche for photography, Mr. Robinson was an agreeable second.

She stepped back to examine Mrs. Goring, who had obviously been ill a very long time if the deep worry lines and blackened crescents beneath her eyes were any indication.

"Quickly, Mrs. Harper, before she sags."

Violet hurried over to Mrs. Goring's dressing table and rummaged through an earring box. It had been a week since Violet's examination of Roger inside his coffin, and it was good to forget what was not a crime—she had to remind herself repeatedly—and return to simple undertaking.

She found what she wanted in a pair of teardrop-shaped pearl bobs. She took one and affixed it to Mrs. Goring's exposed ear. The earring's shape represented mourning, and she knew that the family would appreciate the perfect symbolism.

"Ready," she said, and stepped out of the way.

Violet waited while Robinson did his work; then, when he arose from behind the camera box, she moved Mrs. Goring again, this time turning the chair so that she faced the camera. Violet rearranged the shawl again to completely cover the rope around her shoulders and attached the second ear bob.

From inside her large black undertaker's bag, Violet withdrew a slender block of wood. Positioning herself in front of Mrs. Goring so that Robinson could not see what she was doing, she unbuttoned the woman's shirtwaist, inserted the block of wood beneath her chin to prop it up, then buttoned her shirtwaist all the way up once more.

"Now with your pretty little cheeks and your head held high, you will make a perfect portrait, Mrs. Goring," Violet said warmly.

"What?" came Robinson's voice behind her.

"I'm just chatting with Mrs. Goring," she replied.

Robinson made a half-grunting, half-choking noise to indicate his opinion of Violet's talking to corpses, but she didn't care. She'd always done this, from the time she'd started undertaking sixteen years ago. It soothed Violet, and if there was any chance the departed's soul was still floating about, she thought maybe it assured the soul that the body was well cared for so it didn't need to stay and worry over the burial.

With Mrs. Goring rearranged once more, Robinson took several more pictures. He pulled each plate from his camera box and set them one at a time over a heated cup of mercury. The mercury's vapors were noxious but soon resulted in a visible image on the plates. Once each image was finished, he slipped the plate into a developing box to inspect the image through a special glass window to determine when to stop development, then "fixed" the image onto the plate by dipping it into a saturated salt solution. After drying, the photographs would be ready to be sealed in glass cases evacuated of air and filled with nitrogen to stabilize the images.

Violet had always been amazed by this procedure, the creating of an image from thin air. Despite Robinson's failings and his tendency to overcharge customers, she couldn't deny that he did do fine work.

Once Robinson was done, he loaded up his van, painted dark green and emblazoned in gold lettering with "Henry Peach Robinson, Quality Photography to the Middle and Upper Classes." Meanwhile, Violet shifted Mrs. Goring's chair next to the bed, undid all of the rope and props, and moved the woman into the bed. With a few more words of comfort to the family and confirmation of funeral details, Violet went on to her next destination, that of Mr. Ambrose's rooms in Surrey.

She found the doctor's rooms in a quiet side street in Woking, just a few blocks from the train station. Violet twisted the bell latch, and in moments the door was answered by a frazzled middle-aged woman wearing a gray dress. It wasn't quite a uniform, but it wasn't quite a day gown, either.

"Have you brought the new stethoscope?" she asked.

"Pardon me?" Violet replied. "My name is Violet Harper, and I am here to—"

"My apologies, madam. I thought you had brought round the new binaural stethoscope Mr. Ambrose ordered. He's been dealing with several cases of pleurisy and bronchitis up in Pottery Lane and was hoping his new listening device would arrive today. How may I be of help?"

Pottery Lane was a slum in the London neighborhood of Notting Hill. He was quite a distance away for treating patients.

"Mr. Ambrose sees patients that far away?" Violet asked.

The woman smiled. "My cousin is fascinated by every new outbreak or unusual condition he can find. He hopes to one day find a cure for everything from gout to scarlet fever. His mind is so caught up in his research that I do swear if I didn't come by on occasion to cook and clean for him, he'd starve to death. He rarely—Ah, there he is now."

The woman opened the door and permitted Violet to enter. The doctor was right on her heels. Before noticing his guest, Ambrose kissed his cousin on the cheek. "Has it arrived, Maddy?"

"Not yet. Byron, you have a visitor."

Ambrose turned to Violet, who said, "Mr. Ambrose, do you remember me?"

He frowned, then recognition dawned. "Yes, I do. Mrs. Harper, isn't it? You were the undertaker at Brookwood on that very odd day...." He removed his hat and tossed it on his desk, which dominated this front room. As he sat behind it, he invited Violet to sit down on a leather chair whose seat was ripped and cracked, but at least wasn't as heaped with clothing and papers as the furniture in Violet's parlor.

Violet proceeded without preamble. "That's why I'm here, sir. Do you know who he was? What happened when you assisted him?"

The doctor shrugged. "He came back to my rooms in my brougham with me, babbling nonsensically the entire time. I examined him, could find no physical ailment other than his disorientation. Thank heavens we haven't adopted that abominable American practice of embalming. It would have killed the man."

Violet winced. She was an advocate of embalming. Done properly, it preserved bodies to extend visitation time and eliminate the more . . . objectionable . . . aspects of a body laying in for more than a couple of days.

"Did you have him sent home?" she asked.

"I had no opportunity to do so. He refused to give me his name, and eventually barged out to parts unknown. He was fascinating to me in the extreme, though. Imagine what knowledge about life and death the medical profession could have learned from him. Just his insight into what the great passing over is like . . ." Ambrose ended on a note of wistfulness.

Maddy gave Violet an "As I told you earlier" look. Violet could hardly suppress a laugh at the loving exasperation the doctor's cousin showed.

Ambrose returned to his previous, businesslike demeanor. "Why do you inquire, Mrs. Harper?"

Violet figured she may as well tell him everything and proceeded to detail the second live body she'd discovered on the station platform. She thought it wise to leave out the mysterious Roger, who was a different sort of Gordian knot altogether.

Ambrose shook his head sadly. "Had I known this would happen again so quickly, I would have given chase to the man I assisted. How is it possible that two men have arisen from the dead in so short a time?"

"My thoughts exactly, sir. Have you experienced this before?"

"Never. I've been picking up bodies at both stations for years now and have never encountered such a thing."

Violet stilled as she remembered her conversation with Mr. Vernon. "Pardon me? Are you involved in the selling of bodies for anatomical experimentation?"

"Sometimes. I also perform anatomical experimentation myself in one of my back rooms, and it distresses me deeply to think there may be something unscrupulous going on. Surely, as an undertaker, you understand that few bodies 'appear' to be dead. They are or they are not."

Violet nodded. "Yes, my thoughts exactly."

"I applaud your tenacity at discovering what happened. If only my own skills were as proficient as yours." He put his hands together as if in prayer. "Well, perhaps we have seen the last of these resurrected bodies and can return to our daily practices. My fervent hope is that if another comes to light, we will be able to discover what is causing it, so that doctors are not declaring living people to be dead, and undertakers are not preparing people who are just deeply asleep. These occurrences cast a bad light on both of our professions."

Violet couldn't agree more. In any case, whatever undertaker was mistakenly putting live bodies in coffins should at least be chastised for incompetence.

"May I inquire, Mr. Ambrose, as to whether you have ever received bodies from James Vernon? He's an undertaker back in London."

Mr. Ambrose mulled over her question and shook his head. "No. I deal with several undertakers, but he isn't one of them."

Violet sighed inwardly. Another dead end.

Violet returned to Morgan Undertaking.

Outside the shop, she noticed a grubby boy hawking newspapers and purchased one, wondering why all paperboys seemed to wear ink like a second set of clothes. Did they end up ingesting it, too?

Inside, Harry was cutting lengths of muslin to be used as winding sheets while Susanna folded them. Thus far, Harry had made no comment about Susanna's continued presence, but it occurred to Violet that she should ask him if he minded. She resolved to talk to him the next time Susanna wasn't there.

Whenever that might be.

He also hadn't asked about the progress of her investigations. Hopefully, Harry had forgotten all about it.

She tossed the paper onto one end of the counter and moved to assist Susanna by moving the folded stack into the storage room. Harry stopped what he was doing to retrieve the paper. Opening it up and immediately smudging his thick fingers with ink, he began flipping through it until he found what he wanted.

Harry was a gentle bear of a man, and Violet trusted him implicitly. She smiled as he pronounced, "Here are the obituaries."

He had recently taken to doing a daily reading of the obituaries, wondering if there were any deaths requiring their services. Although many obituaries were placed by the undertakers themselves, some were not. Typically, though, even if a family was placing the obituary, they had already secured an undertaker's professional help. Nevertheless, Harry had found several customers this way, so Violet couldn't fault him for it.

"I see here a Mr. Peter Chudderley of Hammersmith has gone on to his reward. Fell from the exterior walkway on St. Paul's Cathedral while visiting." Harry paused to speculate. "Hmm, wonder if he didn't jump. Family receiving visitors at their home from Thursday through Saturday—so on and so forth. Let me see . . . Ah, undertaking services by Clyde and Wickham. Hmm," he repeated as he continued perusing.

Susanna returned to her work as he read snippets about London's latest deaths and Violet went through the contents of a small crate that had been delivered while she was gone. The obituaries were the usual daily mix of death from old age and disease, occasionally punctuated by a tragic accident, such as that suffered by Mr. Chudderley.

Sometimes obituaries were accompanied by an engraving of the deceased, but those were expensive to purchase and generally only within the grasp of society members.

"Mrs. Delilah Porter of Hampstead died a few days after giving birth to her eleventh child. Hmm, Mr. Porter is planning to announce his engagement to the family governess after the funeral."

Harry's commentary on that was accompanied by a loud snort. "He'll need such a woman to take care of that lot. And do we have . . . ?" Harry scanned the rest of the obituary. "Yes, undertakers are Bishop Brothers and Company. What's this? 'Mrs. Porter died a death that points out the tragic destiny of women, that of mother and angel on the same day.' Hmm."

Violet stopped listening as Harry went on through the death notices, retreating into her own thoughts, but eventually he said something that pierced her consciousness. "Wait, what did you just say?" she asked.

Harry looked up from the paper in surprise. "What? About the demented old man who fell off the omnibus?"

"No, before that. The death of the young woman that wasn't explained."

Harry frowned and ran a finger back through the obituaries. "You mean this? 'Miss Margery Latham, of Knightsbridge?' "

"Yes, that's the one. Read it again."

"'Miss Margery Latham of Knightsbridge, daughter of the Baron and Baroness Fenton, died suddenly last Tuesday. She was the fiancée of Lord Roger Blount, second son of the Earl of Etchingham, who so recently died his own tragic death. The pair were to be wed in September. Miss Latham will be interred at Brookwood, laid beside Lord Blount in his family's crypt so that the lovers can rest together for eter—'"

"Who is the undertaker?" Violet asked, more sharply than she meant to do. Surely Miss Latham had been the hysterical young woman at Brookwood South station whom Mr. Crugg had comforted.

Harry looked curiously at Violet, opened his mouth to say something, then thought better of it and returned to the paper. "Hmm, it doesn't say anything about an undertaker. Do you know the young woman or her family?"

"No," Violet said quickly, then amended herself. "Perhaps. I don't know. Does it say anything further about Lord Blount?"

"Well, no, Mrs. Harper, but it isn't his obituary. What troubles you?"

Violet sighed and put down the tray of tear catchers—glass tubes with which mourners captured their own tears of grief over a loved one—that she had been arranging from the contents of the crate. Susanna was also looking at her questioningly.

"I believe I met this young woman not long ago when I accompanied a body to Brookwood Cemetery. She was at the train station there, and quite distraught by the sight of her fiancé's coffin."

Harry was still puzzled. "Only natural, wouldn't you say?"

"Normally, yes, except it seemed almost as if she was surprised that her fiancé was dead. Yet she had gone there to greet his coffin. Why would someone go to a cemetery's station and then be shocked to find that her loved one had arrived there in a box? It was mystifying."

Harry shrugged. "We've all seen people act in strange ways in their grief. The more they love, the more irrational and raving they are."

Susanna, though, was more pensive. "Why are you curious about the undertaker?"

Violet looked meaningfully at her daughter. "Because Mr. Crugg was there that morning and spent time comforting Miss Latham. He was supposed to return with me on the two fifteen train back to London, but instead went back on an early train, as though something happened to make him forget me."

"Mr. Crugg planned to accompany you? You, the Medusa of Paddington?" Susanna said.

"Susanna, stay on the subject, please," Violet said. "What's important is that Mr. Crugg acted as if he'd never seen the woman before, but now I wonder if that's so."

"Is this part of your investigation into those two bodies—I mean, two fellows—who were coffined alive, Mrs. Harper?" Harry asked.

"I wish I knew," she replied.

Was Roger Blount another one of Crugg's bungled bodies? If so, had he been eager to escort the woman away from Violet before she figured it out? It definitely brought a more sinister specter to mind. Was Miss Latham's death not only "sudden" but also deliberate?

What Violet's mind conjured was unthinkable, yet there it loomed like a graveyard monument. Could Mr. Crugg have had anything to do with Miss Latham's demise?

Susanna must have read her mind, for she said, "Mother, perhaps it is time to visit Scotland Yard. I also recommend that you not travel with Julian Crugg anymore."

Violet nodded. Was this the moment to confess what had happened with Mr. Vernon at his shop? She opened her mouth to tell Susanna, then stopped. Why worry the girl any further? Besides, she had no need to visit him again, as her suspicions once again rested entirely with Mr. Crugg.

It always seemed to come back around to that man, didn't it?

Violet's mind swirled the rest of the day, making her absent-minded and inattentive. She had come out of her own woolgathering long enough to ask Susanna not to mention her suspicions to Sam. Susanna agreed, but only on the condition that Violet go to Scotland Yard as soon as possible.

Her distraction led to several strange looks from Sam at the dinner table, but she managed to avoid any conversation about her day, and it wasn't long before he was snoring in bed with his hands interlocked on his chest as she sat at her dressing table, brushing her hair in long, calming strokes. When she eventually climbed into bed, she unclasped his hands. It was discomfiting to see her husband lying there like a corpse, even if his vitality was strongly signaled in the air lumbering out of his lungs like a train rolling through the Surrey countryside.

Violet lay back against her pillows, but sleep eluded her as she mentally twisted and turned around the events of Brookwood. Was there something criminal going on? Was the commonality Julian Crugg or Brookwood Cemetery itself? Or was it something else she simply didn't understand? She wished she knew whether Crugg was the undertaker for Miss Latham. More importantly, was he the undertaker for Roger Blount? Why, what if he had actually been accompanying Lord Blount's body to Brookwood without telling her? Had he laid claim to the coffin as they stood on the platform? Try as she might, she couldn't remember. Everything prior to Miss Latham's overwrought display was blurry in her mind.

If Crugg was accompanying Roger's body, he had certainly proved himself neglectful. And if he was accompanying Roger, that meant he was indeed the man's undertaker—and therefore it was also a possibility that Miss Latham's family had hired him for her funeral, as well.

The more she reflected on it, the more she thought that perhaps she had more to do to satisfy herself about the situation.

She needed to visit Crugg.

Violet rolled to one side to watch her husband sleeping. She knew he would disapprove of her taking matters into her own hands like this, especially with Miss Latham having died under perhaps peculiar circumstances. She didn't want to disappoint him. However, she had done well enough in solving a couple of crimes while he was off to Sweden and Wales to explore the possibilities of dynamite. This situation wasn't nearly so dangerous as those she had investigated on behalf of Queen Victoria.

Ignoring the voice whispering in the back of her mind that she was making excuses so that she could do as she wished and leave Sam in the dark, she rolled over to her other side, to avoid looking at his face. Although he slept on completely oblivious of her racing thoughts, facing away made her feel less guilty than if he could open his eyes and stare directly into her own eyes, and thus into her wildly speculating mind.

6

Violet stood outside Julian Crugg's shop with yesterday's news-paper in her hand. She was actually nervous about entering the man's premises. He would probably consider her visit an invasion, although he had not honored his own peace offering of a joint trip back from Brookwood together. Swallowing her apprehension, she turned the gleaming knob and entered the shop, accompanied by the jangle of bells that could have awakened any corpse.

The shop was silent except for a tapping noise floating from a back room that suggested someone was attaching memorial plates to coffins. Presently she was joined by a man in ill-fitting clothes with hair hanging low across his brow, with no pomade to keep it tamed back and out of his eyes.

"Birdwell Trumpington at your service, madam." He bowed graciously. Yes, Mr. Crugg called him "Bird," wasn't that what Susanna had said? Now that she was face-to-face with the undertaker's assistant, Violet took an instant dislike to him, although she couldn't identify why. There was nothing particularly the matter with him; perhaps it was just that he was Crugg's assistant that made him unpardonably objectionable.

"My name is Violet Harper, and I wish to see Mr. Crugg," she said.

He frowned, as if her name was familiar to him but he couldn't quite place it.

"The name of your loved one, madam?" he asked.

"I'm not here about a funeral but to discuss some business."
Did she sound official enough?

He bowed again. "Of course, madam," he said, and disappeared
into the back, where the tapping soon stopped and the indistinct
muttering of voices replaced it.

While waiting, Violet spent her time examining Crugg's shop.
As she had recalled from last time, the man's shop was filled with
the tricks and devices Violet loathed. Prominent in the center of
the shop was a sample bell coffin. How very interesting. She was
bent over, searching for a maker's plate on it, when the man himself appeared from a back room. "Mrs. Harper!" he barked.

Violet bobbed up and cleared her throat, knowing she was be-
having as if she were guilty of something. "Good morning, Mr.
Crugg. I came to talk to you about Miss Margery Latham."

Something flickered in Crugg's eyes. Was it fear? Uncertainty?
Guilt?

"And who might that be?" he asked, clasping his hands in front
of him in his best undertaker's pose of confidence.

"I think you know. She was the hysterical young woman on the
Brookwood South platform last week. The one in terrible, raging
grief." She handed him the newspaper, which she had folded open
to the obituary.

He glanced at it and licked his lips. "Right you are. Yes, I believe I do remember the lady in question. I encounter so many
mourners each week, you understand. . . ."

"I hardly think you could have forgotten Miss Latham, given
how you practically had to carry her into the station. What did she
tell you about Lord Blount?"

"Tell me? What should she have told me?"

Crugg was stalling, Violet was certain of it.

Trumpington emerged again from the rear. "Sir? I'm having dif-
ficulty with something, if I might have your assistance."

Crugg shot his assistant a look of gratitude as he excused himself.

"I'm happy to wait," she said.

Crugg handed the newspaper back to Violet and followed
Trumpington into the rear. The loud whispers ensued once again.

So his assistant was trying to save his employer from questions. How interesting. Violet was determined to remain until Crugg answered her questions, and returned to examining his shop's artifices while she waited. As she glanced around, she had to admit that Crugg maintained a properly organized and welcoming shop, even if it was laden with items Violet didn't like.

Crugg had several miniature coffins in his shop, arranged artfully on a freestanding case with individually slotted niches for them. Each coffin was about six inches wide and ten inches long. It saved space in a smaller shop not to have the floor littered with full-size specimens, and enabled the shop owner to carry examples with him when he visited a grieving family, rather than just showing pictures in a catalog.

Naturally, most of the samples were outfitted as miniature safety coffins.

She was holding one of the samples in her hand with the newspaper tucked securely under her arm when Crugg and his assistant finally reemerged. Crugg was openly disappointed to find Violet still there.

"Yes, Mrs. Harper, is there something else I can do for you?"

She put the coffin down on the counter and handed the paper back to him.

"This obituary states that Miss Latham died suddenly. I thought you might know how a perfectly healthy young woman died suddenly?"

"How would I know? I'm not her physician. You should talk to her family."

"I'm asking you because I suspect you knew Miss Latham. In fact, I suspect you were Roger Blount's undertaker, which is why she fell upon you at the station. Don't you find it interesting that these two young lovers died so closely together?"

There was that look of uneasiness flitting across Crugg's face again. Mr. Trumpington spoke up. "Are you now an official detective inspector, Mrs. Harper? No? Then what right do you have to question my employer?"

Trumpington's defense served to give Crugg more courage. "Inspector or not, I have nothing to hide. Surely you don't believe that every Londoner who dies comes under my care, Mrs. Harper? That every corpse shipped on the Necropolis Railway is mine?"

"No, but there have been some curious coincidences between your presence and the mysterious . . . condition . . . of bodies being sent to Brookwood."

Crugg laughed incredulously. "Need I remind you that you have been present for more of these strange sightings than I have? Using your logic, *you* should be the one to explain Miss Latham's death."

Crugg was turning the tables on her, manipulating her.

"That may be true, but I maintain an honest business, without resorting to trickery or shameful practices." She picked up the coffin once more and shook it at him before slamming it back on the counter.

"I give my customers whatever they desire," Crugg retorted. "It would seem that you moralize and preach and screech about what is legitimate in the eyes of the perfect and pure Violet Harper, who is the only undertaker in the queen's empire who has knowledge of such things. Besides, by your own admission, you yourself have witnessed the value of the safety coffin on two occasions."

Their short interlude of peace at Brookwood notwithstanding, Crugg's outrage was expert and biting. And constant. Violet tried another approach.

"Have you ever experienced anything odd with a corpse? Perhaps had one become . . . shall we say damaged? Or gone missing?"

"Only once. When you stole Lord Raybourn's body." Crugg said this smugly. Apparently that raw wound was not healing well.

"Perhaps your choleric temper causes your customers to abandon you," she shot back. "Typically there should only be one party wailing and moaning during a funeral."

"Your insinuation is insulting, Mrs. Harper. Shame on you."

"I hardly think I am the one to be shamed. I am convinced that you knew either Roger Blount or Margery Latham, if not both of them, and that I will learn of your connection to them if I dig down far enough."

"Careful, dear lady, that you don't dig yourself an early grave."

Was that a threat? If it wasn't, why did Violet feel a February chill run up her spine in the middle of August? If only she were better at interrogation than this. Instead, she always just managed to irritate and provoke. She would like to be as subtle as Detective Chief Inspector Hurst was blunt.

In evidence of her poor questioning, which had resulted in absolutely nothing of substance, Crugg offered an even nastier rejoinder as he pointed to the door. "Next time you have business with me, send your daughter in your stead. She is at least a little less odious."

Once more, the door's bells jangled loudly behind as she departed, as if berating her on behalf of Julian Crugg. She felt Crugg's and Trumpington's eyes on her until she was out of view of the shop.

Violet sighed in frustration. Well, that hadn't gone as planned. She wasn't sure, though, whether she considered Julian Crugg more or less guilty than before.

Violet and Mary stepped down from a cab in front of the temporary hippodrome erected to house the circus at the southeast end of Hyde Park, while Susanna and Benjamin emerged from one behind them. A gas-illuminated sign proclaimed that this was "Sanger's Hippodrome."

Knowing that Sam had plans for dinner with one of his bankers—Violet was losing track of their names—Susanna had suggested attending an evening circus performance. Violet enthusiastically embraced the idea and sent word to Mary about it.

The circus had entered London two weeks ago in an impressive parade that featured decorated and gilded coaches pulled by elephants and camels. The animals now made soft snorts and snuffles, cloaked behind brightly painted walls that reached at least thirty feet into the air.

Although Susanna had remained in her borrowed black dress from Violet after a day of working in the shop, Violet had actually shed her customary black and made a pleasant transformation into a bronze gown accented with a cream collar and matching lace cuffs that peeked out of flared sleeves. It seemed ironic that Violet was hiding her newfound elegance tonight in a darkened performance venue.

Mary was surprising in her charcoal-gray dress, a color she customarily wouldn't wear until her year and one day of mourning was over—if she didn't go into second or third periods of mourning, and Violet doubted she would—adorned with several strands of jet and a pearl brooch. It was amusing to see Mary exhibiting such rebellion. Although Violet loved mourning traditions, she wasn't too distressed that Mary was abbreviating her grieving period for George, who had proved himself most unworthy of the title of husband.

The area in front of the circus was bustling with patrons, performers in brightly colored stage garb, trinket sellers, food vendors, eight-year-old cutpurses, and a couple of garishly dressed prostitutes selling their own special wares. An itinerant preacher stood atop an overturned crate, exhorting passersby on the evils of gin.

As Violet waited for the circus's curtained doors to open, she saw a dirty, rumpled man in a tattered overcoat stumble toward the preacher and kneel down before him, as if receiving benediction. Other patrons in line also turned their attention to the drunkard bowed before the preacher, who curtailed his sermon, stepped down, and laid a hand on the man's shoulder.

But Violet and the others gasped as the man recoiled from the preacher, removed a bottle of clear liquid from somewhere inside his overcoat, unstoppered it, took a long pull . . . and proceeded to spew it from his mouth, spraying the preacher in the face with what was presumably the very liquid the reverend had just admonished against. They all held their collective breath to see what the preacher would do.

The man of the cloth never acknowledged that he had liquor dripping onto his clothing and matting his hair. Instead, he squeezed the other man's shoulder, then pulled a few coins from his pocket and handed them to him before stepping back onto the crate and asking everyone to pray for the poor soul before him.

Violet was greatly sobered by the preacher's reaction. Why couldn't she be so placid when faced with such unexpected vitriol?

She forgot the scene as they paid for admission and entered the cool, darkened hippodrome, with its extraordinarily tall ceiling that drew warm air from the ground and sent it out through several holes in the canvas roof. Various wires and trapezes dangled from the ceiling like old cobwebs. The circus ring, which was strewn with sand, bales of hay, cones painted with stars, and a curved stage at one end, was surrounded by tiered seating. They settled onto wood benches that had depressions marking where each rear end should be placed. Violet supposed the depressions were intended to prevent overcrowding on the seating, but they did nothing for comfort.

Violet estimated that the makeshift hippodrome held nearly a thousand people on five tiers of benches. The program listed tonight's activities, which included trick riding, jugglers, aerial acts, and comic pantomimes; with the performance to be concluded with something called "air walking." Whatever that was, Violet looked forward to it. The program promised that attendees who returned on Friday would be treated to an aquatic circus, with the ring flooded with water and horses executing dance steps with riders standing on their backs.

Violet leaned over to Susanna and pointed to the description of Friday's event. "Should we return?"

"Do you have the time?"

"I think so. There is certainly nothing notable with my supposed investigation. I imagine Sam would like to come along."

Susanna nodded and the show began. They gasped and aahed and oohed with the rest of the audience as clowns tossed balls in the air and caught them while running in between and around prancing horses. They cheered a reenactment of the Battle of Waterloo. They clapped over aerialists who gracefully released their trapeze bars and landed on the backs of elephants whose trunks were wrapped around children whom they swung backward and forward.

When a pair of comic tramps were caught stealing jewelry and ran away from comic policemen, the pair ended up stuck in a tree, while the police tripped over hay bales into a mud puddle. The audience all laughed uproariously until Violet was certain she would pop the buttons off her dress.

It was good to clear her mind of everything that had to do with Brookwood Cemetery.

The humor was nearly ruined by a woman sitting nearby who sniffed in disapproval and said, "This is ridiculous. I've been to

America, you know, and Mr. Barnum's museum is vastly superior. He has Siamese twins, a giantess, and even Commodore Nutt—a perfectly miniature man. Such freaks and eccentricities to entertain the mind. This is all so, so"—she wrinkled the nose that was already sweeping the air—"so common," she finished with a satisfied nod.

Violet and Susanna exchanged glances and rolled their eyes heavenward. They had lived in America, and everyone in America knew about Phineas T. Barnum and his famous museum of oddities.

The final act was the air walking, and it stunned even the snobby woman into complete silence. A man with rubber suction pads attached to his feet walked up and down the makeshift walls of the hippodrome over the heads of the audience, who squealed in delight. At the conclusion of the show, the owner, Mr. Sanger, came out wearing a shiny top hat and diamond tiepin and was hugely applauded. "Friends, friends," he cried out, waving his hands, "I trust you have enjoyed this evening. As an expression of your appreciation for the artists and performers, would you consider dropping a token of gratitude into one of the hats being passed around?"

A trio of dwarves in lemon-yellow outfits appeared from nowhere wearing hats that matched Mr. Sanger's and spread out through the audience, teasing and cajoling them into parting with more money, which they willingly did.

When they exited the hippodrome, darkness had completely settled over the city. A half-moon hovered over the cloudless nighttime sky. It joined the few street lamps, along with the lamps dangling from the string of cabs waiting to pick up circus patrons, to illuminate the area. As patrons threaded their way to the cabs, Susanna held back, wanting to visit the trinket seller for souvenirs to take home to Colorado. They all gathered around as Susanna dawdled over circus postcards and picture books of London. Once Benjamin finally made her purchases for her, they turned to hail a cab but, to their dismay, discovered that they had all departed with other circus passengers. Now they were the only people left in front of the hippodrome, except for the trinkets man and a few circus workers who were closing up the venue.

"Shall we wait?" Mary suggested. "Surely there will be another cab along soon."

"I have a better idea," Benjamin said. "Why don't we walk back along the Serpentine? Mrs. Cooke, we can drop you in Bayswater Road and continue on to Queen's Road. A walk through the park to Paddington will be invigorating."

Violet put a hand to her waistline. She could certainly use the exercise. "Yes, let's."

Benjamin was right. The night was warm but not stifling, and there was enough moonlight that they could make their way on the pathway north to the top of the park. The Serpentine lake was to their left, and the moon's glow off the still surface was both spectral and eerie.

Gravel crunched beneath their collective boots and shoes, and soon Benjamin was whistling a catchy ditty he'd learned during the farce of the two tramps, as the male tramp wooed the female into their life of crime. Laughing, Susanna joined him by stomping hard on the gravel as she walked to create a beat, then singing to his whistling.

Come into the garden, Maud,
For the black bat, night, has flown,
Come into the garden, Maud,
I am here at the gate alone.

Violet and Mary joined in with both the stomping and the singing. Violet imagined they sounded like a clowder of howling, tortured cats, but it was fun nonetheless, acting silly in the park with no one else around to hear them.

Violet heard scuffling from nearby. She paused, holding out an arm in the dark to stop Mary, too. Were Susanna and Benjamin behind or in front of them? The scuffling resumed.

"Benjamin," Mary called out, "have you now added dancing to your list of talents?"

"What do you mean?" His voice came from up ahead on the trail.

Mary cupped her hands around her mouth and called forward.

"You whistle, you sing. Now it sounds as if you are waltzing or perhaps doing the tarantella. It's so difficult to know in the dark. May I have a spot on your dance card?" She actually giggled. How good it was to hear Mary enjoying herself, taking pleasure in—

Wait. Something was wrong. "Susanna?" Violet said tentatively. There was no answer, and Benjamin's steps against the gravel also ceased.

"Susanna?" Benjamin repeated after Violet. "Dearest?"

Silence. Dread crept over Violet's shoulders, replacing the gaiety that had been there just moments before. She shook it off. "Susanna, darling? Enough with your hiding. We need to get Mary home."

Violet knew, though, that Susanna was not one to play silly tricks. She tried to keep her voice even and steady and said, "I think we may have lost Susanna along the way."

That wasn't what she thought at all, but it disguised her growing panic.

More crunching, and Benjamin was looming next to her. Even in the dark, Violet saw panic and worry in his eyes. He probably saw it mirrored in her own eyes.

"Why would Susanna hide from us?" Mary asked, completely oblivious to what was silently transpiring between Susanna's mother and husband.

"Benjamin," Violet said quietly, "why don't you return to the circus and see if you can borrow a lamp? Mary and I will stay right here."

"Yes, Mother Harper." He ran off in the direction of the gaslit hippodrome sign. Violet felt a hundred years old when he called her Mother Harper, but right now she felt as though she might be two hundred. How in the world had Susanna simply disappeared?

She and Mary held hands tightly as they waited for Benjamin's return. Within a few minutes, they saw him outlined in the steady flame of his lamp.

"I think you should take Mary home and I'll look for Susanna," he suggested. Violet heard the grimness in his voice.

"Absolutely not," Violet said. "I'm not going anywhere without our girl."

With Benjamin holding the lamp high overhead, they stumbled on and off the pathway looking for Susanna, like a trio of gin drinkers desperately searching for a bottle. Violet despaired of ever finding the girl and was on the verge of suggesting that they stop their search and instead go to a police station for help. Suddenly, Benjamin made a strangled noise and rushed forward into a wooded copse between the path and the lake.

He threw himself on top of a prone figure. Still holding hands, Violet and Mary followed, but Violet shook Mary off to kneel down next to Benjamin, and her worst suspicions were confirmed.

It was Susanna.

Benjamin was mumbling uncontrollably. "My love, my dearest, oh, my sweet." He rose and pulled her into his arms, her head against his chest, as he finally broke into a sob over her.

Violet picked up the lamp that her son-in-law had hastily dropped to the ground. She held it high and beheld the gruesome tableau before her. Her heart nearly stopped beating when she saw that Benjamin was covered in Susanna's blood, which openly streamed from a wound on the side of her head.

Her beautiful daughter's hair was clumped in a dark, bloody mass, and she lay limp and lifeless in the tight clutch of her husband, whose grief Violet wanted to join, though she was in too much shock to do so.

Benjamin turned to Violet, a look of utter self-contempt spreading quickly over his face. "We should have gone back to Colorado weeks ago. I should have never agreed to remain longer, but she wanted to stay. Why did I listen?"

Violet was hardly paying attention to him, so caught up was she in the sight of Susanna. She was vaguely aware of Mary standing behind her. Clouds passed before the moon, casting the area not directly illuminated by the lamp into utter darkness. A bat flitted overhead, squeaking and flapping.

For the first time in her life, Violet was so overcome by shock that she was completely unable to form a word of distress, much less a coherent sentence of comfort for her son-in-law. Mary laid a hand on her shoulder and murmured, "My dear friend, how terrible."

Mary's simple act of comfort nearly caused Violet to drop the lamp. She put it down carefully and took a deep breath, ready to release it in a flood of tears, when she noticed something. Had Susanna just moved? It was so hard to tell with Benjamin rocking her back and forth. Perhaps it was just a postmortem reflex.

"Stop!" she commanded him. He did so instantly, looking at Violet in confusion.

Violet held out her arms, and Benjamin handed Susanna over, like a parent handing over an infant. Violet had no thought for her own dress as she cradled Susanna's shoulders and crimson-spattered head in one arm. She carefully examined Susanna with her other hand, trying to pretend Susanna was simply an unknown body she was inspecting prior to preparation for burial. It was nearly impossible to maintain composure with Benjamin gasping for air next to her.

She pressed a hand to Susanna's cheek. Still warm, of course. Next she held a finger over the girl's lip, as though making a mustache. Could it be . . . ? Violet thought she detected the faintest flow of air from her nostrils. Perhaps it was just the night breeze.

Steeling herself for whatever vacant look she would find, Violet used her thumb to gently raise an eyelid. Susanna's eye rolled backward. Violet couldn't help it—she laughed. If Susanna were dead, her eyes would be glassy and unmoving. Releasing the lid, Violet bent her head down and whispered into Susanna's ear, "Dear girl, can you hear me? It's your mother. Susanna? Susanna?"

Susanna's eyes fluttered briefly, and she moaned. Benjamin uttered a cross between a yelp and a squawk. Violet wasn't about to return her to him yet, lest he start fussing again and upset Susanna. Instead, she continued cooing and whispering in Susanna's ear. Within a couple of minutes, Susanna's eyes were fluttering open while Benjamin stared in disbelief and Mary's jet beads clacked together inside their owner's nervous hands.

Finally, Susanna's blue eyes fully opened and she looked directly at Violet. She spoke distinctly and with an unruffled calmness. "Mother, I could use a cup of Earl Grey."

Violet kissed Susanna's forehead, which was caked with sticky blood. "Of course, anything you want. We'll get you to the hospital."

With great effort, Susanna shook her head. "No, I wish to go home, please."

"Dearest," Benjamin began to cajole, "you need to be seen by a phys—"

"No," she said again, more firmly. "I refuse to be poked and frowned at by some lump of a man with nothing but foul breath and a jar full of leeches. I'm fine, I promise."

Violet looked at her daughter's lacerated head, which at least was no longer bleeding, and had her doubts about the idea that she was "fine," but the firm set of her lips told Violet there would be no arguing. Benjamin looked ready to jump to the moon if that was what Susanna demanded.

With Susanna once again ensconced in Benjamin's arms and Violet leading the way with the lamp, they made their way home with a quick detour to see Mary to her home in Bayswater Road.

Back at their flat above Morgan Undertaking, Sam opened the door in horror at the bloodied, rumpled trio before him. Before he could ask the first question, Violet swept in, extinguished her lamp, and curtly issued instructions to Benjamin for placing Susanna in the tub and finding her nightgown and wrapper. Violet went to work at getting Susanna out of her blood-encrusted clothing and washing her. Ruth would have to take the dress somewhere to be burned.

Once Susanna was finally cleansed of all traces of her attack, except for a lingering bruised and purpled eye, they made room for themselves in the parlor, scooping up clothes and other belongings from chairs and settees and piling them on the floor so they could sit down. Mrs. Softpaws kept a safe distance on top of the display cabinet, grooming and licking herself and pretending not to be interested in the proceedings going on below her.

Benjamin and Sam sat in chairs across from the women on the settee. Benjamin wrung his hands and gazed at Susanna as though her staying alive was predicated on his keeping her in his sight. Sam, though, was like a tightly wound tiger, leaning forward and back and perpetually shifting in his seat as though looking for the right moment to leap. The perpetrator was fortunate he wasn't here at the moment, Violet thought, lest Sam tear him apart with his bare hands.

Violet sat next to Susanna and, with her daughter's camel-hair brush, began brushing Susanna's damp hair as the girl told them what had happened. Unfortunately, there wasn't much to be told.

"I was just marching along with all of you when I felt someone grab my arm. I thought it was Benjamin, simply cutting capers with me, so I let the man guide me off the path."

Sam interrupted her. "You know it was a man?"

"Certainly it was not the grip of a woman." Susanna rolled up the lace-edged sleeve of her wrapper, displaying bruised oval depression marks on her arm.

"That's why you didn't cry out," Violet said, making another long stroke through Susanna's hair. Susanna winced visibly, and Violet immediately withdrew the brush. "I'm sorry, dear. I got too close, didn't I?"

She had tied a bandage over Susanna's wound, which had bled much more than the actual gash suggested it should have. The location of it on her temple so close to her left eye was probably what had resulted in the bruised eye.

Violet resumed brushing, more gently this time and avoiding any area near the bandage.

"As the man's grip on me tightened, I realized it wasn't Benjamin, but before I could open my mouth to shout, I felt—Well, I felt nothing. I was just suddenly tumbling to the ground, and then there was nothing until I woke up to your whispering, Mother. Those mystery novelists all write that the victims who are coshed in the head see stars, or their lives flash before them, but that's not true. There's just a swift nothingness."

"We must go to the police first thing tomorrow," Sam said.

Susanna protested again. "Father, really, I'm fine. Besides, what can they possibly do? Put an advertisement in the newspaper asking all head coshers to put themselves up for inspection?"

Sam wasn't having any of Susanna's lightness. "I'll not have thugs pouncing upon my daughter. At first light we go to the police. Maybe there is a street gang working the area."

"In Hyde Park?" Violet asked incredulously. "I can hardly believe that. Next you'll tell me there are opium sellers waiting for the queen on the lawn of Buckingham Palace."

Sam was insistent, though. "Only a member of a bunch of ruffians would be bold enough to snatch a woman from her husband. Predators. The worst sort of filth."

Violet had a thought. "Did he take your reticule?" she asked.

Susanna looked at Benjamin. "I don't know."

Benjamin shook his head. "No, I carried it back along with you. It's . . . What did I do with it?" He rose and searched around, eventually pulling it from beneath a stack of newspapers that had been tossed down to the floor.

Benjamin handed it to Susanna, who untied the strings and went through it. "Everything is here. Either he looked through it and didn't find anything interesting, or he wasn't a thief."

"But why would someone cosh you in the head and not steal your valuables?" Violet said. "It doesn't make sense."

"I think there is a deeper question," Sam said. "Did he bash her in the head to rob her, to warn her, or to kill her?"

Violet considered this. "To warn her away from what? And to actually *kill* her? For what reason?"

Benjamin started in again on his lament. "We shouldn't have stayed this long. Everything is much more peaceable in Colorado. I should have insisted that we return sooner. I don't—"

Susanna stiffened under Violet's touch. "Quite the contrary, it is vital that we remain, Benjamin. We can investigate for ourselves what happened."

"I don't understand. You don't want the police involved, but you want to—what—prowl through dark alleys, asking who the local bludgeoners are?"

"Do you think I'm not capable?" she asked, the tone of her voice suggesting that unyielding resolve was settling in.

Violet hid a smile of admiration for her daughter's backbone, which appeared to have been stiffened, not wilted, by her experience.

"Capability has nothing to do with it. You're just a tourist here, honeymooning with your new husband. It's time to return home, back to your safe and contented life there."

Susanna set her lips in a thin line. "Of course," she replied, and said nothing further on the matter. Violet suspected Benjamin would rue his words, and Sam must have thought so, as well, for he said, "Careful, my son, on tangling with an undertaker. You aren't as experienced with it as I am."

He turned and leaned toward Violet. "Wife, listen to me. You are not a detective. Our girl is not a detective. A criminal has attacked her for reasons we don't understand, and we are going to the police at dawn's light if Benjamin and I have to throw you over our shoulders and haul you there like fussing babies. Is that clear?"

"Hmm," she replied. She hadn't realized Sam would choose to leap on *her*.

"Violet . . ." he warned.

"Very well. I have no objection to reporting it to the authorities, it's only proper. But we'll go to see Inspector Hurst, not the local police."

"That's the detective who helped you on your other cases, isn't he, Mother?" Susanna was already springing back to life.

"I wouldn't exactly say they were 'cases,' Susanna. It was more like I stumbled into a few unfortunate situations and was able to provide Scotland Yard with some assistance."

"Assistance!" Sam cried. "I can't even count how many times you've nearly been killed. Violet, you make undertaking the most deadly profession in the world."

Susanna laughed at her father's overblown pronouncement, but Benjamin shook his head. "Far beyond time to go back to America," he muttered.

Violet made a few final brushstrokes through Susanna's hair, then gathered the hair up and began braiding it while she contemplated the evening's crime.

If it wasn't a random attack, who would have wanted to injure a sweet girl like Susanna? An image of Julian Crugg flashed through her mind. Hadn't he just mentioned Susanna yesterday during Violet's meeting with him? But why would he feel the need to attack the girl? Other than pay him a visit, she hadn't done anything to him. In fact, Crugg had even suggested—sarcastic though he may have been—that Violet send Susanna in her stead next time. And how would he even know they would be at the circus this evening?

Who else could possibly wish the girl harm? Hardly anyone in London knew her given that she'd been living in Colorado the past four years. Unless it was one of the other undertakers Susanna had visited on Violet's behalf. Perhaps one that they weren't even considering.

The only thing Violet knew for certain was that there would be no return trip to the circus on Friday.

7

The next morning, the four of them crowded into Detective Chief Inspector Hurst's cramped office, while Second Class Inspector Langley Pratt took his usual position with his pencil and notepad.

Susanna looked much better today, despite her eye, which was still very swollen and discolored. Benjamin sat slumped with his arms and ankles crossed. The young couple's heated voices had floated into Violet's bedchamber last night, and it seemed to Violet that Benjamin was still suffering the ill effects of it.

Susanna, however, appeared invigorated by whatever had transpired. Perhaps they really did need to return to Colorado. Violet hated the thought of strife growing between them because of their honeymoon trip. Should she talk to Susanna about it?

"Now, Mrs. Harper, what seems to be the problem this time?" This was Inspector Hurst's way of conveying grudging respect to Violet. She knew she was a constant source of aggravation to him, but she had rescued his own investigations more than once and he couldn't quite bring himself to dismiss her anymore. At least, not completely.

Especially now that he had met the lovely and fragile Mary Cooke. Magnus Pompey Hurst resembled a snorting bull and looked like he swallowed criminals during afternoon tea, but he was a soft, gelatinous mess whenever he was around Mary. Violet had shooed him away from her friend—who was officially in mourning, for heaven's sake—but she suspected she hadn't seen the last of Hurst's mooning eyes.

Sam was no less restless and impatient than he'd been the previous evening, despite a night's worth of sleep, and he jumped right in. "Inspector, I am completely outraged by what occurred last night. My daughter was nearly killed! Do you realize I am a lawyer? As is my son-in-law here. We will seek all remedies possible in the English courts—"

Hurst held up a hand. "Mr. Harper, I'm not following your story. Perhaps if Mrs. Harper would care to . . . ?"

Violet began her explanation of what had happened the previous evening, telling him of their visit to the Sanger circus performance and their subsequently noisy—and treacherous—walk through Hyde Park.

Sam interrupted. "Violet, remember to tell the detectives that you thought she was dead. That she'd been struck so hard it was difficult to revive her. Someone tried to extinguish our girl."

"Yes, as my husband says, Susanna appeared to be dead."

Hurst turned to Susanna. "Mrs. Tompkins, you didn't see who grabbed you?"

Susanna shook her head. "It was past ten o'clock and quite dark."

"Did the assailant say anything to you? Give you a reason for his attack?"

"No. It all happened so quickly."

"And it was just the three of you?"

"No, my mother's friend Mary Cooke was with us."

A sappy smile spread across Hurst's face, as though he'd lumbered into an unexpected hive of honey. "Is that so? Is Mrs. Cooke socializing now? I thought you said she would be in mourning for quite some time, Mrs. Harper."

Violet's protective instincts for Mary controlled her next words. "Yes, she is. She went out for just an evening at my urging. Otherwise, she is mostly still in seclusion."

"Quite understandable." Hurst nodded. "She enjoyed the circus, did she?"

"Yes," Violet said cautiously.

He nodded again. "Splendid. A fine lady like that deserves a bit of happiness. I hear that the Theatre Royal is bringing back Joseph Lunn's *Family Jars* farce this December. I'm sure Mrs. Cooke would enjoy an outing to see it, don't you, Mrs. Harper?"

That was four months away. Perhaps he would have forgotten his crush on Mary by then. Of course, she wasn't being fair to Mary. Perhaps her friend might welcome Inspector Hurst's attentions. But . . . Violet shook her head. The thought was too much to stomach. Mary being courted by Magnus Pompey Hurst? However, his attitude toward Violet might have no bearing at all on his demeanor as a suitor or a husband.

A husband! Mary's husband? No, Violet had to quell the very notion right now.

"Perhaps she would. It's so hard to know, what with her grieving still being so fresh."

Hurst, for all of his quirks, was astute, and took her point immediately. "Of course. You'll pass along my salutations, won't you?"

"I will." Actually, it might be interesting to see Mary's reaction.

The room had quickly grown stuffy with six people wedged into it. Hurst either didn't notice it or was used to it, for he casually put his elbows on his desk and templed his meaty fingers together. "So what we have here is possibly a random attack on a young woman by some tramp or gin addict or cutpurse. Perhaps he was even confused and thought Mrs. Tompkins was a prostitute. Begging your pardon, of course, madam. This is probably not a case for Scotland Yard since there has been no unusual murder or other crime committed. I presume Mrs. Tompkins has no known enemies here in London, given that she has only been a tourist here for several weeks?"

"I believe there is more you need to know, Inspector," Violet said. "I have experienced some curious episodes while transporting bodies to Brookwood Cemetery in Surrey. Strange as it may seem, on two occasions I have witnessed supposedly dead bodies rise up out of their coffins at the train station."

Pratt stopped scratching notes as his eyes widened. "Truly, Mrs. Harper? I've read magazine stories about people getting buried alive, and now here you have witnessed them in the flesh. So to speak, of course. May I ask what you—"

"Let the woman tell her story, Pratt," Hurst said impatiently. "Don't interrupt with silly flapdoodles."

Poor Inspector Pratt. He was eager, if awkward and unpolished. He had always been kind to Violet, and always on the receiving end of Hurst's irritability.

Violet continued. "I wasn't able to talk to either of the two men who rose from their coffins, but it seemed to me that their undertakers had performed extraordinarily sloppy work. Both of them had been placed in safety coffins, and I was able to get a reasonable list of London undertakers who purchase the particular type of coffins they were in. I'm afraid that a couple of these undertakers I visited, Augustus Upton and James Vernon, did not, shall we say, prove to be particularly helpful."

Hurst separated his hands and held them palms up. They shone with sweat. "And you believe these episodes are related to last night?"

"Possibly. Susanna interviewed several of the undertakers on my behalf since she does undertaking work herself back in Colorado, and—"

Sam interrupted once more. "I didn't take stock in what Violet told me about some of these undertakers, but now I'm not so sure. There was the one—Croog? Crum?—that my wife suspected. Have her tell you about him." He rose, his eagle-headed cane in hand, and began pacing, not an easy feat inside Hurst's small office.

Violet drummed the gloved fingers of one hand against the palm of the other, wishing desperately she could shed the gloves. What had gotten into Sam? Why was he so talkative? So relentlessly agitated? Like Mrs. Softpaws with an empty food dish. This was so unlike him. He had seen his share of battle and death and terror, and very little rattled him. Of course, this was Susanna they were discussing. Violet understood his feelings and shared them, but really, if only her husband would sit down and be calm, they might get somewhere.

"Who is Mr. Croog?" Hurst asked.

"Crugg," Violet said. "He's an undertaker who deals in safety coffins. He is not fond of me, as he is of the opinion that I stole away Lord Raybourn's funeral."

Hurst nodded. They had worked together on the case of Lord Raybourn's stolen body. "I recall him. Thin and ill-tempered."

"Yes. I—Susanna and I, actually—have our suspicions of him, that he might be mistakenly putting bodies that are not dead into coffins, and was responsible for the two I discovered."

"Do you have proof of this?"

"No." Violet shifted uncomfortably in her seat. It seemed so foolish when she talked to anyone but Susanna about it. She glanced over; Susanna continued looking rejuvenated, while Benjamin was wilting with each passing minute.

"No, I have no proof. And, as my husband has said, what crime has been committed when a dead body comes to life? I can only—"

Sam stopped pacing long enough to interrupt Violet's train of thought again. "And there was the third body, the dead one. Remember to tell the inspector about that."

Violet sighed. Didn't Sam realize she was used to dealing with Inspectors Hurst and Pratt? "Yes, there was a third, separate incident in which I discovered a dead body in a coffin arriving at Brookwood."

Hurst laughed and stared at her incredulously. "Are you telling me you found it suspicious that a corpse was shipped on the London Necropolis Railway, and indeed arrived in a dead condition?"

"Sir, that is my wife you are addressing," Sam growled.

"Sam, please," she said. "We are all distressed by what happened."

Sam snorted and resumed his caged pacing.

Violet resumed her story. "As I was saying, this particular corpse was indeed dead, but his fiancée was waiting for him on the platform and seemed positively surprised that he was dead. She was nearly beside herself, and Mr. Crugg had to comfort her."

Hurst refrained from laughing this time, as Sam was still on edge, but his voice was still full of disbelief. "So are you reporting to me that a young woman met a *funeral* train and was surprised to find an actual *corpse* in a *coffin?*"

"Yes, Inspector, that's what I'm saying. It's as though she actually expected him to walk off the train, not be carried out in a box."

Hurst sighed. "Mr. Pratt, make a note to investigate who this corpse was."

"I already know that," Violet said. "It was Roger Blount, second son to Francis Blount, the Earl of Etchingham."

Pratt's pencil scratched heavily across the page.

"And you said this Crum person—"

"Crugg."

"Crugg was the undertaker?"

"I'm not sure." Violet explained what had happened with Margery Latham on the platform. "Crugg didn't seem to know her, but maybe he did. Even stranger is that we discovered Miss Latham's obituary in the newspaper, which reported only that she died suddenly, just like Lord Blount."

"And you suspect foul play for both of them?"

Violet bit her lip. "Well, no, I'm not sure I have reason to believe so."

Hurst threw up his hands, leaned back in his chair, and rolled his head in exasperation. "Mr. Pratt, can you read back exactly what we have here?"

As Mr. Pratt read from his notes, Violet realized she'd left out the part where Mr. Vernon had shoved her into a coffin and then acted as if he had no recollection of it. She glanced up at Sam, who now stood in a corner, tapping his cane on the ground. Perhaps it was best to continue keeping that to herself for now.

Sam finally sat down once more, but he was far from finished spewing his wrath. "I must say, Inspector Hurst, I find it appalling that you have such contemptible critters running about, attacking young women at will. I mean, what are your men doing?"

Hurst raised an eyebrow. "Sir, do you know what you're gumming about? You are aware that this is London, the largest city in the world that I'm aware of at three million souls? Not some upstart little town in the American West?"

Sam didn't hear a word Hurst said; he kept pressing on. "My wife suspects this Mr. Crugg of something. Why don't you arrest and interrogate him? See what he knows about my daughter's attack. Even if he didn't do it personally, he may have hired some thug to do the deed for him."

"Mr. Harper, this is not ancient Rome, where we go to the forum and stab whoever we think is our enemy. I must have some sort of reason to arrest him. I cannot see a possible motive. Quite frankly, if I were to point to any possible crime being conducted here—beyond the very obvious one of your daughter's attack, for which we have no suspect—I would look to this Vernon fellow, since we can at least discover whether or not he is doing things properly. Although even if he isn't, he still isn't breaking any laws. You understand, I am entertaining this only on behalf of my high regard for your wife."

Violet smiled and wiped her brow. Her gloved finger came away wet. High regard for her, indeed.

"I agree with my father-in-law," Benjamin said, speaking up for the first time. "I met Crugg, and I thought his demeanor toward my wife was coarse and loutish. I nearly had the man on the floor, I tell you."

"Unfortunately, Mr. Tompkins, we also cannot arrest men for insulting our wives. That is best handled by you in a manner we need know nothing about. However, I'll make you a promise, Mr. Harper. Inspector Pratt and I will visit Mr. Vernon this very day and see what we can find. We'll also talk to our informants to see if any gangs have been working in Hyde Park. Will that satisfy you?"

Sam nodded curtly.

They finally escaped into the open air, which was hot but not nearly as stifling as Hurst's office. Sam's mood lightened considerably, although Violet wasn't sure if that was because Hurst had promised to take some sort of action or because he was able to breathe again. Susanna and Benjamin, too, looked relieved.

Violet, though, was more disturbed than ever. She doubted that Hurst and Pratt would try that hard to do anything. After all, relaying her thoughts to the two inspectors had made her suspicions about her fellow undertakers seem absurd. And an investigation into local thugs wasn't likely to turn up anything, either.

All this visit had done was to arouse Hurst's interest in Mary again.

By the time they reached home, Violet had decided upon two things. First, that she would follow through and visit Hurst again tomorrow to see what, if anything, he'd learned. Second, any further probing on what was probably a wild-goose chase would have to be done by her without Susanna's assistance.

In the meantime, her primary concerns were to keep her husband calm, her daughter safe, and Inspector Hurst at bay.

8

Some visits to customer homes were more difficult than others. Today's was simply revolting. Violet cringed as she set down the bone china teacup into its saucer. Rowena Westbrook, daughter of the newly deceased Charles Westbrook, was proving to be quite a bitter pill.

"Mama," the overly primped young woman in black silk said to the serene matron seated across from Violet in what was obviously a lesser parlor in their home, "isn't that too much expense for his funeral? After all, he will just end up in the crypt. It seems such a waste."

Children, even adult children, were frequently the most broken up over a parent's demise. Not in the case of Miss Westbrook, who eyed the undertaker's book in Violet's lap as though it were a dead rat. It was opened to the Society section; perhaps the girl thought Violet should have flipped one more section over, to Titled, but that was beyond their station, no matter how much Mr. Westbrook may have made from his cotton mills.

"After all, we have my birthday party next month to think of, and the holiday in Paris. Surely we will still go? Please, Mama? It is my first trip to the Continent."

"Well," Rowena's mother said hesitantly, "the trip was planned for mid-October. . . ."

That was merely two months away! An indecent mourning period by any standard. Even Mary, whose husband had been loathsome, wasn't this callous. Violet had to step in. "Madam, if I may, the timing of such a trip might be viewed poorly by your neighbors and friends. Perhaps in the spring?" Even that was still obscenely early.

"Yes, I'm sure you're quite right, Mrs. Harper. We don't want the neighbors' tongues wagging, do we, Rowena dear?"

Rowena put her lip out in a spoiled way Violet had seen many times before. "Can't we just tell them that we are going to France to mourn out of the public eye? That we're going into seclusion in a little seaside villa in Saint-Tropez?"

"I suppose that might work." To Violet's horror, Mrs. Westbrook was visibly working out the idea in her head.

"Madam, would you not be more comfortable mourning here, surrounded by your friends and family, instead of alone in a far-off land?" Violet prompted.

Mrs. Westbrook opened her mouth to speak, but Rowena interrupted. "Here? It's so boring here. Besides, I'm sure Papa would have wanted us to be happy, right, Mama?"

"Of course, of course."

Rowena smiled with greater satisfaction than Mrs. Softpaws after triumphing over a cornered rat. "It makes sense then, doesn't it, that we shouldn't spend so much for Papa's funeral, because he would have wanted us to pay for new dresses, and opera boxes, and cathedral tours."

"Yes, you're right, my dear," replied her mother, with an air of distraction. She turned back to Violet. "Have you something less pretentious?"

These two were nothing like the red-eyed butler who had solemnly answered the door, or the sniffling maid who had brought in tea. Even the household cook must have been in mourning, for their lemon cakes had black-sugared crosses atop the white icing.

It was never a good sign when the servants were in deeper mourning than the relations. Violet presumed that Mr. Westbrook was probably kind and generous to a fault with anyone he met. His servants obviously loved him for it, whereas his wife and daughter despised what they perceived as weakness in the man.

Violet loathed funerals such as this. Her first husband, Graham, who had taught her the undertaking business, had once told her these were the best funerals, for there was very little comforting to do since the undertaker was responsible only to the family, not the servants. Violet, however, did not see it this way. What kind of earthly departure was the deceased receiving when the relatives were too bored with the proceedings to agonize over what clothing to bury their loved one in, to worry over whether there were enough lilies surrounding the coffin? Would Mrs. Westbrook and the spoiled Rowena slave tirelessly over a hair bracelet so that it would be ready in time to wear for the funeral?

Did they not consider what their loved one must think if he were looking down upon them?

Violet shoved the thought from her mind and flipped back to the Tradesman section of her book. Most people sought to move ahead inside her undertaker's book, not go backward. "Of course, madam."

For the next half hour, she helped Mrs. Westbrook, with plenty of commentary from her daughter, plan a funeral for her husband that was insulting and ill-suited to Mr. Westbrook's station. Violet left with her temper barely intact. She worked off her irritation as she walked to Scotland Yard to see Inspector Hurst.

Her temper wasn't much improved after seeing the detective.

"Yes, we visited James Vernon's shop. Not very impressive, is it? Hard to believe he has as much business as he says he does," Hurst said, looking to Pratt for confirmation.

Pratt nodded. "Not nearly as well equipped as yours, Mrs. Harper."

Violet already knew the condition of Vernon's shop. "Did you learn anything?"

Hurst shrugged. "Except that he might be a shoddy undertaker, which isn't illegal, I don't see that he knows anything about the bodies that have you upset. I think you've got your dander up about nothing."

Wasn't that what Sam had said? Still, she knew something was amiss in the situation; she just didn't know what.

"That's all?" she pressed.

She noticed that Pratt shifted uncomfortably. Were they holding something back?

"Nothing of importance," Hurst said. "I hope you've passed on my felicitations to Mrs. Cooke."

Violet gritted her teeth. "I haven't seen her yet, Inspector. It has, you understand, been barely twenty-four hours since I was last here."

"Yes, of course. Right you are."

Between her visit with the Westbrooks and Inspector Hurst, Violet's day was proving most unsatisfactory.

Violet spent most of the next day in a manner most unusual for her, but it was a good distraction. While Harry handled moving the counters and display items out of the way while the men from Morris, Marshall, and Faulkner worked, Violet supervised them as they cut, glued, and smoothed new wallpaper on the walls of the shop. She hadn't realized before how uneven the walls of the building were, which she estimated dated back at least to the turn of the century.

Nevertheless, the men deftly matched up the pattern on all of the walls, except for in a small area above the entry door.

The glue was pungent and used in great quantity, leaving Violet with a headache that evening that not even a cup of clover-root tea could banish. At Susanna's insistence, she lay back on a settee in the parlor while Benjamin read articles to her from the stack of old newspapers Violet kept on hand next to the fireplace for turning into spills. Ruth regularly made up a dozen or so of the twisted pieces of paper and kept them stored in a ceramic jar on the mantel. The jar was nearly hidden among all of Susanna's things, but poor Ruth managed to find it and keep it filled so that spills were always available for starting fires.

Susanna looked much better after a couple of days of rest. She no longer wore a bandage, and her hair didn't quite cover the scabbing wound, but she was alert and smiling. Benjamin, too, looked much happier. The two of them must have made up from whatever argument they'd had. Hopefully there would be no further squabbles.

Sam returned home while Benjamin was in the middle of a story about an upcoming event, the first international boat race on the Thames. After inquiring as to everyone's health, he kissed Violet and sat in a nearby chair. Benjamin continued with his reading, but Sam's mind was obviously elsewhere, perhaps as far away as the moon.

Violet asked if he would like to talk about his day's visit with bankers, but he merely shook his head and waved Benjamin on to continue.

Their son-in-law stumbled across the news that on August fifteenth, the Red Sea had joined the Mediterranean under Ferdinand de Lesseps's plan to build the Suez Canal through Egypt. If the two bodies of water were now flowing to each other, Violet assumed things were presumably on schedule for completion in November.

Benjamin turned the page and, knowing his wife's and mother-in-law's interests, began reading from the obituaries. He scanned the usual listings of childbirth deaths, those expiring of diseases in the lungs, and those who had died suddenly in accidents.

A special section was set aside to list workhouse and factory deaths, those deaths relegated to London's poorest. On the next page—the editors taking care that they not be adjacent—were obituaries for the upper class, complete with engravings of the deceased and lengthy platitudes about their ancestry, clubs, and heirs.

With her eyes closed, Violet only half listened, as though Benjamin were reading a bedtime story to lull her to sleep.

Until he uttered Roger Blount's name.

"What?" she said, sitting straight up. "Who is that again?"

Benjamin backed up and started again. " 'Lord and Lady Etchingham deeply regret to announce the sudden death of their son, the Honorable Roger Blount, which occurred August sixteenth at Etchingham House in Mayfair. He was seized with a fit shortly after dinner, between six and seven o'clock, and was taken by the angels before a physician could arrive. Lord Blount was engaged to the lovely debutante Miss Margery Latham, daughter of the Baron and Baroness Fenton. Miss Latham was presented to the queen last Season, and the grand society wedding between her and Lord Blount was to have occurred in September.' "

Violet frowned. "May I see?"

Benjamin handed the paper over. Indeed, the engraving was of the dead man Miss Latham had been in shock over.

This made no sense. Roger Blount had died at home, so surely Miss Latham had been aware of it. Why was she so shocked to find his dead body at Brookwood?

Violet returned the paper to Benjamin and returned to her own thoughts while he continued reading death notices. Everything she'd experienced lately had been undeniably odd and disturbing, and yet, as her husband and Inspector Hurst had pointed out, there was no crime being committed. Except against Susanna, of course. Was she crazy to think that the Brookwood happenings had anything to do with the attack on Susanna? Perhaps they were merely coincidental. Maybe Susanna had simply been the victim of a terrible prankster, or a would-be robber who had been frightened off for some reason.

Or had Susanna angered anyone since arriving in London? She had interviewed several undertakers about Brookwood; had one of them been so irate that he followed Susanna until he found a moment to attempt to murder her? If so, what in the world had he thought she had discovered? The only funeral man she had mentioned expressing temper was Mr. Crugg. It always came back to Mr. Crugg, didn't it?

Or was it someone Susanna had overlooked?

"Mother Harper, is anything wrong?" Benjamin asked, looking up from the paper. Susanna, too, had a worried look in her eyes.

How worried the girl would be if she really knew Violet's thoughts. She cast her eyes down and pressed two fingers to her forehead. "No, no, I'm just woolgathering, as they say. Please tell me more about Mrs. Frances Burke and the work she did with the Charity for the Houseless Poor."

As Benjamin once more bent his head over the paper's obituaries, Violet, too, returned to her original reclined position, her headache forgotten amid her troubled thoughts. For her closed eyes could not erase the image of what she'd noticed a few moments ago. Atop a trunk in front of the fireplace lay one of Violet's black gowns, one of the dresses Susanna had borrowed upon arriving in London and assisting Violet in the shop.

Just like the one she had been wearing when she was attacked.

Had someone actually been after Violet and grabbed Susanna by mistake in the dark, knocking her out when he realized his error? The idea was a source of relief that Susanna wasn't the target, but was simultaneously chilling. But if it was true, who was the attacker? Whom had Violet antagonized to the point that he would harm her? Mr. Upton? Or, again, was it the infamous Mr. Crugg? Or had Mr. Vernon's deranged state of mind returned again, causing him to stalk and attack the woman he thought was Violet?

Violet's head ached more than ever now. And she dreaded tomorrow, for she had yet another accompaniment to make to Brookwood in the morning.

Violet practically collapsed off the train onto the platform at Brookwood. Poor Captain Pagg deserved better than an undertaker who was distracted beyond reason and could hardly remember whether he belonged in the Anglican or nonconformist cemetery. Her headache had abated by morning, but her fear of trains had welled up much stronger than normal, and she had been nervous the entire hour-long, rail-clacking trip.

Now standing on the South platform, for she had remembered that the good captain was to be buried in the Anglican cemetery, she took a deep breath. She was becoming too troubled over what might or might not have been an actual crime. Or crimes. It would do no good for Violet to lose focus on what was important in her life: her family and her work.

She would have to settle her hash, as Sam would say. Resolve the situation or forget about it. She mulled this over as she rode with the driver of the hearse van to the Anglican chapel. An idea came to her as she made the short trip to the chapel with the driver, who was nearly sullen in his desire not to talk and seemed satisfied with the noise of creaking equipage and his horse's snuffles for company.

Once Captain Pagg was in place in the center of the chapel, Violet asked the man if he knew where Miss Latham was buried. He frowned, then uttered his first words. "Somewheres near the double willow tree, I'm thinkin'."

Violet thanked the man and set off on foot to find it. She had plenty of time before the captain's relatives arrived.

The double willow tree was a large, two-trunked tree with great clumps of trailing leaves. They swayed over gravestones, statues, and vaults, as if the tree were standing guard, waving a magical shield of protection over its charges. Violet traversed the area under the tree's massive canopy but couldn't find the grave she was looking for. She finally paused near a sepulcher near the base of the willow, dedicated to "the memory of A.G., 1802–1857." Where was Miss Latham buried?

She scanned outward from the willow. The day was already getting quite warm, but it was cooler here under the branches. It was no wonder people wanted to be buried under trees. It was like stepping into a private, silent retreat where one could share a moment with God without interruption among the graves.

Violet tilted her head. That looked like a fairly recent grave in the distance, in a copse of yew trees just outside the reach of the willow's arching branch. She walked between the randomly arranged markers under the willow tree and reached a winding gravel path that led to the copse. Yew trees were a common sight in graveyards. One medieval legend had it that yew thrived on corpses and then made excellent wood for making archers' bows. Another story said that because the heartwood of the yew is red and the sapwood is white, the tree was symbolic of the blood and body of Christ.

Regardless, they made for enormous, majestic trees, even if they weren't as graceful as the willow, which, of course, symbolized mourning. Violet certainly had to credit Brookwood's planners for the care they took in landscaping. Or for finding a property that already contained a selection of cemetery-appropriate foliage.

She reached the fresh grave. It was inside a mostly empty gated enclosure, with only two other graves currently sharing the space. The grave had a temporary marker that indeed showed that this was where Miss Latham had been laid to rest, inside the Latham family enclosure.

Roger Blount was not here with her. Didn't her obituary say that she would be buried next to him? Shouldn't she be in the Blount crypt? Everything about this was very peculiar.

Well, it was none of her business if the Latham family had decided to bury their daughter with their kin at the last minute. It was certainly odd, though, that they would have gone so far as to have announced it in the newspaper, then chosen not to bury her with a prestigious family like the Blounts. Yes, it was very, very odd.

Violet glanced at the watch pinned to her dress. She still had plenty of time before the funeral, so she walked back to the chapel and asked a couple of gardeners if they knew where the Blount family crypt was. They both shrugged, so Violet proceeded to walk all the way back to the South station. With all of this exercise, perhaps tonight she could have a morsel of whatever pudding Mrs. Wren had planned for the family.

Violet went straight to Uriah Gedding's office, where she found the man at his desk without his cat draped on him or demanding his attention. He looked up and said, "Ah, Mrs. Harper, how is the funeral business for you today?"

"Well, as I trust it is with you. Mr. Gedding, can you tell me where the Blount family crypt is?"

"Blount?" he asked. "I can't possibly know personally where every corpse is buried in such a vast cemetery—"

"I understand that," Violet said impatiently. "But you undoubtedly maintain records of when families purchase burial tracts. Can you please look in those records and let me know where the family plot of ground is? I'm sure such a family would have a fairly large area set aside."

Gedding rose and went to a file cabinet, but before opening a drawer, he turned back to Violet. "Is there a problem regarding the family? Something that I can assist with?"

"No, I simply wish to visit Roger Blount's grave. He is—was—second son to the Earl of Etchingham."

He still didn't open the file drawer. "As you know, Mrs. Harper, we are very sensitive to anything that might cause the public's apprehension over burial here, so if there is some sort of trouble, I really must know about it."

Would the man never pull on the oak handle and look for the information? Violet felt a faint pounding in her temples again. "Mr. Gedding, I have a funeral to conduct in the next few hours, and I simply wish to pay my respects to the young man, whom I remember seeing here at the station two weeks ago."

"That's all?" Gedding finally opened the drawer. "I'm sure I have the information somewhere here. Let me see . . ." He leafed through several papers in the middle of the drawer and pulled out the one he wanted. "Here we are. Section four, east of the double willow. Do you know where that is?"

Violet looked skyward. Had she really been that close? She left Gedding's office and returned to the same location in the cemetery, this time moving to the right of the willow until she found the Blount family tomb. A full piece of Mrs. Wren's dessert was in order after all of this activity.

The tomb was, unsurprisingly, an imposing Gothic masterpiece of sandstone and granite, resembling a mini-cathedral with its pointed arches and turrets, set in an elevated position in the cemetery. Violet wondered if the rise was natural or if the family had paid to have wagonloads of dirt brought in. She walked completely around the tomb, which was set on a large plot of pristinely maintained grass enclosed by a three-foot wall, like a green moat protecting the family members ensconced inside. It didn't look as though it had been opened recently. She stepped out of the confines of the tomb and walked around the exterior of the wall, stopping periodically to gaze up at the magnificence that the Blount fortune had purchased.

At the rear of the exterior wall, Violet halted in her tracks, disbelieving what she saw. It was a grave with a newly installed headstone, inscribed:

ROGER BURTON BLOUNT
JUNE 4, 1844–AUGUST 16, 1869

"FOR WE MUST ALL APPEAR BEFORE THE
JUDGMENT SEAT OF CHRIST;
THAT EVERY ONE MAY RECEIVE THE THINGS DONE
IN HIS BODY, ACCORDING TO THAT HE HATH
DONE, WHETHER IT BE GOOD OR BAD."
—THE BOOK OF II CORINTHIANS, CHP 5, VERSE 10

Violet was dumbfounded. Not only was Blount buried all the way out here, instead of in the family tomb, but the wording on his headstone was puzzling. Did it suggest that Blount had done good deeds in his life . . . or bad? Most families selected comfort verses from the Psalms to adorn monuments for posterity. This one was enigmatic and highly unusual for a prominent family like the Blounts, who would want everything associated with them to appear respectable and proper.

Burying a family member outside the tomb and inscribing his stone so strangely was anything but respectable and proper. Lord Blount would have had to have committed the most heinous of crimes for the family to justify exiling his body, and there was no evidence that he had done anything other than drop dead after dinner one evening.

Was this why Miss Latham's family hadn't buried her next to him? Because he wasn't actually in the tomb, or at least on the grounds of it? Had they decided that Miss Latham was better off in their own enclosure than relegated to an ignominious location next to Blount?

Violet was also puzzled that the heirs to an earldom would choose to purchase a plot at Brookwood at all instead of having their burials in a churchyard near their country estate. Unless they viewed Brookwood as fashionable. Maybe their estate was nearby in Surrey.

Violet leaned up against the Blount tomb's outer wall, thinking through everything. She couldn't come up with a single reason why Roger Blount should be buried this way. But she did know who would have the answer.

Perhaps it was time to pay a bereavement call on the Blount family.

Violet received her standard greeting from the Etchingham House butler after she twisted the front bell of the stately home whose windows were swathed in black crape: first, a critical glance at her working-class clothing, followed by a frown of disapproval that she was arriving at the front door and not the servants' entrance, both concluded with a disdainful "Yes?"

Violet had experienced this so many times that she no longer took offense. She was also not cowed into entering by the basement servants' door. It was her opinion that undertakers became part of a family for a short time and therefore deserved the privilege of entering by the front door.

Not that she was this family's undertaker, but she wasn't about to change her policy today.

To further put her in her place, the butler held Violet's calling card like it was the tail of a dead mouse and told her to wait in the entrance hall without inviting her to be seated anywhere. She didn't mind. With what she had to discuss, she might find herself quickly escorted out the door, anyway.

After a fifteen-minute wait—undoubtedly more of the butler's doing—he returned and escorted her upstairs into a tiny study filled with collections. The walls were so full of deer heads she could barely see the blue wallpaper beneath. Tables groaned under the weight of glass-covered display cases full of stuffed grouse, pheasants, and ducks. A pair of shotguns hung above the door. The shelves of a wide bookcase contained not a single book but were instead crammed with pocket watches under domes on one shelf and silver spoons on another. A cluster of clocks occupied two entire shelves, all of them ticking, ringing, and bonging furiously, the cacophony not even remotely absorbed by the thick, somberly patterned carpet on the floor.

It even smelled like a museum in here, musty and pretentious.

Violet didn't consider herself to be claustrophobic, but this room made her long for the seaside air of Brighton, where her parents lived.

After several more minutes of waiting under the gaze of probably every avian species in existence, the door opened and a regal woman in mourning entered the room. Violet had expected to be seen by the earl or one of his sons, given the room she was seated in, but perhaps her placement was merely meant to make her uncomfortable.

"I am Lady Etchingham. I understand you are here about my son." The woman was pale and tired-looking, but was not, in Violet's estimation, grieving the way a mother suddenly losing a child should. She did not sit down, her silent signal that Violet's visit was to be a short one.

"Yes, my lady. I am Violet Harper, an undertaker in Paddington."

"So Chapman told me. I find it displeasing that you have entered my home, seeking trade when all of London knows our son was buried two weeks ago." The countess crossed her arms across her black crape bodice and scowled. "Please state your business."

Standing like that in the middle of the bird-choked room, the woman looked like a mongoose protecting her young from a snake.

"I was at Brookwood station when your son's body arrived there, madam, and I wished to talk to you about it."

Lady Etchingham pursed her lips, as if still considering whether Violet was there to steal from her or not. Finally, she relented, even if her invitation was ungracious. "Won't you sit down?"

Violet found a spot on a leather chair that sat so high her feet did not touch the ground, even though she perched herself at the edge of the cushion.

"Forgive my intrusion, Lady Etchingham, but I have recently accompanied several bodies on the London Necropolis Railway down to Brookwood, and have noticed some oddities at the station on three separate occasions, the oddest being when your son arrived."

Lady Etchingham sat straight in her chair, every bit the proud and stately countess. "What was so strange about my son?"

"He was met at the station by Miss Latham, did you know that?"

The countess's lips were now a thin, nearly invisible line in her ashen face. "Miss Latham was his fiancée," she said.

"So I read in the papers. Wasn't she supposed to be buried next to your son? I was at Brookwood yesterday and noticed his unusual placement outside the family mausoleum. Would you be willing to tell me why he is located outside the walled area surrounding the tomb?"

Once again, Lady Etchingham did not directly answer Violet. "Why were you poking around the cemetery?"

Violet replied as vaguely as the countess had. "I am an undertaker. Burial places interest me."

Lady Etchingham's look was frosty. "And somehow your obsession with graves means I must answer ridiculous questions? This household has hardly entered its first period of mourning, and we are not taking visitors. I made an exception for you, Mrs. Harper, as I thought that as a funeral woman you might have been coming in some sort of comfort capacity. If you're actually here under some pretense in order to secure gossip about my son, I'll have you run out of London."

That was certainly an interesting reaction. "My lady, I trade in funerals, not slander. Actually, I was wondering who the family undertaker is who prepared your son."

"Of what importance is it? How could it possibly interest you?"

Violet chose her next words carefully. "When Miss Latham met your son's body at the station, she seemed . . . distressed over his condition. I, too, was a bit shocked."

"What do you mean?"

"In my estimation, he was not properly prepared."

Lady Etchingham huffed. "As though the opinion of some stranger is of importance to us. It is obvious to me that you are seeking information so you can tattle to the newspapers some sort of salacious detail about my son's death."

"Why would you think I wish to tattle to others about Lord Blount?"

"Doesn't everyone want to gossip about their betters? Especially when they find out—"

"Mother, are you in here?" came a deep male voice from outside the door. "I hear an undertaker came to see—Oh, pardon me for intruding." A man of about thirty years of age entered, obviously Roger Blount's older brother. He was stunningly handsome, with auburn hair in a longer, curling fashion that she'd never seen before on a man and sea-green eyes that invited a woman in for an unchaperoned swim. For a moment, Violet wondered why Margery Latham would have chosen Roger instead of this brother.

His lopsided grin suggested that he was well aware of the effect he had on women, and Violet immediately realized why Miss Latham might have shied away from him.

"Won't you introduce us, Mother?" he asked as both women rose.

"Son, may I present to you Violet Harper? She is a London undertaker—"

"Ah, and here I thought she was some neighbor coming to pay respects." He winked at her. Violet felt a flicker of revulsion. This was no way for a sibling to behave when his brother was not yet relegated to the realm of fond memories. This man seemed no more saddened than his mother.

"—who has some questions about Roger. Mrs. Harper, this is my son and the heir to the earldom, Jeffrey Blount, the Viscount Audley."

Audley nodded at Violet. "I would be most pleased to entertain these questions you have, Mrs. Harper."

Mother and son exchanged an unfathomable look; then Lady Etchingham swept out of the room without a backward glance at Violet.

He sat down casually, stretching his legs out in front of him and crossing them at the ankle. Sam sometimes sat the same way, but on Audley the posture was somehow more arrogant—almost insolent—in its air of superiority.

With an elbow on the chair's arm, displaying his black mourning band encircling a well-formed biceps, he rubbed his chin. "Please, Mrs. Harper, do sit down, and tell me what it is you need. I crave your pardon if Mother was rude to you at all; it's just that she's just lost a son, you understand."

"As you have lost a brother," Violet replied as she avoided the leather monstrosity and sat in a smaller armchair across from Audley. How did so much furniture fit in this room?

"Yes, yes, of course. The family is most devastated, but there are other matters that require attention, and so one must forge ahead, yes?"

"Other matters? Such as the death of your brother's fiancée?"

At that, Audley turned serious. "What of Margery?"

He referred to her by first name, not entirely inappropriate, depending upon how close she was to the family already.

"I was just telling your mother that I was present for Lord Blount's arrival at Brookwood, and was just as surprised by his condition as Miss Latham was. I'm sure you know she was there to meet his coffin."

"What? Oh, of course. Yes, right. What surprised you?"

"That he didn't seem well prepared by your undertaker. I was just asking Lady Etchingham who your family undertaker is."

Audley shrugged. "I don't know. I don't keep track of such things. An undertaker is not a man you summon that often, or at least you hope you don't."

Violet blinked. "You seriously don't know who the family undertaker is?"

"It's hardly in my sphere of concern. Mother knows, I'm sure." Except Audley didn't seem inclined to ring a bell and have a servant go after her. "Please, dear lady, surely you have other, more interesting questions? How about a glass of sherry?"

"No, thank you, I—"

For this, though, the viscount rose and pulled a knotted rope on the wall, resulting in a servant appearing almost instantly. "A bottle of sherry and two glasses, and be quick about it."

While they waited, Violet continued to press him. "Were you fond of your brother?"

"As much as two brothers can be, when one is set to inherit a title and the other is not."

Audley must have inherited the ability to sidestep questions from his mother.

"You knew his fiancée well?" she asked.

His eyes took on a distant cast, as if he were an old man reverting to the past. "Ah, Margery, a woman like no other. She would throw a barb of quick wit at you, but her blue eyes—deep like virgin pools of water—and her upturned mouth always softened the blow, so you never took offense. Instead, you couldn't help but share her joy. Roger didn't deserve her." He spoke like a sentimental poet.

"Did your brother know you were in love with his fiancée?" Violet asked softly.

Audley shook off his reverie. "What? I wasn't in love with Margery. I am a married man who—"

The servant reappeared with a tray. The viscount poured himself a generous glass and swallowed it in one gulp before offering the bottle to Violet, who shook her head.

"Suit yourself," he said, pouring again and this time settling back in his chair with the full glass.

"As I was saying, I am a married man. Certainly I found Margery an attractive girl. What man with a beating pulse wouldn't? Why would you ask such a thing? Wait, let me guess. You are a self-anointed detective and believe my brother was murdered, despite the fact that he dropped dead of a seizure, and you'd like to blame me for it." His lips curved into a mocking smile.

"What makes you think anyone would consider your brother to have been murdered?" Violet countered. Was Audley voicing the question she hadn't dared ask herself?

"For what other reason would you be here, with your ridiculous questions about the family undertaker and how Roger and I got along. Besides"—he took a long pull from his drink—"you're groping about in a dark room. Roger was—how shall I say it?—an insignificant member of the family. A black sheep, I believe is the euphemism."

Violet disliked the man's disrespectful tone toward his dead brother. "So you hated your brother?"

"Hated? No, you mistake me. I didn't think enough of Roger for it to rise to the level of hatred. My parents, though . . ." He shrugged in a manner that suggested he was eager for Violet to ask him more. She indulged him.

"Your parents, then, were bitter toward Lord Blount for some reason?"

"Yes. You can imagine that a second son with no responsibilities tends to wander into feckless and sometimes harebrained activities. Gambling, married women, that sort of thing. Some even wade into politics, just to take whatever position their parents abhor. Roger was no different."

"He made political waves?"

"No, he was harebrained. He fancied himself a scientist and began performing experiments that started with rocks and plants and eventually extended to animals. When he killed Mother's favorite springer spaniel in his ill-considered attempt to determine whether dogs have souls—and how the hell would he have been able to know that by anesthetizing and cutting the poor beast open?—I thought she would go completely mad.

"Then Father's valet, Digby, nearly died when Roger cajoled the man into an experiment to see if a man could build up tolerance to lily of the valley, which Mother grows in our gardens back in Surrey, if it was crushed up and steeped in tea. When Digby finally recovered and confessed what had happened, I thought Father would murder Roger himself. My brother nearly became a pariah in the family, only mending his name a little when he announced his intentions with Margery."

At least Violet had learned that the family's country estate was indeed in Surrey, which explained the tomb at Brookwood.

Audley swallowed the rest of his sherry. "Sure you don't care for a glass? It's a bit embarrassing to carry on alone."

Violet shook her head again. "So your parents clasped Roger to them once more when he became engaged to Miss Latham?"

"Not at all, though they thought that marrying him off to her might curb his eccentric tendencies. Father even planned to give them enough money to buy their own estate as far away from Surrey as possible. Once he dropped dead after dinner, which we all assumed to be the result of some botched, self-inflicted experiment, my parents were so disgusted that they didn't want Roger to share burial space with the family, lest his polluted spirit contaminate the rest of the Blount clan interred in the tomb."

"But you say you were not angry with him."

Audley poured a third drink. Was he nervous, or was this merely his habit?

"No, I was indifferent. If Roger wanted to waste his life mucking about in a laboratory, what did I care? I have my father's estates and my future title to worry about, and could ill afford to waste time on the health of a dog and valet. I did feel bad about Margery, though. She deserved better than that imbecile."

With no other information to be gleaned from Audley, Violet spent just a few more minutes in idle chat and left the Blount residence, thoroughly unsettled. She was certain that Audley had led her along on a leash, permitting her to stop and sniff at only very specific flowers. Had she missed something important? Had he lied to her? It was impossible that he had no idea who the family undertaker was, and she was fairly certain the viscount was enamored of Margery Latham. Whether his affection for her was reciprocated, or if the two of them had even been involved in an affair, Violet couldn't be sure.

Had Roger really died of a fit of some sort? Was it just an unhappy coincidence that his family wasn't overcome by his death, or was it possible that the earl or the countess had something to do with Roger's death? It was truly unthinkable to contemplate a parent killing his child, particularly a child who has been nurtured into adulthood, but Violet had witnessed plenty of family intrigues and schemes in her years of undertaking.

She didn't quite believe Audley's cavalier attitude toward his brother. Did it hide some darker, more malevolent feeling? Something concerned with Miss Latham?

Violet eschewed a private cab and this time boarded an omnibus headed for Paddington. Midafternoon London traffic bustled, but at least she would return to the shop before the bankers, merchants, and other middle-class workers stampeded out of London on trains bound for points such as Richmond, Harrow, and Bromley.

Violet paid her penny fare and ignored the crying children, exasperated mothers, and harried servants seated around her, lost in thought about her visit to Etchingham House.

What was most frustrating was that she still had nothing on which Inspector Hurst could take action. Roger Blount's family disliked him. So what? There was no evidence of foul play with his body; Violet simply didn't think it had been handled properly.

And what if one of the Blounts had indeed had something to do with Roger Blount's death? Didn't that mean that his body had nothing to do with the first two she'd seen at Brookwood? For certain it had nothing to do with the attack in Hyde Park.

The omnibus came to a sudden halt near Marble Arch, which housed a small police station. The stop was explained a few moments later as an elegant carriage bearing the royal arms went bouncing past one side of the John Nash–designed arch. The arch could only be traveled under by the royal family, and then only during ceremonial events, but traffic stopped even when a royal coach drove past. Violet could not catch a glimpse of the carriage's occupant to know whether it was the queen herself or one of her bevy of children.

Under the driver's constant pestering of his trio of overworked mares, the omnibus gradually picked up speed again and Violet returned to her contemplations, closing her eyes to blot out the din and jangle of London's streets in order to concentrate.

Was there any possible link between the various seemingly unrelated situations? Were some coincidental and others intentional? When it came down to it, how many different investigations was Violet actually working on?

A thought occurred to her. Audley had been reticent to tell her who the family undertaker was when surely he knew who it was.

Violet knew Julian Crugg had many society clients. Were the Blounts among them? Had he asked the family not to reveal that he was Lord Blount's undertaker because of the shabby treatment they intended for their son, which could only harm Crugg's reputation?

Speaking of shabby treatment, certainly Crugg had his own reasons to be angry at both Violet and Susanna, and might have been trying to attack either of them in the park. How would he have known that they would be in Hyde Park, though? Well, it was entirely possible that he had followed them.

Or paid someone else to do so.

Violet hopped down from the omnibus stop in Paddington, her stomach rumbling. She wondered what delicacy Mrs. Wren had planned for them tonight, then wondered if she should stop somewhere for tea. Seven o'clock was so very far away.

As she made her way through the streets after picking up a slice of savoy cake spread with jam, she decided that Margery Latham had clung to Julian Crugg not because he was standing nearby but because she knew him. Perhaps Audley hadn't covered for Crugg to protect the undertaker's reputation but because Crugg knew what had happened to Blount and was protecting the family.

It was an interesting idea. It made Violet even more sure that Crugg was somehow connected to the first two living bodies at Brookwood, although she wasn't sure how.

By the time she arrived back at Morgan Undertaking, Violet had warmed decidedly to the idea that Crugg was not the innocent he protested he was. Despite the outburst she knew she was facing, Violet decided it was time to visit him again.

When Violet announced to Sam that she intended to confront Julian Crugg again, he insisted on accompanying her, stating that his protestations at the wisdom of such a visit were clearly falling on deaf ears. Violet didn't resist his overprotectiveness. She hadn't been too enthused about calling on Crugg, anyway, imagining that he would either forcibly remove her from his shop . . . or do worse, if he was indeed their Hyde Park attacker.

They went together around midday, once Violet had finished

visiting a family who had lost their matriarch. The old woman had just died at the exceedingly ripe old age of ninety-nine, leaving behind so many children, grandchildren, and great-grandchildren that Violet had asked the woman's daughter to make up a list of them for the obituary.

Harry had stayed home to care for his wife, who was not faring well with her unborn babe. The child was already struggling to make an entrance, and its parents were struggling to keep it content a while longer. Predictably, Susanna was quite happy to mind the shop while Violet went on her errand, only cautioning her mother to "Watch for Mr. Crugg's fangs" as Violet and Sam headed out.

The cab dropped them off in Regent Street, and they walked into the alley where his shop was located. Strangely, the "Closed" sign was in the window and no lamps were burning inside.

"Perhaps he's gone for the day," Sam said.

"Perhaps, but you'd think his assistant would be here." For good measure, Violet turned the doorknob. To her surprise, it was not locked and the door easily pushed open.

The two of them stood at the threshold, neither quite sure whether to enter. Finally, Sam made a sweeping motion. "After you, Wife."

"Mr. Crugg? Mr. Trumpington?" she called out tentatively as she stepped into the shop, knowing instantly by the stagnant, undisturbed air inside that there was no one there. A sense of relief washed over her, as she was actually dreading having to confront him.

"I suppose he forgot to lock the door before he left," Sam said.

Maybe so, but it seemed counter to Crugg's fastidious and exacting nature. He was a man who would never forget to lock the door behind him.

While Sam lit lamps out front, Violet wandered into the back area of Crugg's shop and illuminated that room with one of several lamps hanging on the wall. It was neat and tidy, without a pen or sheet of paper out of place. There was no one in the room. Perhaps Crugg really had forgotten to lock his shop before his departure. She would pay him the courtesy of leaving a note so that he—

"Violet!" Sam called, the urgency in his voice startling Violet. "Come here."

She returned to the outer room. Sam stood in the center of the shop's safety coffin display, next to what appeared to be a bell coffin.

"Sweetheart, I believe I've found Mr. Crugg," Sam said grimly, holding open the coffin lid and showing her what was inside.

9

Violet joined Sam and peered into the coffin. She shuddered to see Julian Crugg lying inside, as calmly reposed as if he were merely napping. Violet couldn't be sure, but she guessed he had been dead mere hours. Ironically—and perhaps cruelly—there was a string tied around the forefinger of his right hand, which linked to an alarm bell.

Sam stood by stoically, still holding the coffin lid. His years in the recent war in America had made him as immune to death as Violet was. "What do you think?" he asked, in a tone that suggested he knew exactly what she thought.

"I think I am right in my assertion that something very terrible has been happening." She bit back her thought that Crugg now lay in a coffin much as Violet once had, courtesy of James Vernon. Except Vernon hadn't *really* tried to kill her, had he? And he certainly hadn't tied a bell to her. So was this the work of someone else?

"You think his murder is related to the doings at Brookwood and Hyde Park?" Sam asked. "How could that be?"

Violet held up her hands. "I don't know, but I have a suspicion this was not the act of some random thief who was discovered in the act of stealing money."

Sam lowered the coffin lid, which banged lightly against the box, sealing Crugg up again. "Well, if this was the man responsible for the attack on Susanna, I can't say that I'm particularly sorry at his demise."

Violet agreed, but didn't voice her opinion that the attacker was probably after Sam's wife, not his daughter. Another thought came to her mind. "It's curious that Mr. Trumpington, his assistant, isn't here, either. I wonder if . . ."

"You think something happened to him, as well?"

"Honestly, I'm more confused than ever, but we should consider the fact that he may have gotten in the way of whoever did this."

"Or maybe this is Trumpington's handiwork. It wouldn't be surprising to learn that Crugg was a difficult employer. Perhaps Trumpington was berated to the point that he simply exploded, and this was the disastrous result."

Violet arched an eyebrow. "Exploded, like a bundle of dynamite?"

"Not at all like dynamite, Wife. More like a volcano." Sam gave her his sternest look, which had her smiling inappropriately over Crugg's dead body.

Instantly serious again, Violet knelt on the floor and lifted the lid. "My apologies, sir, for my dreadful behavior. We did not get on well at all in life, but you don't merit derision in death." She began to close the lid again, but remembered something and opened it up again. "And please be assured that your death won't go neglected. I'll not rest until I determine who did this to you."

She felt Sam shift next to her and looked up to see him rolling his eyes. "Do you plan to undertake the man, as well?"

Violet shook her head. "No, that is for his family to decide on. But I will certainly try to find out who did this to him. He deserves at least that much."

Her husband sighed. "We'll have to go see Inspector Hurst again. He won't be able to ignore you now." He put out a hand and helped Violet up.

"You're right. But first, wouldn't it be helpful to have our own look around? Before we summon the police?"

"What are you looking for?" Sam asked.

"I have no earthly idea. Something that would give us a clue as to who might have been here and done this."

"Maybe Crugg was murdered elsewhere and brought here later."

Violet considered this. "No, it would have been too difficult to haul his lifeless weight here without someone seeing him."

"I disagree. All the killer needed was a covered wagon. This shop is far enough from Regent Street for the murderer to have unloaded him into here without detection. The bell string on the finger was a coarse gesture, though. Was it a message?"

The thought sent shivers down Violet's spine. "More importantly, was it a message for me?"

They were silent several moments as they contemplated the gravity of what Violet had said. Finally, Violet turned away from the coffin. "Let's see what we can find."

She and Sam went through the undertaker's shop as unobtrusively as they could, starting in the outer room and making their way to the back. They worked silently but efficiently together, picking up everything and always setting items precisely back in their places. As they searched Crugg's desk, Violet found several items of interest. First was a silver pocket watch, its case filigreed with the subtle shape of a bell on it. Possibly a funeral symbol Crugg had had specially made, or perhaps it was a gift from a safety coffin supplier. Next to it was a woman's hairbrush, a common enough item for an undertaker to possess but not typically stored inside a desk. A half-full bottle marked "Laudanum" also lay in the drawer, with a label glued to the front of it, listing all of its benefits for curing cases of nerves, vapors, and imbalances. It didn't surprise Violet, given how high-strung the man was. She wished he had used more of it.

"Aha!" Sam said triumphantly, holding up what looked to be a journal. It was tattered along the edges, and most unlike something Julian Crugg would use. "Found this cleverly propping up one desk leg. I imagine we'll find something interesting in it."

Violet closed the drawer she was searching through, and together they opened up the journal and stood side by side, poring through it. Violet was soon disappointed. It just seemed to be a ledger listing names and dates of bodies Crugg had handled.

There was nothing detailed, such as type of funeral, cost, or the name of the nearest relative for each listing, but each undertaker had his own way of handling things. It wasn't how Violet would do it, but there was nothing wrong with Crugg's ledger.

Except . . . "Why do you think he would have stored this on the floor, practically as a piece of trash?" Violet asked.

Sam looked perplexed. "To hide it from others? Who would casually walk in here and notice it down there?"

Violet was struck with another thought. "Maybe it belongs to Mr. Trumpington. But I suppose the same question still applies. And why hide the thing? There's no information of any value in it."

Sam shut the ledger and returned it to its place under the desk. "These are questions Inspector Hurst will have to answer."

They departed Crugg's shop to seek out the detective at Scotland Yard, but not before Violet checked on Mr. Crugg once more. A pocket watch dangled from a chain clipped to his vest. Either Crugg had more than one watch, not an unreasonable idea, or the watch in the drawer belonged to someone else. But whom? Mr. Trumpington? Then why wasn't he wearing it? Or did it belong to an unknown party who might know something about what had happened in this shop today?

As they made their way to Scotland Yard, Violet made a bizarre observation. Today she had found the first actual murdered body in the string of funeral oddities besetting her lately, and it belonged to the man whom she had blamed for all of those irregularities.

Sam was wrong; Inspector Hurst was more than capable of continuing to ignore her, despite the fact that she now brought him the news of a dead body. In fact, he laughed outright when she told him of their findings. "An undertaker died inside one of his own coffins? That's a tale worthy of a Poe novel," he joked.

"Inspector!" Violet admonished as severely as she knew how, even though she felt a twinge of guilt over having been recently irreverent herself. "A man has been murdered in his place of business and it is not an amusing matter."

"Mrs. Harper, you say he has been murdered, but you are not expert in knowing the signs of it. Yes, I know that you have had some luck in the past, but you have also been grossly wrong before. Need I remind you of your misidentification of Lord Raybourn's body? Your peculiar passion for your work makes you overly excitable sometimes. You must leave such determinations to us. I'll send a couple of men over to check him out, don't you worry."

Next to her, Sam was tapping his cane ominously against the floor. Violet shot him a look of warning. *Please, Sam, let me handle this.*

"Of course, Inspector. I just think it might be helpful to confirm how he died."

Hurst intertwined his fingers. "Very well, Mrs. Harper, why are you convinced that the man was murdered?"

"Because he was lying inside one of his own coffins with a bell pull around his finger."

"I see. Perhaps he did himself in."

"How would he have done that?" Violet asked, frustration rising that a corpse lay stuffed ignominiously inside a coffin while Hurst toyed with her. Would he never trust her instincts?

"You lot of crows have a peculiar sense of humor. Crugg probably thought that it was a riotous way to go, hanging himself on a rope timed to come apart over a coffin."

Before she could stop him, Sam thundered, "You dolt, that is an insanely complicated way to commit suicide. And there was no rope, just a man shoved into a box with the lid on top of him."

Hurst gave Sam a sharp look, admonishing him without a word to be respectful of the detective's station. "Very well, Mr. Harper, I said I will put some men on it. I would just caution Mrs. Harper not to see nefarious doings in every death she comes across. Lately, she seems to find wrongdoing even in living bodies."

Without even looking over to see his expression, Violet put out a restraining hand to calm her husband before speaking again.

"Inspector, I'm sure you'll do all you can to investigate Mr. Crugg's death. You won't mind if I make my own inquiries, as well?"

Hurst smiled condescendingly. "As you wish. Keep me informed if you find any *real* evidence of criminal activity. And try not to get yourself into trouble."

"Impossible," Sam muttered.

"So you'll send someone right away?" Violet asked, standing.

"Yes, yes. You may rely upon me."

Violet hesitated, words in her mouth she wasn't sure she should utter. Annoyance forced them out.

"Mary will be relieved to know that you are entirely trustworthy in the matter," she said, then wished the earth would swallow her whole for having bandied her friend's name like that. What was she thinking?

However, her words had the desired effect. Hurst sat up straighter and took on a more serious tone.

"Mrs. Cooke need have no concerns as to whether Scotland Yard is working to keep London safe. In fact, I would be happy to assure her in person if she has any worries at all—"

"I'm sure she doesn't. She's been quite busy helping me redecorate my shop."

"Is that so?" Hurst stood, too. "So she's working there currently?"

Violet wanted to be swallowed up for those words, too.

"No," she admitted. "Wallpaper has been installed and Mary is coming on Saturday to hang new draperies."

"Interesting. Well, Inspector Pratt and I will report whatever information we glean on Crugg as soon as possible. By Saturday, for certain."

Violet felt like a complete imbecile as she left Scotland Yard. Hurst would do just enough to help Violet to enable him to seek Mary's company.

Well, at least she had the detective's begrudging blessing to conduct her own investigation.

Edmund Henderson, London's commissioner of police, stood outside Inspector Hurst's office, listening to every word that transpired between Hurst and Mrs. Harper. Apparently, his detective

chief inspector was still allowing himself to get nettled by the undertaker, who was a great favorite of the queen's. In Henderson's
opinion, a favorite of the queen's was not to be dealt with lightly.

He slipped back into his own office when the undertaker and
her husband departed, then went back to Hurst's office, entering
without knocking.

"Sir?" Hurst said, rising from his desk. Hurst's protégé, Langley
Pratt, sat in one of two chairs across from the desk and followed his
mentor's lead by also standing.

Henderson waved at them both to sit down and took the still-
warm seat that Mrs. Harper had just vacated.

"I believe I heard Mrs. Harper's voice in here," he said to see
how his detective would respond.

"Yes, she is considerably worked up about some goings-on at
Brookwood Cemetery in Surrey. Especially since an undertaker
connected to the funeral train there has committed suicide." Hurst
mockingly rolled his eyes to express his opinion of Mrs. Harper's
concern.

Hurst's attitude needed to be surgically removed.

Henderson's primary fixation lately had been on building up his
detective force. Prior to his taking over the London Metropolitan
Police several months ago, the force only had twenty-six detectives and one sergeant, hardly adequate for a city population of
three million people. He'd already grown it by four detectives, but
he had plans to increase the force to over two hundred men. In addition, he intended to consolidate power such that he would determine which crimes could be solved by divisional detectives in
local police departments, and which were notorious or difficult
crimes that required the investigative abilities of his choice inspectors.

Magnus Pompey Hurst was one of those elite inspectors, and
Henderson didn't want him at cross-purposes with anyone who
might have the ear of the queen or Parliament, not when the commissioner might need more money or influence or laws enacted for
creating the best detective force in the world.

"What do you mean, 'worked up'?"

"Honestly, it's impossible to know. Two bodies were shipped down on the funeral train who turned out to be alive. Both literally rose out of their coffins. A third body was dead, but the undertaker thought the circumstances were odd. She's been here a few times to plague me over it, demanding that I interview certain people, but I don't know exactly what it is she wants us to investigate, given that no crime has been committed. Honestly, I think she might be a little . . ." Hurst tapped the side of his head.

Henderson had met the Harper woman on more than one occasion. She didn't seem like a hysterical female, so if she was uncomfortable in a situation, there was probably something to it. Not to mention that she merited attention because of her connections.

"And you, Pratt, what is your opinion?"

Hurst immediately spoke up. "Inspector Pratt shares my opinion."

Henderson ignored Hurst and nodded at Pratt to finish. The second class inspector swallowed and slid a nervous look between Hurst and Henderson, as though not sure which superior to be more fearful of. "Well, sir, she does seem peculiarly . . . attached . . . to her work. I remember when we worked on the Raybourn case with her, she insisted that we make the old Lord Raybourn's body comfortable on the dining table right away."

"Comfortable?"

"Yes," Hurst interjected. "As though the deceased had been lying there thinking about how very cold and hard the tiles were. Mrs. Harper was quite demanding. I expect being designated undertaker by the queen gave her airs."

"You were saying, Inspector Pratt?"

"Sir, yes, I would say she was, well, she may have been a mite confident, but she has always seemed to know her business."

Hurst's disparaging look did not escape Henderson's notice. The commissioner leaned forward. "Here is my opinion of Mrs. Harper. I say she is a valuable asset to Scotland Yard, and you will cooperate in any flight of fancy the woman might have."

Hurst's expression fell. "Why? What is special about her?"

"What is special about her is not for conversation here. Mr. Hurst, you are hereby instructed to assist Mrs. Harper in her concerns. Make sure she believes Scotland Yard is doing everything in its power for her."

"How so? Am I to hand out mourning cards? Water the lily pots set around the coffin? Sit at Brookwood and wait for corpses to fly out of coffins?"

Henderson bit back a sarcastic retort. Excellent detective or not, Hurst might soon find himself on the wrong side of his superior. Gritting his teeth, he said in a halting voice, "Answer. Whatever. Questions. She. Has." Returning to his conversational voice, he continued. "I have no idea of what nature they might be. Is that clear?"

Pratt's head bobbed up and down. Hurst grunted and scratched his side-whiskers.

Henderson sensed that Hurst was being privately rebellious. "By the way, Inspector, I overheard you asking Mrs. Harper about a Mrs. Cooke. Is this Mrs. Cooke a suspect to be investigated?"

Hurst's eyes opened wide. "What? No, of course not, sir."

"Then who is she?"

"She is just, er, just . . . a friend of Mrs. Harper's."

"So you are asking after someone who is not a suspect but have no interest in those persons that concern Mrs. Harper? I suggest you reverse your priorities." Henderson glared at Hurst, determined to get his point across.

The commissioner didn't want anything fouling up his plans, especially not something as laughably ridiculous as one of his detectives being uncooperative in a case, even if it turned out to be no more than a dog chasing his tail. Who knew, Mrs. Harper's matter could end up another laurel for Henderson. He imagined a headline that read "Scotland Yard Quickly Clears Up Mysterious Case of Living Dead. Queen Victoria Bestows Knighthood on Commissioner Henderson." It wouldn't do for the papers to run lurid stories of battles royal between his inspectors and the royally appointed undertaker. Good God, what joy the *Illustrated London News* would take in such a ludicrous story. Scotland Yard would be reduced to complete impotence, and even the savages in the remotest pockets of Australia would be laughing at him.

Hurst would find himself patrolling the streets in St. Giles if that ever happened.

It had been Henderson's observation that detectives got uppity when permitted to work in plain clothes instead of donning a uniform like regular officers. Once he'd hired all the men he needed, the next pressing issue for Henderson was uniforms. Definitely uniforms.

If Violet felt foolish after meeting with Hurst, Sam could only be described as morose the next evening after yet another day with his bankers.

Susanna and Benjamin had left suddenly to visit Violet's parents down in Brighton, with Susanna cajoling Violet and Sam to go with them. Violet had demurred, though, sensing that Sam had much to say to her and also feeling that Susanna and Benjamin needed to spend more time alone together. After all, they were still honeymooning. A few days away for Benjamin to meet Susanna's grandparents would be good for them, and Benjamin seemed eager that they get away.

She kissed Susanna good-bye, only to feel the girl stiffen in her arms, although she dutifully kissed Violet back. Whatever was wrong with the girl?

That evening, their only company was Mrs. Softpaws and Mrs. Wren, who made an occasional appearance to drop dishes on them from above, as though releasing an unwanted mouse from the air. Mrs. Softpaws sat in Susanna's chair, watching the dinner proceedings with an air of disdain for the veal cakes, fried rabbit, and stewed cucumbers, which were entirely unpalatable to her gourmet feline sensibilities. Mrs. Wren eventually coaxed her out of the room with a piece of leftover chicken in béchamel sauce, for which the cat happily left their company.

Dinner was finished off with an almond cake, of which Violet ate only a half slice and then sorrowfully put down her fork. It was only after Mrs. Wren left that Sam spoke in earnest about the day's events.

"I have been hesitant to tell you that I know why these banks are reluctant to finance me, aside from my unforgivable sin of being an American without social position. It's all about that dad-blamed Debtors Act."

Violet listened while Sam explained what Cyril Hayes, from London East Bank, had told him regarding debt dodgers. "So credit is riskier now that debtors can avoid prison?" she asked.

He nodded. "They can sue a man civilly, but how does that compare with the threat of prison for failing to satisfy a debt? Not only that, why would a bank issue a loan to someone as 'risky' as I am, when I can't be counted on not to run back to Colorado at the first sign of trouble?"

Sam looked as though he could break the dining room table in half in his frustration. "Even worse, today Mr. Hayes shared a confidence with me that would be a complete scandal if the newspapers found out about it."

Now Violet's interest was piqued. "What would be a scandal?"

"Remember I said that the law abolishes imprisonment for all debt, except in a few cases? One instance is the owing of money to the Crown. Apparently, the queen and Parliament are a bit crabby about that. More importantly, from my perspective, is that the crime of defrauding creditors is now merely a misdemeanor, not a criminal offense."

Sam was still not sharing any inflammatory information. "So banks are hesitant to give out loans. This is public record," she said. "What is so scandalous about it?"

He dropped his voice as though someone—Mrs. Softpaws?—might be listening to their conversation. "Some of these debtors, most of them once very wealthy, or at least very titled, are disappearing. Mr. Hayes says they have had reports of people seeing them on trains, escaping to places north, like Northumberland or Durham."

Violet was still confused. "Then how has a scandal not broken already if people are gossiping about these men abandoning their debt and fleeing London?"

"Because the gossips don't know what they are saying. In other words, the newspaper might report that Lord So-and-So was recently seen on excursion to the north, where said newspaper knows the family has a country house, or where his Aunt Daisy lives. Or that he has a friend he might be visiting until the next London Season can occupy his mind. It's all just society chatter because neither the papers nor the busybodies know that these men are in troubling debt."

Sam sighed as if that explained everything, but Violet still wasn't satisfied.

"Why don't the banks report the matter to the police?"

"Report what? Escaping the debt is a misdemeanor crime. We can hardly get Inspector Hurst to acknowledge an actual murder, much less something as trifling as a debt dodger. With all of the prostitution, street murders, and gin-related crimes in London, what would Scotland Yard or the police care about a man running away from home?"

What Sam described reminded her of her own troubles: Something seemed very wrong, yet there seemed to be no one to whom responsibility could be attached. There was no actual serious crime being committed.

They continued their discussion in their bedchamber, where Violet sat at her dressing table in her nightgown and wrapper, brushing her hair as Sam took his usual position propped on the bed.

"The bankers believe they are fleeing to points north inside England, but I wonder if they aren't going to Scotland. The Scots have no love for your queen and country, and aren't likely to extradite them."

Violet stopped brushing and turned to look directly at her husband instead of talking to his reflection in the mirror. Had that been sixty or sixty-two strokes on her right side? No matter.

"Are you proposing to assist the bank with rounding these dodgers up?" she asked. "To snatch them off trains and haul them to the bank to remit payment?"

"Of course not." Sam laughed at her proposal. "Can you imagine me, a bumbling American from the West, collaring important British citizens, roping them like steers, and delivering them to bank presidents? Besides the fact that I would soon find myself locked behind iron bars with naught to eat but gruel, I would be the source of all newspaper gossip for the next year. The queen would most certainly rescind our invitation to the opening of the Suez Canal." He cocked an eyebrow. "Wait, it might be worth it just for that."

"Oh, Sam, stop," she said, trying not to smile. Samuel Harper didn't enjoy the public eye, and dreaded the idea of parading about in Egypt with a delegation sure to include members of Parliament and the royal family.

He clasped his fingers on his chest. "I s'pose I'll hold that idea in reserve."

"What will you do then about your financing?"

"What can I do? Now that I know that these debt dodgers are ruining credit for everyone, I reckon I'll have to convince a banker that I'm not a likely candidate for shirking my debt. Maybe I'll ask them to come see your shop so they understand my permanence here. Although they may find an undertaking business off-putting, as well. Such stuffed turkeys these bankers are. I can hardly believe that it is no longer that I have to convince them of the value of dynamite but of the value of my character."

Finally finished with hair brushing and surreptitiously pulling out two gray hairs that had mysteriously appeared without warning, Violet coiled herself against Sam, who lay there tense and frozen, like one of his beloved ice cream cups. What could she say to soothe and comfort him? Especially since she wasn't sure how comfortable she was herself with the idea of her husband setting explosives off in a coal mine, despite how safe he said it was.

She could think of nothing that wouldn't make her sound insincere, and her mind wandered back to Julian Crugg and the events of the past few weeks.

Who had killed the undertaker? Was Inspector Hurst correct in thinking that Crugg had committed some bizarre form of suicide?

No, Violet was certain that wasn't true. The man had definitely been murdered.

Why would someone want to kill him? Violet could think of no reason, and yet she could think of a hundred. Those who mourned could be wholly irrational in their logic. Mourners who thought their undertaker had cheated them, had not carried out their loved one's wishes, or had not produced a funeral reflecting their lofty status might channel all of their anger, sorrow, and pain onto the undertaker.

She remembered the ledger tucked under the desk leg in Crugg's shop. Had the detectives found it? She wished now that she had studied it more closely, or perhaps copied out a few names. She could have visited the families, or at least investigated them to determine whether Crugg had somehow enraged a family member or two, someone with a known bad temper.

Too late now. She made a mental note to ask Hurst about the ledger.

Violet rolled away from Sam, who was finally snoring softly. She curled up on her side, her mind still awhirl with reflections on Julian Crugg's death, Roger Blount's unprepared body and his family's near unconcern for him, and Margery Latham's sudden death on the heels of her fiancé's untimely demise. She also couldn't forget the two men who had popped out of their coffins at Brookwood.

They were all dissimilar events, she reminded herself. They couldn't possibly be related. But what *was* related? What was completely innocent and irrelevant?

There was no solace for her, either.

Violet and Harry took inventory of a shipment of mourning jewelry from T. & J. Bragg the following morning, with Harry unloading wrapped items from the crate, and Violet carefully cataloging each piece in a ledger before setting it in its appropriate place either on top of the long L-shaped counter or under the counter's glass.

"Look, another cracked dome, Mrs. Harper." Harry held up a

mourning brooch whose brass backing and pin were flawless but whose glass covering for the hair design to be placed beneath it was practically shattered. She wondered how many more damaged brooches were in the crate.

"What's this, the third one in this shipment?" Violet said, making a special note in the ledger and setting the piece aside. Harry continued digging through the crate, now unwrapping earrings, necklaces, bracelets, rings, hair combs, hairpins, and fans fashioned from jet, a material that was popular with anyone who could afford it.

Jet was a hard, coal-like material formed when driftwood sank to the ocean floor and became embedded in the mud. A combination of heat, pressure, and chemical action that Violet didn't understand transformed the wood into a fragile, black substance that was lightweight and easily carved. It could be obtained all over the world from places like Spain, Germany, Canada, France, and the United States, but Morgan Undertaking only purchased jet from suppliers who bought it from Whitby, England, where the finest jet in the world was to be found.

The wearing of jet was de rigueur for all ladies who wanted to be funeral fashionable, although the lower classes satisfied themselves with less expensive, glass versions of the valued substance.

Not unexpectedly, several of the delicate jet pieces were broken, as well. A glass-topped brooch or ring made of gold could have its dome replaced; crumbled jet was useless.

All of the broken jet was set aside with the damaged glass pieces as Violet continued her note taking. "It seems we will no longer wish to use T. & J. Bragg, would you agree?" she asked her partner as he unwrapped the last item, a mourning tear vial that was thankfully unbroken.

"Agreed. I'll take care of preparing a return box. If they cannot prepare their shipments properly to avoid breakage for the trip from Birmingham, they shouldn't be in business." Harry scooped the damaged pieces onto a tray and disappeared into the back room, presumably to get them ready for a return shipment.

Violet took the ledger with her as she went to retrieve writing paper. Standing behind the counter, she penned a letter to T. & J.

Bragg, detailing all of the smashed jewelry and stating Morgan Undertaking's intention not to purchase from them anymore. She made a mental note that she would need to pick up a bank draft later to cover the pieces she was keeping. The jeweler would undoubtedly be dismayed, and possibly angry, that Violet was dropping them for sloppy practices. She added that she planned to transfer her business to Asprey & Co., which possessed a royal warrant from Queen Victoria.

As she scrawled out the letter, her mind drifted to what Harry had said, about the fact that if T. & J. Bragg couldn't prepare shipments properly, they shouldn't be in business. Wasn't that what she had said about Mr. Vernon? She'd spent so much time being uncertain as to whether crimes were being committed that she had forgotten that very important fact: If Mr. Vernon was not a proper undertaker, he shouldn't be in business, regardless of whether there was anything for Scotland Yard to be involved in.

She shook her head. It was none of her concern, and she would just be accused of being a busybody to bring it up again.

Yet it kept coming back to her as she finished her letter, rolled the blotter over the wet ink, and folded it carefully. If James Vernon were of a mind to throw Violet into a coffin—even if he supposedly did so unaware of his actions—might he not have done so to other people? Could they possibly have been made unconscious first so that they did not awaken until they were at Brookwood?

But for what reason? What had the others done to anger or frighten Vernon?

She contemplated this idea seriously as she addressed the envelope to the jewelers. Another thought popped into her mind. Had Julian Crugg also become suspicious of Vernon and suffered more harshly than Violet? After all, he, too, had ended up in a coffin . . . permanently. Had Violet just been lucky that day in Vernon's shop? Or perhaps he was willing to simply warn her because he found murdering a woman to be a little too distasteful.

She dug threepence out of a drawer and dropped it on top of the letter to hand to the postman later.

If Vernon was responsible for the bungled undertaking jobs, it explained the first two bodies who popped up from their coffins. Crugg's possible knowledge of his colleague's practices explained his own death, too. Moreover, it might even explain Roger Blount's condition, if Vernon was his undertaker.

Perhaps she should visit him once more, despite the danger of being locked in a coffin. She would need to take along some protection. Violet wondered if she should wait for Sam to return from his club meeting with Mr. Hayes, but Harry's brawn should suffice. Besides, who knew when Sam would be home? He'd spent so much time in the company of bankers that, even though they were hesitant to finance Sam's venture, they'd grown fond of his American mannerisms and speech. They'd invited him again and again to smoke cigars and drink whatever vile liquor was being poured at Arthur's, a gentlemen's club actually founded inside a bank several decades ago.

"Harry?" she called out. He emerged from the back room with a wrapped package. "I'd like you to run an errand with me."

"Sure," he said, depositing the package next to her letter. Dear Harry, he didn't even question what it was. A final thought popped into her mind, and she stopped to write out a telegram message that would help answer an important question that still remained.

With Harry in tow, Violet locked the shop, and they stopped first to send her telegram. The mail could wait for the letter carrier on one of his twice-daily visits tomorrow.

Mr. Vernon was none too happy to see either Violet or Harry arrive, but his poisonous greeting rolled sweetly on his tongue, like clotted cream on a scone.

"Are you my Moses, Mrs. Harper, come to deliver a plague? What shall it be this time? Locusts? Frogs? The death of all the firstborn in London?" His voice quavered at the end, suggesting that his sarcasm was like waves attempting to cover the jagged rocks of fear.

Violet offered a tight smile, ignoring Harry's expression of bewilderment. "I won't occupy too much of your time, sir. I am just following up from a visit Inspector Hurst made to you recently."

"Who?"

Was Vernon's confused look another ploy?

"Detective Chief Inspector Hurst of Scotland Yard. He visited with his fellow detective Second Class Inspector Pratt."

"I've heard of no such men, nor have I been visited by Scotland Yard."

Violet was beginning to believe him. The thought that Hurst had so boldly lied to her about interviewing Vernon, with Pratt nodding his head in agreement, caused her blood to simmer in her veins. She had to stop thinking about it, lest she erupt in outrage. He had sworn he would pay a visit to James Vernon and hadn't, which meant he was probably doing nothing about Julian Crugg. Was he even seeing to the family's collection of the man's body?

"I see that I am mistaken in my understanding. My apologies, sir." She had planned to imply she was there on Hurst's behalf in order to scare a confession from him, but how could that possibly work now? An idea flashed through her mind, and she turned as though to leave, then turned back again, as though something had just occurred to her.

"One thing, though, before I leave. I wrote to Uriah Gedding." Violet watched Vernon's expression, but it was bland. "He assured me that you were the undertaker for Roger Blount." Violet didn't know this but anticipated Uriah Gedding confirming it for her soon enough.

"Who?" Vernon said again, this time blinking slowly like an owl.

"Lord Roger Blount, second son to the Earl of Etchingham, who died very suddenly about two weeks ago and was sent to Brookwood for burial."

"Once again, dear lady, I have no idea what you are talking about." He turned to Harry, whom Violet had not even introduced yet. "Are you her husband?"

Harry tapped his undertaker's hat. "Her partner."

Bless Harry, he was completely baffled by what Violet was doing but pretended to be fully aware of it.

Vernon, apparently dismissing Harry as no threat, turned back to Violet. "I don't know this Lord Blount, although his name is familiar. I'm sure I've read of him in the papers. I also don't know these inspectors you mentioned, and I especially don't know why you're here again."

Violet continued. "The LNR keeps records of the bodies shipped to Brookwood, and you are the undertaker of record for Lord Blount. The condition of his body matched your particular . . . style . . . of undertaking."

"Which is to say what, exactly, madam?"

"That he was nearly untouched. His eyes were not fixed shut. His mouth gaped open. His hands were not folded and secured together. And not a single ounce of cosmetic massage had been applied to his skin. That is your method, isn't it? To charge customers for practically nothing?" Violet heard Harry's intake of breath next to her.

"How dare you accuse me of cheating families through slipshod work?" Vernon sputtered angrily. "I have been undertaking for twenty-three years, and my father had this shop before that, and my grandfather before him." His eyes were back to blinking rapidly in that bizarre way of his.

That was most likely true. Undertaking was a skill usually passed from father to son, and each family maintained its own secret techniques for preparing bodies. The Vernon men, though, did have some rather imperfect methods.

Still, James Vernon claimed no knowledge of Roger Blount's body. Violet tried again.

"I would like to see Lord Blount's record," she said, something she had no right to ask.

"I tell you, Mrs. Harper, I have no record for Blount because I never handled the body."

Hmm. She had expected his guilty defense to be that he was under no obligation to share his private funeral records with her. Instead, he had maintained his ignorance of Blount.

It didn't prove anything, of course, but it made her waver a little bit. He was a dreadful undertaker, for certain, but maybe he wasn't the criminal she had suspected him of being. Or else he was much cleverer than she had thought.

She tried one more tactic. "You do realize that Scotland Yard will be most unhappy to discover you were Lord Blount's under-taker and that you lied about it?"

Vernon pinched his vest hems on either side with his forefingers and thumbs and attempted a smile, which turned into more of a leer, and Violet didn't like the chill it sent up her spine. "My dear Mrs. Harper, Scotland Yard apparently doesn't give a whit for me and what I do. It would be wise if you didn't, either."

10

After a tense cab ride, during which Violet told Harry as little as possible to satisfy his curiosity, they arrived back at Morgan Undertaking. Violet had hardly removed her hat and placed it on a wall peg when a boy in uniform from the telegraph office arrived. She dropped a penny in his hand and took the telegram. How remarkable machinery was becoming, that she could send a missive all the way to Surrey and have a response within a couple of hours. She read the telegram from Brookwood South's stationmaster.

SUBJECT, ROGER BURTON BLOUNT, DATE OF DEATH AUGUST THE 16TH, IN THE YEAR OF OUR LORD 1869, SERVED IN DEATH BY JULIAN CRUGG OF LONDON. RESPECTFULLY, URIAH GEDDING.

Violet was stunned. Was Gedding certain? How could this be? She had been completely sure of her theory this morning of Vernon's guilt in not caring for Lord Blount properly. The condition of Blount's body pointed to Vernon, not Crugg.

But first Vernon's manner of denial and now Gedding's telegram threw her entire supposition into the wind.

She dwelt on it for the rest of the day, even as she met with a family to discuss the burial of their parlor maid, whose own family could not afford any sort of funeral. With her undertaking book held open to the Working Class section as she described by rote an appropriate funeral for the maid, Violet's mind drifted off to her situation.

Everything thus far that she had assumed or determined to be right had proved to be completely wrong. Violet could have sworn that Roger Blount had been undertaken by James Vernon, but instead he had been treated by her old nemesis, Julian Crugg. Was it a coincidence that Crugg was also now dead? Had someone murdered both Blount and Crugg, or was that a fanciful imagining on Violet's part? What reason would someone have to murder the second son of an earl in addition to his undertaker? It was preposterous.

Unless Julian Crugg knew something about Blount's death? In fact, was there something about Lord Blount's death that had frightened Crugg and thus made him imprecise and clumsy in dealing with Blount's body?

As she left her customer's home and returned to the shop via omnibus, Violet warmed to this idea. Now that Gedding had confirmed Crugg was Blount's undertaker, it made much more sense that Margery Latham had clung so desperately to the undertaker at Brookwood. Was there something that both had known about Blount's death?

Which reminded Violet that Miss Latham, too, was now dead. Was someone running about murdering everyone connected with Roger Blount? What in the world was so significant about the young man that he was causing someone so much terrible angst? That would cause Crugg to lie to Violet about knowing Lord Blount and his fiancée?

Perhaps there was something inside Crugg's shop that she'd overlooked. She would return there tomorrow morning and take another look.

If Violet had known what was waiting for her, however, she would have avoided it like a burial in a thunderstorm.

The door to Crugg's shop stood ajar, and several people dressed in mourning were milling inside. Half-filled crates lay around the room, and the shop's display cases were almost completely empty.

She knocked on the door with her gloved hand, pushed it farther open, and stepped inside. All activity ceased as five pairs of eyes—three male and two female—fixated their gazes upon her.

"Pardon me," Violet said. "I am here to . . . I was just . . ." She cleared her throat as she walked farther into the room. "You must be Mr. Crugg's family."

A pinched-looking man whose dour face meant he could be no one other than Crugg's brother said, "Yes, are you one of Mr. Trumpington's family members? He's gone, off to start his own shop somewhere else in the city."

"My name is Violet Harper. I am a fellow undertaker of Mr. Crugg's. I stopped by to, er, pay my respects and to hopefully pick up his shop ledger to—"

"You!" breathed one of the women in accusation. She was an elderly crone whose confection of black feathers, crape, and dangling jet beads wound around her head did little to detract from her beaked nose, through which her next words were emitted like a series of goose honks.

"How DARE you? What DO you think you mean coming here? After what you DID to my nephew?" The woman's hat feathers shook violently. Violet expected her to start flapping at any moment.

"Again, pardon me, madam, I can see that you must all be his family members, and as such I extend my deepest condolences. I shan't keep you. I merely wanted to see—"

The dour-faced man cut Violet off. "You're the crow who ruined my brother's business."

Violet was used to being called a crow, but by another undertaker's relatives . . . ?

"I assure you, sir, that I—"

Another man stepped forward to proffer an opinion, and Violet didn't like how Crugg's family was beginning to circle her.

"You not only ruined his business, you accused him of the most . . . most . . . vile actions imaginable." The man was much younger than Crugg, with fleshy cheeks that puffed out further as he practically spat his words out at Violet.

It was almost as though Julian Crugg was somehow reaching from the grave to torment her. She instinctively took a step back toward the door.

The other woman in the room was thin and choleric. Crugg must have had two siblings. The strands of jet draped around her neck looked like an anchor weighing her down. "How ironic that you've had the nerve to show up here. We were talking about you earlier. My brother here, Malcolm, wants to take you to court. I told him it would be much simpler to push you into the Thames. It would be kinder, too, than what you did to Julian, putting him into his grave."

Violet held up a hand. "Madam, you are greatly mistaken. I found your brother's body, but I had no hand in his death."

"Hah!" said Hat Feathers. "The police tried to tell us he committed suicide. But we know you killed him as surely as if you plunged a knife into his heart yourself. Julian had been complaining of you for months, about how you snatched profitable business from him and then stalked him, accusing him of all manner of wrongdoing. You're shameful."

"You are misinformed of my dealings with your nephew, madam. I have never intentionally taken customers from any other undertaker. The situation for which Mr. Crugg blamed me was unfortunate, but it was the queen's decision that I handle the body in question. As for stalking him, I simply became concerned over the . . . mishandling of some bodies, and I—"

"Yes, we know," Hat Feathers said, holding up a hand to stop her. "Your haranguing and pestering made the dear boy nearly ill with worry. He could hardly sleep at night."

Violet bit her lip. If Julian Crugg was so disturbed that he wasn't resting, it likely had nothing to do with her. About what, then, was he so distressed? Was this more evidence that Violet was correct in thinking that Crugg knew something about Roger Blount's death, something that ended up getting the undertaker killed?

Should she share her suspicions with his family? As Violet looked at the murderous stares they were all giving her, making her skin prickly and hot, she thought maybe not. She offered one more defense.

"I assure you all, any harm Mr. Crugg may have believed I caused him was purely unintentional. I was just—"

"You were just devious." Hat Feathers stepped forward, her hand still raised but now positioned as if she wanted to choke Violet. "You were just devious, and sly, and knavish." With each word she took a step closer to Violet. To Violet's dismay, the woman's relatives were also moving forward, grinning. They looked like leering corpses who had risen from the dead and were looking for another victim to take back to Hades with them.

Except that Violet didn't believe in corpses rising from the dead. It's why she was investigating this matter in the first place.

Deciding that a healthy dose of discretion was in order, Violet simply said, "My apologies for disturbing you all during this sad and troublesome time. If I might just pick up the ledger . . ." She marched purposefully to the back room as though she had every right to do so, wiggled the ledger out from under the desk leg, turned on her heel, and left without looking back. She was only a few steps away from the shop when she heard the door open again and a male voice, belonging to Crugg's bony and forbidding brother, floated out to her.

"Don't bother to return here, Mrs. Harper, or you'll find yourself in the same condition as my brother."

Violet didn't acknowledge the remark but kept walking, cursing herself for not looking closer at Crugg's records after she and Sam had discovered his body. After several blocks, she stopped and looked up, cupping a hand over her eyes. The sun was rising over the building tops—it must be nearly noon. Mary was coming by later today with the new draperies for Morgan Undertaking, so Violet needed to return to the shop and prepare for her friend's arrival.

She walked a few more blocks, then abruptly turned down a side street to go in a completely different direction away from the shop, toward Scotland Yard. Despite what had just happened with Mr. Crugg's relatives, Violet realized they had told her something valuable that required investigation. She needed assistance, and by heavens, Inspector Hurst was going to help her.

* * *

Violet trudged home from Scotland Yard, dejected at having been unable to find Hurst and Pratt. They were "on an investigation," the desk sergeant said, but he would let them know she had visited.

As she walked past Hyde Park, the scene of so much misfortune for her, she contemplated the odds that Magnus Pompey Hurst would actually respond to her plea. If he didn't, she would have to figure out what to do herself.

When she returned to Morgan Undertaking, Harry was practically hopping on two feet, quite a feat for such a hulking giant of a man.

"Emily is feeling poorly. I've been waiting for you to return so I can go pick up her favorite Fry's chocolate bar and take it to her. She likes the ones molded like kittens with the bilberry centers. Have you had them? Not to my taste, but Emily loves them, so I—"

"Yes, Harry, go. I'll take care of things here and see you tomorrow morning."

"Right you are, Mrs. Harper," he said, hurriedly grabbing his hat and lumbering out the door.

Violet was glad for the quiet of the shop so that she could think more about her investigative matter, which seemed to be growing more and more complicated by the day. As she dusted, swept, and generally made ready for Mary's arrival with the shop's new draperies, she puzzled through it all. Roger Blount, Margery Latham, and Julian Crugg were somehow connected together, she was sure of it, but except for Julian's death, was there any foul play involved? Try as she might, she could see no connection between these deaths and the men who had arisen from their coffins, unless Crugg had been their undertaker, too.

Even if he had been, there was no crime there. There was also seemingly no crime in Blount's death, despite his relative youth, and the same could be said for Margery.

So, Violet Harper, the only real murder you are investigating is that of Julian Crugg?

As she knelt down to sweep up some bits of lace that must have fallen off a mourning fan, she heard the door's bells jangle behind her. "Ah, Mary, I've been thinking—"

She stood to find that it wasn't Mary who had entered the shop but Hurst and Pratt. Both held their hats in their hands and nodded graciously as Violet stood to greet them.

"Hot afternoon, isn't it, Mrs. Harper?" Pratt said, mopping his face with a handkerchief that probably had needed laundering at least a week ago.

"Not fit out for man nor beast. I wonder how you manage to keep your shop so pleasant," Hurst said, offering a rare smile. It was unnatural on him, and he looked like a caged circus bear that had just been taught a new trick. However, it was certainly a change in his demeanor from the last time she met with him. Violet wasn't sure whether to be glad or suspicious.

"The desk sergeant told me you came by the Yard, and I just wanted to check on you," Hurst said distractedly as he looked around at the walls and windows. "Are these your new draperies?"

"No, Mary will be here shortly—Ah." Now Violet understood his cordiality. "So, you came by just to look in on me?"

"Yes, yes, the desk sergeant seemed to think you had some urgent news."

Well, if there were ever to be an opportunity to get the inspector committed to this matter, here was the moment. Perhaps it was better not to reveal that she knew he had never gone to see James Vernon. To put Hurst on the defensive might work against her, no matter how besotted he was with Mary. She explained to both detectives what had happened during her visits to both Vernon's and Crugg's shops. As usual, Pratt whipped out a notebook and took notes with his stubby pencil. Violet imagined that he had rows of these filled notebooks in a bookcase somewhere. How was he able to go back and find information pertinent to any single case?

As Pratt scratched away, Violet made her request of Hurst. "I'm not sure now if it was Mr. Vernon who was responsible for the live bodies at Brookwood, or if it was Mr. Crugg . . . or someone else."

Hurst had the good grace to blush. "Ahem, yes, well, I have to admit that I'm not so sure of Vernon's innocence myself. You see, I—that is, we, Inspector Pratt and I—didn't exactly have an in-depth conversation with him."

"No? But you did visit him, didn't you?" Violet was surprised he was confessing to this so quickly.

"Well, as you must realize, we are very busy with many important cases. People are murdered every day in London, Mrs. Harper. Not just in the gin alleys, either. When a high-profile case occurs, it can't just be left to the police, now, can it? No. We spend many days tracking down the most vicious and evasive of killers. So you understand that a careless undertaker didn't garner our, ah, full attention as you might have hoped."

If she weren't so irritated that Hurst had lied to her, she might have found his embarrassment amusing. "How little attention was it, sir?"

Hurst turned to Pratt. "What are you doing? Don't write this down!" he snapped.

Pratt scratched through everything Hurst had just said.

"Er, we didn't visit him at all." Hurst looked around the room again, avoiding Violet's gaze.

Violet made no response. His discomfort was working to her advantage.

Hurst filled the silent void with another excuse. "If it had reached the point that I thought lives were in danger, I would have immediately barged over there."

Yes, Violet could imagine Hurst barging in on someone he thought was breaking a law.

"We came over because the commiss—because we thought you might have discovered something else that we could act upon."

Undoubtedly he would take action if Mary were present. However, now was the time to present her request.

"I would like a favor of you. I stopped in at Mr. Crugg's shop and found several of his relatives there, closing it down. They mentioned that Mr. Crugg's assistant, Birdwell Trumpington, has started his own shop elsewhere in London. I can't begin to fathom where it might be. Can you find him?"

Hurst's expression suggested that Violet was asking for something as simple as lighting coals in a grate. "Of course we can find him. But what of him?"

"It occurs to me that he quit Crugg's shop before the poor man was even buried. In no time, he had his own shop. Had he been planning on leaving for a while? If so, why? Or, did he have some sudden need to vacate Crugg's shop? It would be valuable to know what he has to say."

Hurst was surprisingly agreeable and said they would start a search for Trumpington right away. The two men left Morgan Undertaking, but not before Hurst turned back to say, "Mrs. Cooke will be here soon, you say? I'd hate to lose the opportunity to offer my greetings to her."

"Then hurry, detective, so you don't miss her."

Hurst rushed to obey, with Pratt on his heels, but the junior detective paused at the window outside the shop to look back in and shake his head at Violet and point at his superior's back.

Hurst's love-struck countenance was obvious to everyone except himself.

This time, Hurst wasted no time in fulfilling Mrs. Harper's wishes, although his mind was cleaved in two between irritation over the distinct thought that he was obeying her like a subordinate and the optimistic hope that he soon might have a few moments with the charming Mrs. Cooke.

With Pratt hurrying behind him, Hurst stopped first at Crugg's shop to interview the family for more information about where Trumpington had gone. He almost had sympathy for Mrs. Harper after that, what with the dealing with an aunt whose hat came close to eating him alive. However, they learned that Trumpington had said something vague about St. Paul's Cathedral, and it didn't take long to find the man's new shop a few blocks from the churchyard.

Fortunately, they managed to catch him off guard, and he was clearly startled to have two Scotland Yard detectives barge into his shop, which was still in disarray and not yet ready for customers.

Hurst introduced himself and Pratt, then dove straight into questioning the undertaker, to keep him off balance. "How did you manage the money to open your own shop so quickly after your employer's death, Mr. Trumpington?"

"I—I came into an inheritance from a family member," the man replied. Hurst didn't like the tic in the man's cheek, which he almost missed noticing, what with the man's poorly groomed hair hanging in his face.

Hurst took an instant dislike to him. There was no excuse for a middle-class man neglecting his ablutions. Even if he did poke about with corpses.

"What relative? What was his name?" Hurst asked, insinuating that Trumpington was lying.

"It was from my great-aunt Sylvie, who always told me I had the makings of a great man."

"You made haste in using that inheritance, didn't you?" he shot back at Trumpington. "Didn't bother to undertake your employer, did you? I imagine you didn't even attend his funeral."

Trumpington became indignant. "Sir, it is unseemly for an undertaker to work on his fellow worker or his employer. His family had him sent back to wherever he's from—somewhere south, I believe. He was not my concern or responsibility once he died."

Hurst quickly veered to another topic to keep the man off balance. "What did Julian Crugg know about bodies coming out of coffins on the Brookwood train station platform?"

At this, Trumpington stilled. "Has Mrs. Harper been complaining to you?"

Hurst had nicked open a vein. Now to encourage a bit of blood flow. "Mrs. Harper? What do you mean?"

"She's another undertaker. She accused Mr. Crugg of all sorts of vile things with regard to a Lord Roger Blount and his fiancée, Margery Latham, both of whom Mrs. Harper saw at Brookwood."

Hurst frowned as if he were receiving this information for the first time and needed to digest it. "And so what did your employer know about these bodies?"

"Well . . ." Trumpington shifted uncomfortably. "I didn't want to think ill of Mr. Crugg, but it seemed to me that he had something to hide. He told me that Mrs. Harper's interference was going to ruin him and he had to take care of it. I've never seen him so upset, although he didn't explain to me how Mrs. Harper was ruining him. It wasn't my place to ask."

Hurst dug into the vein to drain the man. "How did you assist him in handling Blount's and Miss Latham's bodies?"

His question didn't catch Trumpington as off balance as he'd hoped. "I assure you, Inspector, that I have no notion what Mr. Crugg may or may not have been doing with the two of them. He never brought it up to me privately. Now, as you can see, I have a great deal of work ahead of me before I will be ready for customers."

Hurst waited until Pratt was finished scribbling Trumpington's statement down; then they took their leave of the man.

"What did you think?" Hurst asked the junior detective as they walked to a nearby cabstand.

"A bit frightened, like most suspects who are interviewed by you, I mean, by the Yard."

Hurst nodded. "But was he lying, either about how he came across the money for his own shop or Crugg's handling of Blount or Miss Latham?"

Pratt reviewed his notes as they stood waiting in the sun. "Nothing he said was incriminating." He put his notebook away. "I saw nothing in his demeanor to suggest he was deceiving us, either."

"Nor did I. Despite the man's unconscionably poor grooming, I see no falsehood in him. The next question is, how do we tell Mrs. Harper this without her becoming hysterical?"

Pratt's expression was quizzical as a cab pulled up and the two of them climbed in. "Do you think Mrs. Harper is hysterical, sir?"

"No, I suppose not. But she is most certainly demanding, self-righteous, and irritating, and unfortunately, I'm afraid I'm under her power right now."

"Because of the commissioner?"

"No, not because of that." Hurst turned his head to look out at traffic, refusing to say more.

Hurst returned to Violet just a few hours later with his disappointing report that he did not believe Trumpington to be guilty of anything.

Hurst's voice was dejected as he added, "I see Mrs. Cooke is not yet here."

"No." Violet was not interested in Hurst's pining at the moment, nor was she dismayed in his assessment of Trumpington, as she was busy with a stack of death certificates she had discovered in the back of Crugg's ledger. How had she missed them when she reviewed the ledger with Sam? And for what reason was he storing them there?

The detectives must have realized that Violet was intent on the documents and joined her at the counter.

"What do you see, Mrs. Harper?" Pratt asked, genuinely interested and concerned. Violet hoped the junior detective never adopted his superior's gruff and self-important airs.

"We have here several groups of death certificates, all signed by various doctors, and some of them from the past few weeks during which all of these mysterious events have occurred."

"Not necessarily mysterious," Hurst said. How many times would she have to hear this?

"You're right, but this is the only information I have, and I want to see how I might be able to link Mr. Crugg to certain bodies headed for Brookwood. The type of deaths, for example, might suggest that he legitimately thought they were dead when they weren't."

"But not all deaths are medically certified," Hurst pointed out. Was he being intentionally obstinate?

"True, but this is all I have to examine."

Pratt picked up one of the certificates. " 'Esmeralda Oxenbrigg, aged eighty-two, of Great Queen Street in Lincoln's Inn Fields. Primary cause of death, old age. Secondary cause of death, angina pectoris. Body sent to Bunhill Fields for burial.' "

He put it down and picked up another one to read. Violet stopped him. "What I'd like to do is to sort out the certificates for bodies bound for Brookwood Cemetery within the past month."

Pratt shook his head. "Not all of them indicate the body's destination."

Violet tamped down her frustration with the detectives. She had to remember that they looked at everything through the specific methodologies they employed for solving cases, whereas she was just clutching at straws, hoping she might find an answer. "No, but some do. I want to compare them to Mr. Crugg's ledger."

"What do you hope to find?" Pratt asked, adding another certificate to her growing pile.

"I'm not sure. Something—anything—that links the bodies to each other. Their supposed cause of death, where they lived, their social status . . . Presumably there could be many connections."

Hurst shook his head. "You could spend months interviewing the—" He was interrupted by the doorbell jangling. He turned and his voice instantly became affable. "Mrs. Cooke, what a pleasant surprise, madam. Is that your cab outside? Why, the second seat is simply loaded with draperies. You must allow me to help you."

Violet and Langley Pratt shared a look with each other and continued working through the death certificates.

"Thank you, sir. Inspector Hurst, isn't it? It's kind of you to help. Violet picked a lovely fabric, but it's so very heavy. They will be just splendid in her shop. We selected a gold fringe that—"

The doorbells jangled again as the two went out to retrieve the draperies from the waiting cab. Violet turned and noticed through the window that Hurst offered his arm to Mary for the twenty-foot walk they had to make.

Inspector Pratt stopped what he was doing and drily commented, "Perhaps I should go outside and help them, if there is such a large load of draperies. It wouldn't be proper for me to stand inside while a lady performs manual labor like that."

Violet laughed. "I suspect Inspector Hurst would be happy to carry them all upon his back to avoid having any male company during his flirtation."

Pratt joined her in amusement. "Inspector Hurst's affection for your friend is one case easily solved."

Violet became serious once more. "It just isn't appropriate for him to follow a woman in such recent mourning like a puppy on a trail scent. Even after she is finished with mourning, I'm just not sure about the inspector and my dear friend in a courtship . . ." Violet let her voice trail off. She could tally up a hundred reasons why it was a bad idea.

Well, she didn't have to worry about it for nearly a year. The more important thing was her investigative matter.

The door jangled again as Mary and the detective entered, with Hurst's brawny arms loaded with lengths of fabric and Mary chattering beside him about the Morris, Marshall, and Faulkner shop.

Violet and Pratt exchanged knowing looks once more. Ignoring Hurst's infatuation, Violet flipped through the culled stack of certificates. "Well, I've already determined one thing. Everyone under Crugg's care bound for Surrey over the past month was a male." She had noticed something else but wasn't ready to share it with either of the detectives yet.

"That's not much to go on, Mrs. Harper," Pratt said, shaking his head.

"No, but it's a start, and I'm determined to find out what is happening with these bodies no matter what."

Hurst didn't hear Violet's resolute proclamation. He was too busy helping Mary hang draperies.

That evening in their bedchamber, Violet spread out on the bed the twenty-two death certificates she had separated from the rest, explaining to Sam how she had come by them.

"So these are Crugg's bodies who went to Surrey over the past month?" he asked, picking one up and examining it.

"For the most part. Some of the certificates were missing information. But look here." She pointed to one of the certificates. "This body went to Royal Surrey County Hospital. So did this one. And this one." She indicated two other death certificates.

Sam frowned. "Why would a body go to a hospital instead of a cemetery?"

"Some hospitals conduct anatomical research, although the government has implemented many restrictions on the practice since the days of Burke and Hare."

"Who?" Sam asked. Violet kept forgetting that he didn't know her country's history that well.

"Two men who were murdering people to obtain bodies for sale to anatomists. Today, anatomists have access to the workhouse dead for experimentation."

"Therefore, these are certificates for workhouse dead? Good Lord, Susanna's birth mother might have ended up with an anatomist."

Quite possibly. The woman had died of illness inside the St. Giles-in-the-Fields workhouse where she had been living with Susanna eight long years ago. The tragedy had created the happy circumstance of Susanna coming to live with Violet.

"Most bodies that go to the anatomists are the workhouse dead or people who couldn't be identified: the indigent, prostitutes, and the like."

"How do they come to Crugg? You don't trade much in workhouse bodies, do you?"

"No, just occasionally will someone alert me to a person who has died without relatives to care for him. Crugg may have come about them in different ways. He might have an arrangement with a workhouse to take away bodies, or he may simply have been well known in his neighborhood for taking care of these sorts of deaths, although Mayfair isn't exactly teeming with indigents."

Sam examined the three certificates Violet had pointed out. He picked up one to scrutinize it closer. "Harold Herbert Yates." Sam paused, as if rolling the name around in his mind. "This is familiar. Where have I heard of him before?" Sam straightened, all perplexity gone. "Wait, I know. Sweetheart, this is the name of one of the dodgers Mr. Hayes told me about. He supposedly fled somewhere north."

Violet took the death certificate and read it again. " 'Mr. Harold Herbert Yates, aged thirty-one, of Bedford Street off the Strand. Primary cause of death, unknown. Secondary cause of death, unknown. Body sent to Royal Surrey County Hospital.' " She read it aloud once more and shook her head. "This makes no sense. How could he have escaped up north to avoid his debts and at the same time have a death certificate ascribed to him?"

Sam pushed aside some of the certificates and sat down as Violet paced the room with Yates's certificate in her hand. Suddenly, she stopped and looked at it again. "This shows his date of death as the thirtieth of July."

"Is that significant?" Sam asked as he stretched out his battle-injured leg, raising his trouser leg and kneading his knee. He must have walked too far today.

Violet went to her dressing table and pulled a bottle of Mr. Johnston's Essence of Mustard from a drawer. She handed the certificate to Sam and then poured some of the pungent oil into her hands and rubbed it on her husband's knee. He grimaced at how the combination of rosemary, camphor, oil of turpentine, and mustard flour felt on his skin but didn't pull away.

"Yates's date of death is three days before I saw the first body come out of its coffin at Brookwood. The timing is right for Yates to have been that body."

Sam covered her hands with one of his own. "*If* Crugg was responsible for those living bodies you saw. *If* the body traveled the third day after death. I think you're putting together too many coincidences, Violet. You're forgetting a crucial point, too."

Violet withdrew her hands from his and rolled down his trouser leg. "What is that?"

"Yates was seen on a northbound train. Mr. Hayes is under the impression that Yates is living under an assumed name in Northumberland, or Durham, or perhaps Cumbria."

"But that's impossible. I'm holding the man's death certificate right here." She took it back from Sam to read it yet again, as though concentrating on it more would somehow cause it to show her something new.

"Moreover," Sam continued, "why in tarnation would a prominent man—no matter how indebted he was—commit his body for dissection? It's unthinkable."

Violet was utterly deflated. Sam was right, of course. She returned to pacing, trying to make sense of so many watch parts that she simply *knew* must fit together into a fully functional timepiece, even though they seemed to be just a jumble of wheels, pinions, and springs on a table. If only she could pick out the central piece around which the others would logically and quickly fit.

She mentally reached out and selected a new part. "I have an idea," she said, pausing.

Sam smiled. "Of that, I have no doubt. What is it?"

"It seems to me the next logical step is to visit Royal Surrey County Hospital."

"I don't suppose you can get into too much trouble there. What do you hope to accomplish?"

"Find out whether Yates actually ended up there. You know, perhaps he escaped north and a substitute body was put in the coffin to make everyone—including all of his creditors—think he was dead."

"Do you realize what you're suggesting, Violet? That Yates murdered someone to have a ready body for his coffin after faking his own death?"

"Or he found a workhouse body that died with good timing."

"But that means . . ." Sam couldn't finish the thought.

"Yes. Julian Crugg used his relationship with a workhouse to obtain substitute bodies for various men fleeing the country. Except his plan went terribly wrong on two occasions."

"But how does that explain his own murder?"

Violet paused and sat on the bed at Sam's feet. "I'm not sure. I expect that if he was supposed to be sending substitute bodies and they kept popping up alive, someone might view him as incompetent and a threat of some sort."

Sam leaned back heavily against the bed frame, causing the fringed canopy over them to briefly sway back and forth. "This theory in no way solves the main problem, though, does it?"

"What do you mean?"

"Roger Blount did actually die, as did his fiancée. How do you connect that to your solution?"

Violet sighed. "I have no idea."

11

Fortunately, the staff of Royal Surrey County Hospital did not view Violet's visit with suspicion when she announced that she was an undertaker come to see about a couple of bodies they might have.

She was ushered into the office of Mr. Nathan Blackwell, the superintendent of the hospital. The room was a strange cross between a museum and a laboratory. It was cluttered with jars containing organs floating in sickly brown fluid, as well as trays of bones presumably belonging to men, women, and children. One contained all the pieces of a foot, another a rib cage, and yet another an arm and a hand. Many other trays were stacked up in haphazard piles on the floor.

Violet knew that medical science was advanced in this way, but her stomach constricted at the thought of what must have happened to the bodies in here to get them into jars and trays.

Mr. Blackwell was pleasant, if a bit mad-looking, with wiry red hair exploding everywhere from his face and head. Small, unruly bushes protruded from his ears, eyebrows, nose, and a small wart that had sprouted near his left eye. The man desperately needed a wife to see to his grooming.

However, Violet supposed she might be a bit uncivilized-looking herself if she were cutting open bodies all day long. Caring for them whole seemed an acceptable service to society. Chopping them up for experimentation was rather . . . repulsive. Violet shuddered.

"How may I help you, Mrs. Harper?" Blackwell asked, one hairy eyebrow raised in curiosity.

"I am wondering about some bodies that you may have received for dissection," she said, pulling the certificates of bodies bound for Surrey from her reticule and handing them to him.

"Indeed? What of them?" he replied, looking through the papers and nodding.

"If you are done with them, I would like to do my own personal identification of them." Violet wasn't sure she would be able to keep down her breakfast when she saw them, but she would do whatever it took to solve this matter.

Blackwell looked down at the certificates. "These are Julian Crugg's bodies. What is your interest in them?"

"I am . . . was . . . an acquaintance of Mr. Crugg's until his recent untimely death."

Blackwell nodded. Crugg's death was clearly of no surprise to him.

She continued. "I am simply following up on some documents that have been entrusted to me from his shop." That was the truth, wasn't it?

Blackwell shrugged. "These are the three you wish to see?" he said, rising with the certificates in his hand. "I'm not sure what their conditions are or if the students are even done with them, but please follow me to the dissection classroom."

Violet dutifully followed behind him, her heels clacking along the wood floorboards, which creaked in a variety of places. Patches of blackened flooring indicated where rushed surgeries had taken place in the long hallway. Violet couldn't help but envision surgeons, aprons covering the lower halves of their own bodies, standing over eviscerated, anesthetized patients, whose blood dripped to the floor in a predictable half circle in the shape of the surgeon's apron.

The hallways reeked of bodily odors and ether, which she supposed was to be expected. She ignored the smell and concentrated on the walls, which were painted a sickly, pale green.

They ended up in a room in the basement. The cavernous room, which reminded Violet of the interior of a railway station, had white tiles on the walls about halfway up from the floor, and the remaining were painted the same feeble green as the hallways.

Wood tables, with small chalkboards dangling from hooks at one end of them, dotted the room. Each table had a crank enabling it to be raised or lowered according to the anatomist's needs, and a body was laid out on each one. The bodies ranged in shade from a mottled white, like dirty snow, to a laundry-water gray. Several young men, whom she assumed were anatomy students, stood over tables with instruments. At one end of the room was an older gentleman instructing them. He stood before his own table with a saw in his hand. Violet blanched.

What is wrong with you, Violet Harper? You've seen victims of drownings, disease, and train wrecks. Why is your backbone crumpling?

It just seemed such a disrespectful way to treat the dead.

The professor's voice was deep and authoritative. ". . . end of this week we will have finished with examination of the brain; then we will move on to—"

Blackwell cleared his throat, and the sound reverberated through the room, causing the professor to stop what he was saying. Blackwell introduced Violet to the room in general, and she found them all looking at her curiously, as though she were the one with a vicious tool in her hand ready to hack through dead flesh!

Blackwell explained what Violet wanted and held up the three death certificates. "Is Harold Yates, Raymond Wesley, or Jeremiah Dormer among the corpses you are working on?"

Each of them, including the professor, examined his table's chalkboard and shook his head.

Blackwell nodded. "Thank you," he said, before escorting Violet out. "These dates of death are far enough back that I assumed they would have already been examined, but I wanted to be sure for you. We'll go to the disposal room."

Violet liked the sound of that even less.

This was an even gloomier room, where dissected bodies were stored in canvas shrouds in a dizzying array. Some lay on tables; some sat upright on the floor along the walls. It was a smaller room than where the dissections were performed, and there was only one gas chandelier in here. Violet felt as if she were in an old church, surrounded by spirits who had been unable to ascend or descend. Spirits who reeked of earth and decay and desolation.

"I'm afraid your best chance of finding any of the three is in here," Blackwell said, handing the certificates back to Violet.

How would she even begin?

"Mr. Blackwell, are all of these bodies from a local workhouse?" It was beyond Violet's imagination that this many people were dying there, despite how deplorable their conditions could be.

"Many, but not all. The hospital produces its own cadavers, of course. We have a small burial ground here for patients who died but were never claimed. Some are exhumed for skeletal examination and then reburied."

And Violet had foolishly thought that remains were safe after the Anatomy Act of 1832. "Is this legal to do?"

"It is. In fact, at one point, Royal London Hospital's school was almost entirely supplied by subjects which had once been the hospital's own patients."

"That is very interesting," Violet said politely, wondering how many bodies were never left to rest in peace.

"Of course, not all of our surgeons want real bodies because of the, er, troubles associated with them."

Violet had dealt with enough putrefaction to know what Blackwell implied.

"Some of them prefer artificial facsimiles, plaster casts, wax models, and sometimes even animal carcasses, although rounding up the beasts has its own problems. It all depends on what is being studied and what the surgeon prefers. Now, if you'll excuse me just a moment . . ."

Blackwell disappeared for less than a minute and returned with an oil lantern, already aglow with light. "I think this might help you." He then exited the room, pulling the door shut behind him and leaving Violet alone to figure out whether Yates, Wesley, or Dormer was in here.

Violet removed her gloves and went to work. Some of the bodies had names pinned to their canvas wrappings; some had a meager description, such as "female, middle-aged, white plague." "White plague" was a nickname for tuberculosis. Some of the bodies had no identification at all. Violet was indignant to think that these people had been unceremoniously buried in unidentified graves, dug back up and mutilated, and would be dumped back into anonymity.

The condition of the bodies also varied. Violet wouldn't be able to stay in here long before the odors she was unwrapping would begin to overwhelm her. She had to be methodical. First, she examined all of the bodies with external identification. None of them matched Yates.

She thought back. How tall was Yates when he came out of the coffin? Making her best estimate, she dislodged the fabric from the heads of those bodies who appeared to have male builds of the right height. Some of their faces were so decomposed that it was impossible to know whether they were the men she was looking for. Violet was despairing of finding anything of promise when she unwrapped a man who was laid out on one of the wood examination tables, which had been shoved to one side of the room.

Pinned to his shroud was a label: "Raymond Wesley."

She hurriedly freed the man's head from the shroud and gasped aloud. This was *impossible*.

Inside the shroud lay the second man who had arisen from his coffin in Brookwood. Violet was reeling not only from the odors drifting upward from the dead man but also from the implication of his discovery as she put the facts together in her mind. Raymond Wesley had apparently died, and Mr. Crugg had written a death certificate for him. He was sent to Brookwood, turned out to be alive, but now here he was, stacked among a cluster of workhouse and hospital dead. He was dead, then he wasn't, now for certain he was.

Provided this really was Wesley.

She untied the rest of the cords that loosely held the shroud around him. *This is odd.* Wesley was still clothed. If he had been subject to anatomical experimentation, why was he dressed? He was fully clothed, in fact, down to his shoes. Were these the clothes he was wearing when Violet saw him at Brookwood? It was hard to remember as it had all happened in such a blur, but it was certainly possible. He now wore an inexpensive Chinese silk vest of emerald green. It wasn't the sort of somber color or high quality that a man of society would be buried in, but perhaps Violet was making an assumption about him.

She checked Wesley's death certificate. No, he was from Piccadilly. He should have been buried in a much fancier suit of clothes.

Unless he was one of the dodgers running away from his debts. But they were all going north, weren't they? The banker said so, had even said some of these dodgers had been spotted on trains up north.

Violet wondered if anyone except the banker could attest to these sightings. She felt an uncomfortable flutter in her chest as a sudden thought struck her. Was the banker guilty of something?

Violet Harper, you're ready to accuse the entire world of madness.

What possible interest could a banker have in murdering a debtor who had abandoned his responsibilities? Surely the loss to the bank wasn't devastating enough for the banker to actually kill such a man. However, such a theory might explain why there was a claim that the debtors were going north when in reality they were merely being dumped at Brookwood for Julian Crugg to dispose of them with Royal Surrey County Hospital.

Violet wondered if she could determine Wesley's cause of death.

"Forgive me, Mr. Wesley," she said softly. "I must inspect you, and I don't wish for you to feel too terribly violated. I promise to be quick about it."

She unbuttoned his jacket and shirt and struggled to remove them. It was always difficult to remove clothing from dead bodies. Violet ran her hands over his skin gently, as it was decomposing and she didn't want to accidentally damage his skin by pressing too hard. She found nothing on his torso or arms to suggest his manner of death.

With even more struggle, she removed the dead man's trousers. "I'll just be a few more moments, sir; then I'll return you back to your coverings. I'm sorry for this disturbance."

She continued talking as she examined his legs. "It's a tragedy, Mr. Wesley, that you will not have a proper funeral, and I'm so very sorry for it." There was nothing obvious on his legs, either.

She stepped back and examined the entire man, trying to see past the eerily pale skin mottled with purple, green, and brown patches. His stomach was swollen, but that was perfectly normal. No, there was nothing out of the ordinary to suggest a particular disease or illness that would have put him in the hospital.

Moreover, he had obviously not been eviscerated by the anatomists. Why, then, was he here?

Violet bolted upright. Wait, if Mr. Wesley was here among these bodies, he ought to have been a hospital patient who had been exhumed. Yet here she had his death certificate, signed by Julian Crugg, with the cause of death noted as "unknown." How had Wesley gone from being in Crugg's custody to becoming, ostensibly, an unearthed hospital body? Had Mr. Blackwell accepted him from Crugg, then had him thrown in here? But if so, *why?*

Violet redressed and reshrouded the body, running through the possibilities in her mind, not liking where her thoughts were ending up. Was Royal Surrey County Hospital paying undertakers like Crugg to bring in bodies for them? Were they running out of bodies in their own graveyard and from the workhouse? If this was true, it was no wonder Crugg was so nervous and tightly strung. It was despicable for an undertaker to be involved in such an effort.

So perhaps Mr. Blackwell was not the innocent, if exceedingly hairy, superintendent he had seemed to be when she arrived at the hospital. It was time to confront him.

Nathan Blackwell wasn't as pleasant the second time when Violet asked him if the hospital was practicing resurrectionist activities. Blackwell's thick eyebrows shot upward as he jumped out of his chair at the accusation and demanded that she leave the building.

Realizing that her direct approach—which consistently failed her, making it inexplicable why she continued using it—was not working, Violet immediately adopted a conciliatory tone. "My apologies, sir. You must understand that seeing all of those unloved bodies made me a bit irrational. Please, I didn't mean what I said. Perhaps I could just ask you a few more questions . . . ?"

Blackwell eyed her suspiciously but eased back down into his wood chair, which creaked under his weight. "It depends upon the questions."

Violet folded her regloved hands demurely in her lap and bent her head, hoping she looked submissive. "There was a body I discovered downstairs, a man of perhaps thirty years, named Mr. Raymond Wesley." She dug the death certificate out of her reticule once more and handed it to Blackwell, who barely glanced at it and handed it back.

"What of him?"

"I was wondering if you could tell me how he died."

He pointed to the paper in her hand. "It says the cause of death was unknown."

"Yes, but since he has been in your care, you may have observed something that the doctor did not."

Blackwell laughed and gasped at the same time, sending him into a coughing fit from which he quickly recovered. "Mrs. Harper, when bodies come to us, they are hardly in our 'care.' We experiment and dispose. Besides, I can hardly remember one body out of hundreds."

Violet maintained her composure. "Nevertheless, perhaps you can come to the basement and have a look."

Blackwell sighed but did as she asked. Once back in the body storage room, she unshrouded Wesley again and waited for Blackwell to look him over. The man frowned, drawing his brows together into a nearly perfect caterpillar as he walked around the body with his hands folded behind his back, sidestepping others propped up nearby.

"Hmm, yes, I see," Blackwell murmured. Violet had the distinct impression that he was stalling for time.

"Don't you find there to be something very odd about the body, sir?" Violet asked, still remaining as calm as possible.

"Odd? Well, he is certainly a victim of misfortune to have ended up here, for certain."

"Indeed. But isn't it strange that he is fully dressed?"

Blackwell hesitated. "Yes, he is, isn't he? Oh yes, I remember this body now. He was determined to have died from swallowing acid. A terrible accident, for certain."

What was certain now was that Blackwell was lying. Violet had dealt with bodies that were victims of acid ingestion. The body always convulsed and recoiled from it, and he should have the telltale spatter marks where acid had flown out of his mouth and hit his chin and upper body.

What was the superintendent hiding?

"Why was he not used for experimentation?" she asked.

He gave her the same condescending look so often employed by Hurst and the now-dead Julian Crugg. "Because of the damage the acid would have done to his innards, of course. We are far more interested in exploring corpses that have been attacked by disease and other ailments not understood by science. A man who has committed suicide and destroyed his body is of little use. Which reminds me, he cannot go into the hospital burial ground, so we'll have to send him to some unconsecrated ground since he is a suicide."

Violet was further irritated by Blackwell's callousness toward the bodies in his charge. "A final question, sir. How do bodies arrive here at the hospital?"

"By hearse or wagon, of course."

"No, I mean, who provides them to you, the ones that you don't exhume yourself?"

"A variety of undertakers. Julian Crugg is one of them, or was, until his terrible demise in London. Any reputable London undertaker can offer to bring us abandoned bodies."

This left Violet in a worse muddle than what she'd been in before she arrived at the hospital. She offered her farewells to Blackwell and headed home. After arriving at Paddington train station, she stopped in at a grocer's to purchase more black tea for washing her hair.

As she perused the shelves, she considered how her investigative matter was just spinning out of control. What had happened to

Yates? Why was Mr. Wesley's body at the hospital, and how had he died after having been shipped to Brookwood in a coffin? What of Roger Blount and his uncaring family? Was he murdered, or did a perfectly healthy young man really drop dead after dinner, followed shortly by his fiancée? What was Julian Crugg's involvement in all of this? Nathan Blackwell's?

She handed money over to the proprietor as his assistant wrapped her tea tin in paper.

Violet had nearly forgotten the attack in Hyde Park, too, which had surely been meant for her. What had she unwittingly uncovered that had necessitated her removal?

And what of the banker Mr. Hayes? Was it crazy to think he was somehow involved? What secret might he be keeping? She would talk it over with Sam tonight.

There were so many possibilities of who might have been involved. But that never-ending question kept clanging in her head like a tolling bell:

Why? Why? Why?

That evening, Mrs. Wren had prepared a dinner of stewed duck and peas, which Violet indulged in fondly. Violet regretted her overindulgence and excused herself almost immediately afterward, going to her bedchamber to fling off her corset and change into her nightclothes. She was seated in front of the mirror when Sam finally joined her, and they discussed what had happened that day. He listened intently without interruption to her story about Royal Sussex County Hospital, while Violet dabbled black tea onto her head and pulled it through her hair with a brush.

As usual, Sam propped himself up in bed. He wasn't rubbing his knee, so it must have been feeling better. "So what do you think?" she asked. "Is it possible that Mr. Hayes is involved?"

Sam shook his head. "Sweetheart, I don't want to say that the theory is crazy, but what advantage is there for the bank to go around murdering its debtors? It's not as though the bank could empty their pockets and thus be repaid."

"But aren't the heirs of an estate responsible for the deceased's debts?"

"Yes, but wouldn't it make much more sense for Mr. Hayes to visit those relatives and ask them to exert pressure on the offending family member? Wouldn't that be more effective than committing a hanging crime?"

Sam was right. Perhaps Violet's imagination was becoming too wild for her own good. And yet . . .

"Maybe Mr. Hayes and other bankers are helping the debt dodgers stage their own deaths. They then make a claim upon the estate and have their loans returned to them without actually having murdered the debtors." Violet warmed to this idea, one she had never even considered.

"And why would the debtors collude on this? If they are dodging their debts to begin with, and there is no threat of jail for them in doing so, why would they help the bankers swallow up their estates?"

Violet frowned. Did Sam have to be so dismally logical? "No, I suppose you're right. The debtors would never help the bankers in this." Violet sighed.

Sam wasn't finished. "Besides, it doesn't answer the question of how Mr. Wesley ended up dead at Royal Surrey County Hospital, nor what happened to Roger Blount and Margery Latham."

That, too, was true. Yet Violet couldn't shake the feeling that Mr. Wesley's indebtedness had something to do with his death. She put down her brush, ready to climb into bed.

"Oh, before I forget," Sam said, rising and searching through his coat, which he had earlier hung on the hook on the back of the door. "We had a letter from Susanna."

"Samuel Harper! How could you hold that back from me?" Violet got under the coverlet. "Come and read it to me."

Sam changed into his own dressing gown and joined Violet, removing Susanna's folded missive from its envelope. "She and Benjamin are well. Your mother seems to have adopted Benjamin as her own grandson and has him escorting her all over Brighton so she can show him off to her friends."

Eliza Sinclair, recently recovered from a serious illness, was probably enjoying the new zest brought into the household by Susanna and her husband.

"How is my father?" Violet asked.

"Relieved to have your mother's attentions distracted away from him. He is also having a grand time with Susanna. They are reliving her childhood, with trips to buy candy floss and other sugary treats."

Violet smiled. If she weren't so busy with her investigative matter, she would have suggested to Sam that they take a few days and head to Brighton themselves. It would have been good to spend a few days away with her family, especially now that her mother was no longer convalescing and was presumably much less discontented and fretful. "What else does she say?"

"That if she stays much longer, eating as much as they are, she will need new dresses."

Violet put a hand to her waist once more. Perhaps they would go dress shopping together.

"Does she say when they will return to London? I'd like to visit Mary's shop with her."

"Doesn't she specialize in mourning wear? Why don't you both buy some more colorful gowns instead of that perpetual black?"

" '*Et tu, Brute?*' " Violet quoted. "No one understands an undertaker's comfort in wearing black."

"Hmm," Sam said, returning to the letter. "Now for the most important part. They are returning in a week."

"Marvelous!" As much as Violet had felt constrained by having Susanna under her roof for so long, now that her daughter was gone, she missed her terribly. Did all mothers have such wildly divergent feelings?

Sam turned down the gas lamp on the wall over the bed. "Talk to Mrs. Wren about a special dinner when they return, will you?"

"An excellent idea. Maybe we'll even get a special treat for Mrs. Softpaws. I'm sure she'll be relieved to have Susanna back again." She curled up against her husband, hopeful that easy sleep would come to her on the news that her daughter would be back soon.

Unfortunately, it didn't. She had a dream—bordering on a nightmare—about dead, moldering bodies, a very rare occurrence for Violet despite her daily work with them. After a few hours of fitful sleep, she left the bedroom so as not to wake Sam and spent an hour pacing in her cluttered sitting room. By the time she returned to bed to attempt a few more hours of sleep, she had decided to return to Hurst and Pratt again. Surely they wouldn't mind a visit to Royal Surrey County Hospital with her.

12

As expected, Inspector Hurst was more than willing to accompany Violet back to the hospital in Farnham Road in Surrey. He talked incessantly of the "elegant Mrs. Cooke" the entire way, cloaking his admiration in a discussion of Violet's shop renovation. Violet was exhausted after the hour-long train ride, and as she stumbled out of the carriage, she wondered whether it was time to talk to her friend about the detective's attentions and whether they were wanted.

"Again?" was Blackwell's curt greeting upon seeing Violet in the doorway. Once he realized she'd brought along someone from Scotland Yard, though, he was much more amenable, courteously escorting them back down to the storage room when Hurst barked for it in his most authoritative Roman-centurion voice.

As the superintendent opened the door, he said, "It may interest you to know that Crugg Undertaking delivered two more bodies last evening. Given your interest in Crugg yesterday, we haven't done anything with them yet."

How was that possible? "Pardon me," Violet said. "Did you say Crugg Undertaking? His business no longer exists. I watched it being packed up myself. Are you sure it wasn't another undertaking firm?"

Blackwell shrugged. "The two men said they were from that shop. I assumed you knew them. Don't all of you undertakers know each other?"

Although Violet had darkened the doorsteps of many of London's undertakers in her recent investigations, it wouldn't be correct to say she actually knew them all. What she did know, though, was that Crugg Undertaking no longer existed.

Unless Birdwell Trumpington was carrying on in his former employer's name.

"Show us those bodies," Hurst commanded.

Space had been cleared on the floor for them, a pair of elderly people, a man and a woman. Neither was even shrouded yet. As usual, Violet felt bile rising in her throat at the callous treatment of these corpses.

As he stepped back into the hallway, Blackwell said, "I'm not sure what you're looking for, Detective Hurst, but be assured that all of the staff here stand ready to assist you in whatever way possible. Shall I post someone outside the door to summon me if you have need of my assistance . . . ?"

Violet didn't remember such a generous offer yesterday. Hurst might be tiresome and bearish, but his stiff-necked demeanor and his association with Scotland Yard certainly made people jump to carry out his wishes.

Could Mary possibly tame Magnus Pompey Hurst? Turn him into a gentleman? Violet rolled her eyes at the thought that Hurst could be made over into a gentle human being. Mary Cooke was far too timid to shoulder the effort required to make Hurst agreeable. After all, the poor thing hadn't been able to do anything with that scoundrel of a husband, George.

Hurst wrinkled his nose and put up a hand to cover his mouth and nostrils. "Smells like the Thames in July in here," he said, his voice muffled.

Violet ignored him and knelt down next to the woman's body, going through her usual routine of examination. As she did so, Hurst took a deep breath from behind his hand, then knelt down himself next to the man, employing his own detective skills in looking him over.

At almost the exact same moment, they each stood.

"This woman died of old age," Violet said.

"As did this man. I expect they were a married couple. When one went, the other couldn't take it and stopped breathing."

Hurst had a marvelously delicate way of putting things.

"Their clothing—" she began.

"I'd say they were of the lower classes. You can see some patching on her dress. Her fingernails are none too clean," Hurst said with authority.

Violet agreed, but that wasn't really where her mind had wandered. Who was doing business under Crugg's name? From what location was he operating? Blackwell had mentioned two men. Who was the second man? If she asked the superintendent, would she receive more than a shrug? Should she ask Hurst to interrogate him over it?

"Inspector, perhaps I should show you Raymond Wesley, who Mr. Blackwell said committed suicide by swallowing acid. In my estimation, there are no marks on him to suggest this is true, but perhaps your expert eye will result in a differing opinion."

Hurst puffed at the compliment as Violet led him to the table upon which Wesley's shrouded body lay. Violet removed the wrapping quickly and, at seeing what lay before her, cried out, "No!"

She dropped the shroud, hardly noticing it flutter to her feet.

Hurst cleared his throat. "I can say with certainty that his death wasn't caused by ingesting acid."

Wesley lay before her, mutilated and completely unrecognizable, as though someone had charged in here with a knife and gone to work on Wesley, treating him like no more than a dinner roast. It was unspeakable.

Violet picked the shroud up from the floor and began covering the body up again. "Dear Mr. Wesley," she said quietly, "I'm so sorry I wasn't here to prevent this happening to you. I know nothing about you, but I'm positive you didn't deserve this, sir." She completed her task by pulling the shroud over his face.

Putting her hands on either side of his disfigured face, Violet patted him gently through the cloth. Behind her, Hurst huffed impatiently. Violet ignored the detective.

"You may rest assured, sir, that Inspector Hurst and I will not rest until we see justice done for you. You may rely upon me." With a final pat, she turned away from the corpse, only to find Hurst rolling his eyes at her.

"Is there a problem, Inspector?" she asked, arms crossed, practically challenging him.

"No, it's just . . . never mind. I wonder who did this?" Hurst said, presumably to change the subject.

"I know who did it," Violet said resolutely.

Hurst raised an eyebrow at her.

"Whoever came here with the two elderly bodies, ostensibly representing Mr. Crugg's shop, did so for the express purpose of getting into this room and destroying some sort of evidence on Mr. Wesley."

"That makes no sense. Why wouldn't they have dealt with the body before bringing him here?"

Violet made no reply, afraid to voice her thoughts. Whoever it was knew that Violet had been down here yesterday, and was either angry or afraid. Either way, Violet was probably in grave danger.

"What will you do now?" she asked.

"I plan to head back to London. I think Crugg's assistant may have had something to do with this, so Inspector Pratt and I will go see what he has to say about the old man and woman there," Hurst said, pointing at the corpses. "And you?"

"First, I plan to make the gentleman and his wife more comfortable." More eye rolling from Hurst. "Then I'm going to talk to Mr. Blackwell once more. Perhaps he hasn't told me all he knows."

Violet just hoped it was safe to be alone with the man. At this point, she didn't know who was friend or foe. Or lunatic.

"More questions, Mrs. Harper?" Blackwell waved off a student who appeared to be presenting a report to him.

The student gave Violet a curious glance as he hurried out of the room.

"Just a few," she said, refusing to be intimidated yet hoping she carried Hurst's shadow behind her.

Blackwell invited her to be seated, but Violet was too full of nervous energy. Instead, she paced as she sorted through a morass of questions and selected the most important one.

Just as she was about to ask it, Blackwell said, "Where is Inspector Hurst?"

"He's gone back to London."

"Ah, how disappointing." Violet wasn't sure if his voice was tinged with deep sincerity or sarcasm.

"Yes." She paused, standing directly in front of his desk and clasping her hands together. "I am of the impression that you didn't personally know the undertakers who brought in the elderly bodies yesterday."

"That is correct."

"May I ask you to describe them to me?"

Blackwell looked at the wall behind Violet, as though trying to conjure up their images. "One was a young fellow, rather short and slight. It actually surprised me that he had the strength to carry the weight of the dead, even if it be that of papery-thin old people."

Violet compressed her lips tightly, hopefully her only outward sign that she disapproved of his description.

"The other one was middle-aged, nondescript. No, wait, I do remember that he had an abnormally tall hat and wore a light-colored coat. Oh yes, and he had some of the densest mutton-chop whiskers I've ever seen."

This was saying something coming from a man whose own facial growth was—

Violet's heart raced as she stared at Blackwell, openmouthed. "Did you say he had thick muttonchop whiskers?"

"Yes, why?" The superintendent's own furry features contracted as he frowned.

"Oh my. Thank you for your time, sir. I must be going." Violet spun on her heel without explanation as the explanation was too chilling to put into words.

What in heaven's name did Mr. Ambrose have to do with this situation? Did he hold the key to this entire situation?

13

Mr. Ambrose answered the door personally, and his face registered genuine surprise to see Violet again.

"Mrs. Harper, what a surprise. Do you have news to report about the bodies at Brookwood?"

Violet held out a hand, and he shook it in a firm grip, then invited her inside. His office, despite being loaded with shelves of medical books and instruments, was once again spotlessly neat. Violet couldn't help but feel admiration for someone who kept his working place so tidy, even to the point of having his cousin help him.

A disastrous home was perfectly fine as long as someone who dealt with the dead—or the seriously ill, as Mr. Ambrose did—was immaculate at work.

Violet shook her head at such ridiculous approval. She was here to ferret out a killer.

A closed door at the rear of his office led to another room, presumably his anatomical examination room. Was it as tidy as this one?

There you go again, Violet Harper. A man's innocence isn't measured by the lack of dust on his shelves.

"I was wondering if I might ask you a few questions, sir," she said, once again playing a demure and retiring lady.

"Of course." Ambrose didn't sit behind his desk this time but instead stood in front of it with Violet. Was he eager to go somewhere? Violet would have preferred to have the expanse of the desktop between them.

"You already recall that there were two bodies who were shockingly alive at Brookwood. I have been looking into some peculiarities around them, and my investigation led me to Royal Surrey County Hospital."

"Yes, I have had many bodies delivered there and have taught the occasional seminars in anatomy and diseases. I understand Nathan Blackwell is a most competent superintendent." Ambrose smiled as if to encourage her to go on.

"I just left there a short while ago. The bodies of an elderly man and woman were dropped off yesterday. Was this your doing?"

"Indeed it was," Ambrose said. "As I told you, I occasionally purchase bodies for my own experimentation, but I also periodically handle them on behalf of undertakers who cannot accompany them down here and handle the transfer to the hospital. They telegraph me, and I come to Brookwood to meet the necropolis train and transport the coffins in a wagon I keep at the mews a few blocks away."

So that was why Ambrose was poking about the coffins at Brookwood, as an agent for undertakers shipping bodies there. Violet thought the undertakers should accompany the bodies themselves as a sign of respect for the dead, but it certainly wasn't illegal for them to pay Ambrose to do so.

"Mr. Blackwell said you were there with another man," she said, remembering that the superintendent referred to a second man who was short and slight.

"There are several young men in the neighborhood I hire to help me. Most of them have little ambition but are willing to do a night's work for a few coins."

"Who, then, was the undertaker for the elderly couple?" Violet was almost afraid of what the answer might be.

"Let me see . . ." Ambrose went behind the desk, opened a drawer, and shuffled through some papers, eventually nodding and pulling one out. "It was for Augustus Upton."

Violet blanched. How had she gone so completely off the train rails as to forget about the puffed-up, greasy undertaker? Trying to recover, she said, "But Mr. Blackwell said that two men from Crugg Undertaking were the ones who brought in the bodies."

Ambrose shook his head. "Mr. Blackwell was mistaken. There have been no body transports from Julian Crugg since he was, ahem, carried off last week. Actually, a funny thing happened with yesterday's transport. Upton sent me a telegram asking me to pick up the bodies, and later, when I returned from doing so, I had another telegram from him, attempting to cancel my involvement, saying he was planning to come on the next morning's train to take care of them. Of course, it was too late by then, and I telegraphed him to say so."

Violet blinked rapidly, digesting what the physician had told her. Upton must have wished to cancel Ambrose's involvement so that he could come to Surrey himself, accompany the body, and mutilate Mr. Wesley. But that meant . . . that someone had sent him word that Violet was poking around. Who was it? Mr. Blackwell? Who else could it have been but the hospital superintendent?

Violet couldn't believe that she had been so blind about the conceited Mr. Upton. What she couldn't understand, though, was why he had chosen such an unsavory sideline. She had many more questions, too. Had he attacked Susanna in the park? Was there any connection between him and the banker, Mr. Hayes, or was Violet's theory that he or other bankers were murdering their debtors a completely ridiculous idea?

Well, she might not understand the *why* of what was happening, but apparently Violet had learned the *who*. The most pressing problem now was how to stop Upton before he stopped her.

Violet was worried that Augustus Upton's shop would be closed for the day by the time she arrived, but as she approached it, she could see through the door's paned window inset that Upton was still there. In fact, he was comforting a woman dressed in black silk with expensive ebony lacing around the hem. How odd. Violet would expect a society lady to command the undertaker's presence at her home. Only the middle and lower classes would take themselves to the undertaker's shop.

"What am I to do? How could my sister do this to me?" The

woman's wailing cut clearly through the glass and probably down to the next block. "Clemmie, how I hate you."

Upton patted the woman's back with one tentac—*hand* and offered her a handkerchief with the other. "There, there, Mrs. Harrison. You've had a terrible shock is all. You will forget what your sister did in time."

The woman dabbed daintily at her nose with it, as if all of a sudden remembering her position in life.

The undertaker looked up as the door's bells jangled upon Violet's entry, his expression changing from curiosity to one of relish as he realized who had just entered. He held up a hand to Violet, a signal for her to wait while he tended to his customer.

Violet walked to the other side of the shop, pretending to examine a portrait on the wall. The photograph employed a technique that exploited grieving family members who were also interested in spiritualism. In the picture, a photograph of the mourner sitting in a chair was superimposed with an image of the deceased, artfully arranged to appear to be looking down upon the mourner, almost like an angel watching over his charge.

Sometimes photographers superimposed a picture of the deceased such that the body appeared to be ascending upward, into the arms of an angel welcoming the new soul into eternity. Photographers charged nearly double for these sly but enthralling pictures, which were frequently hand-tinted. Violet wholeheartedly approved of postmortem photography, but not these . . . these . . . hoaxes, which probably convinced people that every death entailed a direct entry into heaven, when many probably resulted in the complete opposite.

Still ostensibly concentrating on the framed photograph, Violet turned slightly to see that Upton had escorted Mrs. Harrison to a plush chair of sea-green velvet. Mrs. Harrison twisted the handkerchief through her fingers while Upton retrieved a tray of mourning jewelry for her to look through. The woman's tears ceased as she was instantly distracted by the baubles. The handkerchief fluttered to the floor as she picked out a locket and tried it against her shirtwaist.

Upton now crossed the room to Violet, smoothing down his hair and straightening his jacket. "More questions today, Mrs. Harper? I am obviously quite busy, but am more than happy to assist you shortly. In fact, I have remembered a story about a man I once buried in the most unusual coffin—" he said in a low tone.

Violet was still concentrating on Mrs. Harrison and nodded toward the woman. "She is mercurial in her grief."

He shrugged, making him look like a penguin in his tightly corseted frame. "Her younger sister was a bit wild. Still unmarried at twenty-four, she decided to explore the streets of St. Giles on her own one evening, which was bad enough as it is. But a gent mistook her for a prostitute, and when she refused his advances, well, she ended up like many a fallen woman. The family is mortified. In times like this, I wish I had some laudanum to give them to calm their nerves."

That explained why Mrs. Harrison didn't want Upton coming to her home, which would only serve to pique the neighbors' interest and thus make public the news of her sister's indiscretion.

"I can only imagine how distraught she is," Violet said. She was having a difficult time concentrating on anything but the tormented woman in the chair, who had just bent over to retrieve the handkerchief and now held it to one eye even as she continued pawing through the jewelry tray with her other hand.

"Indeed, but she will recover. I know how to use charm to soothe them in their grief," Upton said with great confidence.

"I suspect she needs sympathy, not charm." Violet doubted, though, that he had a genuinely sympathetic suction cup on his tentacles.

As usual, though, Violet was not approaching her subject in a winsome or tactful manner, although Upton was too self-absorbed to notice. "You may one day serve the likes of Mrs. Harrison. I can show you some clever approaches for attracting society to your shop."

Violet didn't have the heart to tell him she had served the queen herself. Besides, she was here for answers, not to enter a mourner-handling contest. She decided to be direct right now rather than wait for him to finish with his client.

"You may be interested to know that I am well aware of the two elderly bodies you asked Mr. Byron Ambrose to accompany to Brookwood, later telegraphing him and stating that you would go down yourself to take the bodies on to Royal Surrey County Hospital."

Upton's eyes goggled, as though he had transformed from an octopus into a frog. "Mrs. Harper, you are truly daft. I have no idea what you speak of. What elderly bodies? What do they have to do with me? As you know, I am a well-respected businessman who—"

"Plenty, sir. You were eager to take Mr. Ambrose's place in delivering the bodies to the hospital, for you needed to visit another body there, Mr. Raymond Wesley. He had survived being installed in a coffin by you, rising alive from it not two weeks ago. You were panicked, were you not, to realize that I had discovered him lying in the storage room. You had murdered him and needed to return to cover up your method of murder. Accompanying two new bodies to the hospital provided you with that opportunity, did it not?"

Upton's normally jovial expression went blank. "Madam, I believe you may have lost your senses. Why did I need to murder anyone, much less this Mr. Wesley you're making such a fuss about?"

"I believe that after this man rose from his coffin, he realized that he had been there due to your incompetence. You told me yourself that you can have a body buried in no time." Violet snapped her fingers as Upton had once done. "Someone who buries hastily is bound to make serious errors about his customers. Mr. Wesley came back to you, perhaps you argued, perhaps he demanded a bribe to remain quiet about your ineptitude. You became enraged and murdered him. His body was largely unmarked, so I suspect you somehow choked him, perhaps by stuffing something in his throat. I didn't think to check there on my initial examination of him."

"These are the ravings of a Bedlamite. How could you imagine that a revered man of undertaking such as myself could be involved in such a villainous scheme? It is complete nonsense." Upton was glancing nervously over at Mrs. Harrison, who seemed to be taking an interest in the raised whispers across the room.

Violet continued. "Somehow, you discovered that I had taken an interest in Wesley's body. Perhaps you and Mr. Blackwell are in league with one another. You were desperate to return to mutilate the body to cover up what you had originally done to him. After all, desecration is a far lesser crime than murder, isn't it? You already had plans to ship a couple of bodies through Mr. Ambrose to Royal Surrey County Hospital, hence your ill-fated plan to take Mr. Ambrose's place. Undaunted, you simply went later and did your heinous work."

"Mrs. Harper, clearly you are more hysterical than Mrs. Harrison. That is the most preposterous, ridiculous story I've ever heard, and I have been an undertaker for nearly twenty years."

Violet refused to be mocked. "You should know that Inspectors Magnus Pompey Hurst and Langley Pratt, of Scotland Yard, are very interested in this case."

Upton shook his hands out as if ridding himself of Violet's accusation. It was a disturbing sight. "Dear lady, what case? Is London so devoid of thieves and murderers that Scotland Yard is concerned with two decrepits who have ended up at a teaching hospital for dissection? Or another body that some inebriated medical student ravaged?"

Violet hadn't thought of that possibility. Surely Wesley's destruction was not the result of a medical student having experimented on it overnight. Upton was attempting to distract her. "No, they are concerned with a case of possibly three murders, most likely caused by an undertaker who is being careless with the bodies in his charge."

Upton glanced back at Mrs. Harrison once more. "I am not careless, merely efficient. Now if you will excuse me . . ." He started to return to his client, then turned back to Violet, his expression contrite.

"See here, Mrs. Harper, I'll admit that I sell bell coffins and other safety devices for a large profit, but there's no crime in that. A man of my stature has to offer whatever it is the public wants and is willing to pay for. And perhaps I drop hints to customers that Brookwood Cemetery requires that safety coffins be used for any burials there so that they feel obligated to purchase them."

This was a surprise. Violet held her expression steady, as if she already had known this piece of information.

"There's no harm in them, is there? In fact, you've already seen them work twice in recent days." He rubbed his palms together. Violet wondered how badly he was perspiring beneath his corset. "You've made a mistake in accusing me. I think perhaps I should lodge a complaint with—who were they?—Hirsch and Katt over your harassment of a man as well respected as I am."

From across the room, Mrs. Harrison was weeping and snuffling again, the jewelry tray's interesting contents forgotten in her lap. Upton contemplated Violet sadly as though she were responsible for his customer's renewed outburst. "As you can see, I have a customer who needs me. If you would please find your own way out . . ."

Upton hurried away from Violet, slowing as he approached Mrs. Harrison and opening his tentacles wide as if welcoming her for the first time. "Ah, I see you are admiring the Beautiful Memories ring, an excellent choice. You will be able to insert not only styled hair under the dome, but some lovely pearls and miniature ribbons. You can remember your sister as she used to be, before the unfortunate incident . . ."

Violet moved to the door. This was the second time in three days that she'd been thrown out of an undertaker's shop. Would her reputation suffer from all of her snooping and accusations? Perhaps she should visit Hurst tomorrow morning about Upton and ask the detective to make an *actual* visit to the undertaker. Hurst would be far better at extracting a full confession from the man.

As she gently opened the shop's door to let herself out, careful not to let the bells jangle too much and draw attention to herself, Violet reflected upon the fact that she needed to improve her skills of interrogation and accusation. For the moment, she was proving to be a dismal failure at it.

Not only that, something was bothering her. It was something Upton had said—what was it? It had been important, perhaps critical, to the situation. She shook her head, unable to remember, but wondering if it further bolstered the case against him . . . or established his innocence.

Back at home, Sam had left a note for her. He and some new banker were taking the train to Nottinghamshire to walk over the coalfield Sam wanted to purchase. It was the closest Sam had gotten to a "yes" with one of the finance men. He would return on the morrow.

Mildly irritated that her husband wasn't there for counsel, especially given her upset state, Violet paced back and forth inside her bedchamber. At dinnertime, she refused Mrs. Wren's meal to the cook's great annoyance, instead requesting that tea and toast be brought to her, which were produced with grumbling and a sour look.

Violet drank the tea and nibbled halfheartedly at the toast, which she knew would vex Mrs. Wren even more. It wasn't often that Violet refused plates set before her. However, Mrs. Wren's temper and her own waistline were irrelevant at the moment. Violet needed to think.

She had been so sure Upton was guilty, but as usual, now she was uncertain. Just as she had been suspicious of Crugg, Vernon, and Ambrose. She was running out of suspects. Twenty minutes of hair brushing didn't calm her mind or help her to see things any more clearly.

Hours later, restless and unable to sleep, Violet retrieved her copy of *Lorna Doone* from the bookshelf in the parlor. Ruth had made great headway on returning the room to normal upon Susanna's departure. Mrs. Softpaws was even at ease enough to have made her bed on the settee, where she now lay curled up in a tight ball. Other round spots of fur on the other chairs in the room proved that the cat was probably quite comfortable now that she had so much space to call her own with Susanna and Benjamin gone.

With the book under one arm, Violet stopped to scratch behind the ears of the sleeping cat, which she'd found as a kitten, loitering outside the basement door of the townhome she'd shared with her first husband. She smiled to think of how she used to parade about the streets of London with the orphaned waif Susanna, who would walk the young cat on a lead. Violet had been an oddity then, and she supposed she still was now.

Mrs. Softpaws's fur wasn't as thick and luxurious as it used to be, probably due to the cat's aging. Violet sighed in sympathy. The cat looked up at her so sleepily and incoherently, it was as if she'd been drugged.

Violet's hand stopped in midscratch, eliciting a cross between a meow and a yawn from the feline. She wasn't sure what was racing faster, her heart or her mind, as she quickly put together everything in her head. She now understood everything: what had happened with the bodies at Brookwood, what the circumstances were surrounding Roger Blount, why Margery Latham had died, and why Julian Crugg had been murdered.

It was a ghastly, horrific chain of events, and she had been completely blind to the obvious. How could she have missed the unmistakable clues that had loomed so large in her path that she should have been tripping over them?

"Thank you, Mrs. Softpaws," Violet said gratefully, giving the cat a final scratch under the chin. "You've been very helpful."

14

Violet stood outside the door, nervously mustering up the courage to knock.

After a sleepless night, she had finally risen around eight o'clock, dressed quickly, and, on a whim, removed a fish knife from the kitchen while Ruth was puttering around in the study. Then she had raced to Scotland Yard to rouse Inspectors Hurst and Pratt with her explanation of what had happened.

The two men weren't in yet but would be within the hour, the desk sergeant told her. Violet had paced for several minutes while debating what to do, and finally decided that there was already too much risk that the murderer had left town and wouldn't be stopped.

She told the desk sergeant where she was going, leaving a message for Inspector Hurst to meet her there.

Had she been foolish not to wait for the detectives before coming here?

There was no help for it now. Violet put her hand inside her reticule to assure herself that the short but wide blade that regularly cut through fillets of haddock and trout was still there.

Would she be able to cut through human flesh with it if someone tried to murder her? She wasn't sure. She had spent her adult life caring for bodies, not destroying them.

Finally summoning the will to do so, Violet rang the bell but received no answer. Hearing movement from within, though, she tried the door latch, which gave way easily. She pushed the door open and stepped over the threshold.

A small travel trunk lay open on the desk, half filled with books, papers, and medical supplies. Should Violet really be surprised that he was gathering up his valuables to leave town? Where was he planning to go? America, maybe? Australia? A remote, deserted island?

A door at the back of the room opened, and he stepped out, carrying a vial full of caramel-colored liquid littered with oddly shaped flakes and wearing an expression of surprise at seeing Violet standing there. In the moments that the door was open, Violet saw what she had expected behind him: several coffins, a portable examination table, and the tools of the anatomist's trade. She steeled herself for what was to come.

"Mrs. Harper, what a surprise to see you again so soon." He tossed the vial into the trunk and went to a bookcase, searching through the shelves until he found a stack of papers, which he also added to the trunk.

"Are you going somewhere?" she asked.

"Just a little holiday. I've been working entirely too hard."

That was an interesting way of characterizing the murder of at least four people, if not many more. He continued to toss items into the trunk.

"Were you successful in your investigation?" he wanted to know.

"Yes, although not in the manner that I expected. I had time to think things over last night and realized that I hadn't been pursuing matters in the most fruitful way possible." She stared directly at him, daring him to hold her gaze. He dropped his almost immediately, returning to his packing.

"It was last night, as my daughter's cat looked up at me from where she lay sleeping, that I realized it all. Does that surprise you, sir? That a feline held the answer? It's true, Mr. Ambrose. It made me realize how you were transporting the bodies to Brookwood. Before you killed them, of course."

Ambrose stopped what he was doing and glanced up with a look of near admiration. "Is that so?"

He came from around the desk and locked the door. It bolted with a disturbing finality. His smile as he turned back to face her was equally disturbing. "I see no point in dissembling, madam. I must compliment you on not being thrown too far off the scent when I sent you to Augustus Upton. He's so odious that I was certain you'd be chasing him for at least the next week."

"My apologies for disappointing the good doctor." Violet felt her pulse racing beneath her skin. What was he going to do next? To her relief, he went back to packing, removing some items and substituting them with others. It seemed a random mix of belongings, but who knew what went on in the mind of a murderer?

"And what did your dear kitty tell you?" he asked lightly, although Violet was certain he was trying to determine if she really did know anything.

"It was what I noticed in her. She was sleepy, and it reminded me of someone who has been administered a sleep tonic. That made two things jump out at me."

Ambrose flipped through a medical book, as if considering whether to take it or not. "And what two things were they?"

"I remembered finding a bottle of laudanum among Mr. Crugg's belongings. At the time, I assumed he took it himself, given how high-strung he was."

"Hmm, a reasonable assumption, Mrs. Harper."

"Yes, but now I know that wasn't true. When I went to see Mr. Upton yesterday, he commented to me that he wished he had laudanum to give to his more hysterical customers, to calm them. After seeing Mrs. Softpaws in such a tranquil state last night, I realized that Crugg's laudanum wasn't for himself but for calming his customers. His customers inside coffins, that is. Crugg obtained the laudanum from you, didn't he?"

"There are hundreds of places to purchase the drug. He didn't need me to give it to him." Ambrose seemed unperturbed by what Violet said, addressing her condescendingly, as if she were a mere child. "So you think he was embalming them with it? How could Crugg possibly be administering opium tinctures to corpses?"

"He wasn't, sir. He was offering it to living people on your behalf. Instead of the usual dose that would be used to suppress a cough or calm someone's nerves, you instructed Crugg to give a dose that, while not fatal, would ensure unconsciousness for a period of time. With their slowed breathing, the bodies could endure the hour or two necessary inside the coffin to make the trip to Brookwood without running out of fresh air. Also, they wouldn't experience the panic that comes from being shut inside a cramped box like that.

"You couldn't ask for air holes to be drilled into the sides of the coffin, lest your cabinetmaker be suspicious, so you had to be sure the body could survive with just the coffin's air. Ironic, isn't it, that with so many safety coffins available, you couldn't use most of them, lest some unsuspecting railway worker—or nosy undertaker—notice a living body inside too soon."

"That's quite an interesting theory." The doctor sat down in the chair behind his desk, pushing the trunk to one side so that he could fully view Violet. "You seem to be quite astute. Why don't you tell me the rest of your thesis? I'm sure it is every bit as fascinating as this fabrication about laudanum." He smiled, and it reminded her of a wolf salivating over a heedless doe that was stepping precariously close to him.

Violet began pacing, her usual nervous activity as she thought through a knotty problem.

"I think that a banker, specifically Mr. Cyril Hayes of East London Bank, was informing you of aristocratic young men whose debts were considerable, but who still had plenty of assets that could be easily turned into cash. For a fee, he referred them to you, although some, like Roger Blount, found you on their own. You helped them devise an escape, as they were ostensibly dying, but in reality they would end up going south, perhaps ultimately to Spain or France. I imagine the rumors of these men being spotted on trains were merely a happy coincidence of gossipy reporters stretching the truth to come up with stories."

"I see," he said, leaning back in the chair.

"The desperate dodger would first transfer his assets into your name. You would sign a fake death certificate and arrange for the dodger to go to Julian Crugg, who, for another fee, would enact the charade of a workman's funeral, then drug the client enough to make the journey to Brookwood inside the coffin comfortable."

Ambrose's smug expression told Violet that she had guessed correctly.

"You would meet the coffin, usher it off the platform to your office, then help the dodger start his new life. But your plans took a darker turn."

The doctor raised an expectant eyebrow but still said nothing.

"I had suspected Mr. Upton early on, but was not truly led to him until your misleading suggestion. I also suspected James Vernon, as I know he is a very sloppy undertaker and might have been responsible for shipping off live bodies, not realizing they were dead. Even you, sir, passed through my list of suspects. But it was only last night that I realized it all. I should almost congratulate you on such a cleverly executed plan and your calm demeanor. If not for Mr. Crugg's death, which removed him from my list of suspects, you might never have been caught."

There was that dreadfully patronizing smile again. "But, Mrs. Harper, I haven't been caught. You are telling me a fine story, and when you're done, you yourself will take some of my opium tincture and fall fast asleep. You need have no fear of pain, just as my other patients felt none. I only regret that I will have no access to your fortune, although I suspect that, as an undertaker, you don't have one worth considering. I use Sydenham's formula for my opium tincture. It takes two weeks to macerate the opium, saffron, cinnamon, cloves, and sherry, but it creates a very palatable formula for administering it in large doses. You will enjoy the taste."

Ah, that explained Mr. Wesley having the odor of cloves on his breath.

"And, yes, you were correct in your earlier assertion. I attempted to have Crugg use prefilled syringes to ensure the right amount, but he was squeamish about injecting a living body, so I had to rely on him to dropper the right dose into their mouths. He was quite hopeless at it."

Violet started to understand why Crugg was so keyed up all the time. She would be, too, if she were involved in such improprieties.

"Mr. Yates must have awoken during the train's journey," she continued. "Probably a combination of the noise and motion of the train, and an inadequate dose of laudanum, made him confused, so he rang the coffin bell."

"Stupid Yates. I told him the bell was only for me to ring when everything was clear, not if he merely woke up on the platform before I had secured him. Of course, it would have to be *you* waiting on the platform with me, wouldn't it? Ultimately, though, you proved a minor inconvenience once I realized you hadn't heard what the man said."

Violet was puzzled. "What he said? I only recall that Mr. Yates was muttering something nonsensical."

"No, he was confused in his drugged state, and was saying that he had to find a bank. I ushered him away on the pretense of checking him over, to get him out of your presence as quickly as possible."

Violet still didn't understand. "Why did he want a bank?"

"He must have thought he was still in London. All of my customers were required to sign over their monetary assets into an alias of mine. Once they arrived in Surrey, I would sign everything back over into whatever new name they had adopted for themselves, less my considerable handling fee, naturally."

"Naturally." Violet was amazed by the man's arrogance.

"But I am not a stupid man, Mrs. Harper. It came to my attention that I could demand much more than twenty percent of their money, and that they would be in no position to refuse me. If they did, well . . ." Ambrose spread his hands apart. "Yates was smart enough not to refuse me, but Mr. Wesley wasn't quite as intelligent.

"First, he jumped out like a madman when you rang the bell on his coffin. I suppose he couldn't be blamed for assuming that was my signal, but it was most inconvenient. Then he threatened to sue me for increasing my price." Ambrose shook his head. "Foolish."

Violet realized something else. "Your arrangement with Royal

Surrey County Hospital enables you to easily dispose of the bodies of those who don't pay you what you want, meaning you get paid by your victims, then again by the hospital."

"As I said, Mrs. Harper, I am a very successful physician."

"Physician" was hardly what Byron Ambrose could be called.

"Once you realized I was poking about at the hospital—presumably because Nathan Blackwell mentioned it to you—you immediately went there to mar Wesley's body so that I wouldn't figure out how he had died."

"Blackwell is a ninny, hardly worthy of his position, although he does stay out of my way."

"He isn't that much of a ninny, sir, for he implicated you. Not by name, of course, but by giving me a description I was sure to recognize."

Ambrose harrumphed in derision. "Then he isn't a ninny, he's a nitwit. Not that it matters much."

Blackwell's personality defects were irrelevant in Violet's mind. "He tried to tell me that Wesley died from swallowing acid."

At this, Ambrose laughed. "He probably thought you were accusing him of a crime against Wesley, and he didn't have the courage to stand up against the little lady undertaker and tell you to mind your own business."

Violet wanted to know more about Wesley. "I admit I was confused. There were no apparent marks on him, and he was fully clothed, which made no sense if he was an indigent body taken there for dissection."

"I asked Mr. Wesley to join me for a friendly drink to celebrate his departure after he had refused my request for more money. It was no hardship for him to take the opium-laced drink. In fact, we could almost say he did it to himself, so readily did he accept the glass."

Poor Mr. Wesley, he had had no idea that his plan to start a new life had ensured his death.

"Mr. Wesley was from Piccadilly but wore cheaply made clothes, and I—"

"Yes, I always tell the fools to dress in middle-class clothing for their coffin journeys, just so they do not draw attention to themselves in case things go awry, as you can see they sometimes do. Most listen to me, but some dolts cannot resist their silks and brocades. At least Wesley was obedient in that respect."

"What of Jeremiah Dormer? Was he a successful escapee, or will I find him in the hospital's burial ground?"

Ambrose's smile was both enigmatic and chilling to behold. "I don't think he's anyone you need to worry your little head over. I am quite good at taking care of those who don't listen to me."

Poor Mr. Dormer.

"But Roger Blount was a different case, wasn't he?" Violet asked, dreading to learn what may have happened to him before he reached Brookwood. "It was his death that really had me confused. He was escaping London, but not for debts, and engaged your services."

"Yes, he was the closest I came to making a mistake. He came to me on his own, no doubt referred by some other wastrel friend. He wanted to be rid of his family, and the feeling was mutual on their part. His plan was to fake his death, be sent to Brookwood, meet his fiancée, and together they would go on to France. The family paid me for my services in advance, but I assumed I could squeeze him of a bit more when he arrived at Brookwood. But that nitwit, Crugg, gave him entirely too much laudanum and he died en route. Or else he gave him far too little, and the man awoke en route and suffocated to death." He shrugged in a cavalier manner. "Who can be sure?"

"How did they avoid having the coroner do an inquest when he died?"

"Really, Mrs. Harper? You don't think that a family as prestigious as the Blounts could avoid an inquest by merely telling the police that their boy had died naturally? That he had been ill for some time, or that he choked to death on a chicken bone?"

Violet had to admit that that was possible.

Ambrose continued dispassionately. "Crugg came to me later and told me about Miss Latham's hysterical breakdown at the station, in front of the inquisitive Violet Harper. He was able to escort her away from you, but the damage was done."

Violet knew what had happened next. "You then murdered Miss Latham."

"What choice did I have? I couldn't have that grief-mad woman divulging any secrets now, could I?"

"You did it in such a way that her parents and the coroner thought that she, too, died of natural causes." Violet could hardly believe the callousness with which Ambrose went after his victims.

"Must I remind you that I am a terribly talented physician? I am quite proficient in my use of opium tinctures."

Indeed.

Ambrose was enjoying his story, probably elated to have an opportunity to share it with someone almost as intimately familiar with it as he was. "After you interfered once more and went to Crugg to accuse him of killing Miss Latham, he nearly fainted dead away. I told him to kill you before you ended up reporting our little arrangement to the police, but Crugg was like a frightened little boy. He informed me that he was fine with extortion, but he drew the line at murder. What a squeaky little mouse. With great bluster, he said he was finished with our partnership, but I had no other undertaker lined up and told him so. He insisted he be freed from his duty to me, and I obliged him. He no longer has a duty to me. He was entirely too weak to be associated with me."

"But first you followed me and attempted to kill me in Hyde Park. Only you confused my daughter for me, and nearly killed her."

"No, no, I realized my error soon enough. It was an excellent opportunity to send you a warning, though. One you didn't heed. You should be grateful to me for being so kind to your daughter."

"You would call bashing the girl on the head to be *kind?* Are you—" Violet stopped her thought. Of course he was mad, the complete opposite of the kindly physician she'd spoken to on other occasions. Shouting at him would not save her, either. She had to remain calm. She changed the subject.

"The Debtors Act must have been a great disappointment to you, sir, since the elimination of jail for them meant that fewer dodgers would feel the need to escape punishment."

"Not really. It was easy enough for Mr. Hayes to convince them that they would be better off with a fresh start in a new country, even if they could no longer be jailed for their debts here."

"But their debts would have passed on to their estates. They didn't absolve their families of them after their supposed deaths."

"And how would that concern me? That was the problem of their loved ones, not me."

Of course.

She returned her attention to Ambrose. "Among Mr. Crugg's belongings, I also found a pocket watch engraved with a bell on it. That was a gift from you, wasn't it?"

Ambrose smiled. "Ah, you discovered my little conceit. The bell was a clever touch, wasn't it? Yes, that was a gift to Crugg. It was my pretense for getting into the shop and having him show me the back room. When he turned to put it in a drawer, I took the opportunity he presented to . . . take care of him."

"You forced him to overdose on laudanum." No wonder Hurst thought the man was a suicide. It was doubtful there was any evidence of murder on Crugg.

Ambrose shrugged. "He had become a liability to me and my work."

"You mean, to your ambitions?"

"They are one and the same, Mrs. Harper."

"Where was Mr. Trumpington in all of this?"

"Crugg was sworn to secrecy, so Trumpington was of no concern to me. Although I suppose he might have made a good partner after Crugg died, given how ridiculously loyal he was to his employer. Hmm." Ambrose appeared to contemplate this, as though it was some angle he had overlooked.

The physician stood again, searched through his trunk, and pulled out the vial Violet had seen him pack earlier. He tucked it into his jacket pocket and crossed the room to a table, which held an assortment of bottles and flasks. His back was to her, but she saw him pull the vial out of his pocket, and she knew what he was doing.

"What is your plan now, Mr. Ambrose?" Violet asked, slowly reaching into her reticule and grabbing the knife's handle. Was this the wisest course of action? Should she simply flee? Surely she could unlock the door and get out of his office and to the train station without his catching up to her.

Without turning around, he replied, "Oh, I do believe I will head over to the continent somewhere. I should be able to easily start my practice again. I imagine there are plenty of places where young spendthrifts have the threat of debtors' prison hanging over their heads."

"My apologies, Mr. Ambrose, but I cannot allow you to do that."

He glanced briefly over his shoulder. "And you believe you're going to stop me?" he said, returning to his work of pouring what she knew was laudanum into a glass. The scent of cloves and cinnamon drifted over to her, before being quickly diluted by the splashing of spirits into the glass.

"I will do what I must." Violet pulled the knife out of her reticule and tossed the bag onto Ambrose's desk. He turned around with the short glass in his hand. It was only half full, so she could only imagine the high ratio of his opium tincture in it.

Ambrose laughed in derision. "Do you think you will stop me with that silly little thing? Come, let us be reasonable, Mrs. Harper. We both know you are no match for my superior strength. Also, I am much more valuable. There are hundreds of undertakers in Great Britain, but only one man with my particular skills."

How had this monster managed to hide behind such a kind and meek façade? How many men had he fooled with his genial demeanor? Did they all die in disbelief that a physician—a healer—was actually intent on murdering them? Or did he overdose them before they realized what was happening, and thus they passed on swiftly?

Am I about to die swiftly? The thought stiffened her resolve. *No, absolutely not.*

Violet rushed forward with the knife in her right hand, instinctively raising it up in the air as she bore down upon him. Ambrose's immediate reaction was to set the glass down carefully—as if he knew he'd still need it—then bring his right fist up in a wide arc that landed squarely on Violet's left jaw, completely knocking her off her feet. She landed hard on her right side, and the knife went clattering across the floor. The pain in her jaw radiated throughout her head, and she worked to maintain consciousness.

She was aware of Ambrose, the glass of laudanum in his hand once more, casually stepping over her to retrieve the knife.

No, she couldn't allow this to happen. She couldn't . . .

Ambrose pulled her roughly to her feet and stood over her, the handle of the knife held between his bared teeth. He moved it to his free hand. "Now, Mrs. Harper, as I said, you must be reasonable. Take this"—he held up the glass of opium tincture—"or take this." Violet's knife, an instrument of protection thirty seconds ago, now gleamed threateningly in her face.

"I'll do neither," she said, with far more bravado than she felt.

He shook his head, a headmaster disappointed in an errant pupil. "I much prefer that you drink the laudanum; there's no pain to it for you and no mess in it for me. But if you insist on it being this way . . ."

Ambrose put the glass on the desk behind Violet. He grabbed her throat with one hand, and for a moment, Violet thought he was about to kiss her. But when she saw the feral gleam in his eye as he raised the blade above his head, she knew she was about to be his next victim.

And, for certain, a fish knife was sharp enough.

15

"We'll have none of that, will we?" Hurst's voice boomed so loudly as he crashed through the door that even though Violet was rapidly losing consciousness thanks to Ambrose's hand squeezing her windpipe, she was able to hear him clearly.

At Hurst's forced entry, Ambrose let go of her. Or, rather, he pushed her out of his way. Violet stumbled backward to the ground, gasping. The centurion in Hurst had taken command of the situation in an instant, and he was shouting at Ambrose as if the doctor were a lowly legionary soldier. Coming in behind him was Inspector Pratt, who was dangling iron manacles from one hand.

As Hurst roared at the physician, Violet rose clumsily to her feet by grabbing the edge of Ambrose's desk and pulling herself up. The pain in her jaw made her wonder if she had loose teeth.

She heard the grinding sound of a key inserted into a lock, and knew that Mr. Ambrose was secured. All of a sudden, Inspector Pratt loomed over her. "Mrs. Harper," he said, his voice full of concern, "your face . . ."

She could only imagine the bruise that was forming. Before she could answer, Ambrose stumbled across the room, with Hurst pushing him from behind. "Mrs. Harper, anything you'd like to say to this cretin before I—What happened to you?"

"I'm afraid I had a little spill." Violet refused to give Ambrose the satisfaction of hearing how badly he had hurt her.

Hurst looked pensively at her, and Violet knew he understood exactly what had happened. "Well, the desk sergeant at the Yard told me you were off to Ambrose's office here in Surrey and wanted us to join you. It sounded suspicious enough, so we jumped onto the first train we could. Good thing we did, else you might have been another of the good doctor's victims, eh, Ambrose?" Hurst cuffed the doctor against the ear and was rewarded with a grunt.

"Augustus Upton filed a complaint against you, Mrs. Harper," Pratt said. "I thought you might like to know, as we will have to ask you a few questions about it."

Violet nodded. "I understand. I probably owe that man an apol—"

Ambrose broke in. "I would like to join Upton's complaint against Mrs. Harper. She is a carping busybody and a—"

"Be quiet, will you?" Hurst growled, cuffing the man's other ear.

Ambrose went silent but glowered at them as if hoping they might all drop dead from the intensity of his stare.

"Mrs. Harper," Hurst said, "I presume you now know what happened with all of your disappearing bodies?"

"I know everything, Inspector."

The detective sighed in capitulation. "Naturally. Come on, both of you. We'll get Ambrose here to a cell where he belongs; then we'll return to the Yard to make a report. I believe I will need several drams of whiskey to hear it all."

Violet suspected that Hurst would be plying her with questions about Mary, not Ambrose, long before they ever reached Scotland Yard.

16

Violet sat in Etchingham House's tiny, overfilled study once more. Byron Ambrose had been taken to Newgate, where he awaited trial for numerous counts of murder and embezzlement. Violet doubted the doctor would be able to intimidate a jury with his black scowl. Mr. Hayes, too, was awaiting trial on lesser charges. Now she wanted to clear up some remaining details.

At least Audley had the good grace to act a little sheepish.

Inspector Hurst had decided that pursuing the family for fraud was pointless, given that their son had died in the execution of the fraud. Violet, however, wanted questions answered. Lady Etchingham was indisposed, the butler said, an obvious lie, but Audley was willing to see her.

This time accepting his offer of a glass of sherry, she explained everything she knew. Audley took a gulp of his drink. "Yes, that is all correct."

"So the grave next to the family crypt was a fake?"

He nodded. "It had to look as though we were burying him, but we didn't want to open the crypt for an empty coffin. His body would be placed in there far in the future when he really died, not that he deserved a hallowed place with us. Except that he—" Audley choked on the last word, and took another swallow from his glass. "Except that his plan was an unmitigated disaster, as most of them were. I should have known better than to go along with it, but it seemed the best way to save the family's reputation."

"And what was that plan?" Violet wasn't sure she really wanted to hear Audley's version of things.

"He would fake his death, meet up with Margery, and together they would start a life elsewhere on the three thousand pounds we gave him to never resurface."

Violet shuddered inside to think of having such dreadful familial relations that you would be paid to never return nor acknowledge your family again.

"I remember his gravestone," Violet said. "It had a verse on it: 'For we must all appear before the judgment seat of Christ; that every one may receive the things done in his body, according to that he hath done, whether it be good or bad.' Why did you choose that?"

"It was a reminder of how Roger had so fouled up this family as to make us coconspirators with him. I, for one, would never forget it, and I didn't want anyone passing by what was ostensibly his grave to forget it, either. It also served to shore up our position that we heartily disapproved of my brother, and weren't sad at his passing."

The whole situation made Violet almost glad she had no siblings.

"You lied when you said he dropped dead after finishing a meal."

Audley looked at Violet as though she were an imbecile. "Well, of course I did. Did you think I would confess all of our family doings to a mere undertaker, and one I'd never met before, at that?"

No, she supposed he wouldn't.

"Why didn't Miss Latham's family bury her with him?"

He shrugged elegantly, a move he had probably learned in the past while on the Grand Tour. "We haven't had contact with them since it all happened, but I suspect they didn't want to be associated with our tainted family, no matter how much wealth we might offer."

Unlike Ambrose's other victims, Lord Blount needed a way to escape England for reasons other than dodging a debt but was still able to pay handsomely for the assistance. Almost to herself, Violet said, "If Mr. Crugg hadn't bumbled up the laudanum dosage, perhaps Lord Blount wouldn't have died in the coffin before arriving in Brookwood."

"Yes, Julian Crugg assured us he had everything well in hand. Obviously, he didn't. Now we learn from Scotland Yard that Roger would have fallen into the hands of that demon Mr. Ambrose even if he had survived the railway trip, meaning it was never even possible that Roger's plan was going to work." Audley shook his head in disgust. "Why did we listen to him?"

Violet ignored the rhetorical question. "You also lied about not knowing who the family undertaker was."

The viscount shrugged. "It didn't seem important. And I had no idea Crugg would be targeted himself."

Violet's next question was irrelevant, but she had to know. "As for Miss Latham—"

"Of course you would ask about her." Audley cut Violet off before she could even finish her query. "Yes, yes, yes, I was in love with the dear girl. Does that satisfy your curiosity? I hardly think my wife needs to know about it, do you? Margery was—Well, Margery was exquisite. I can hardly believe that madman, Ambrose, snuffed her out like that. My brother didn't deserve her, and I was shocked that she agreed to his plan. My only hope now is that she rests in heaven while my brother is tortured with the flames of wrath." Audley's eyes welled up, but he quickly blinked back his sorrow.

Society men were trained not to demonstrate grief. Violet found it interesting that the Earl of Etchingham's heir was far more broken up over his brother's fiancée than over Blount himself. She would intrude no further on the man's sorrow. Putting her nearly untouched glass on a table, she rose and thanked him for his time, then fled Etchingham House as quickly as possible.

Roger's foolish experiments and ideas had cost him not only his own life but that of Margery Latham, as well. What a terrible web of lies and deceit this entire affair had been, with Byron Ambrose sitting in the middle of it like a vigilant, patient, and monstrous spider.

* * *

At the sound of the shop's bells jangling several days later, Violet put aside her ledger, which seemed to be growing heavier each year. She glanced at her fingers, as covered with black ink as Inspector Pratt's were always coated with graphite. She'd heard about some new invention in the States called a type-writing machine. Supposedly it used a foot pedal and keys to put words on paper. Could such a device help her with her correspondence and keeping her books?

"How may I be of service to—Oh, Mr. Vernon," Violet said, surprised to see the man entering her shop and not quite sure what to say to him.

"Mrs. Harper," he said shyly, removing his hat and twisting it in his hands. "I've come, er, to pay my respects to you."

She stepped out from behind the counter. "Your respects, sir?"

"Yes, madam. You see, I—I—" Vernon stopped and frowned, as if he'd forgotten his line and was waiting for a whispered cue.

"Would you care to sit down?" Violet offered.

"No, that won't be necessary. I, yes, I just wanted to inform you that—" Vernon took a breath and seemed to find his place in his script. "I'm leaving London. A bit of rest and relaxation, you understand."

"How very pleasant for you," Violet said cautiously. Why was he reporting this to her?

"Yes, indeed. My daughter lives up in Rutland. She wants me to stay with her awhile. You know how children can be."

"They are our greatest joy and our greatest worry, are they not?" she replied.

Vernon still twisted his hat nervously, as if the action would summon up a well of courage.

"I do hope you have a pleasant journey," Violet said. "Are you sure you wouldn't like to—"

"I'm asking for your forgiveness, Mrs. Harper," Vernon blurted out. "I apologize for what I did to you in my shop that day. I confess I was a bit . . . strained . . . at the time. I never did mean you any harm."

Violet suspected the man's mind was probably still strained, and not entirely whole, and that he would remain with his daughter permanently. For the sake of grieving families all over London, Violet was glad.

Ignoring that thought, she instead responded to him graciously, "I accept your apology as if the matter never occurred, and I will never think on it again." She meant it. Why dwell upon the actions of a man who was not evil, like Ambrose, but merely disturbed?

Vernon gave her a weak smile and ceased the mauling of his hat. "I'll leave you now, Mrs. Harper, with my thanks that you didn't ever send the police after me." He planted his crumpled hat back on his head and departed.

No, Vernon was no criminal, just a poor soul who needed to be as far away from the undertaking profession as possible.

17

September 20, 1869

Violet hated trains, yet here she was at St. Pancras, ready to board one for Nottinghamshire. Around her were Sam, Susanna, Benjamin, piles of trunks, and the once-again displeased Mrs. Softpaws, who occasionally yowled from inside her wicker cage, which Susanna held by its leather handle. Susanna and Benjamin were leaving on a later train for Southampton and would then board a ship for America.

The trip to see Violet's parents had done little for Susanna's disposition. She seemed resentful that Violet had managed to solve the matter of the bell coffins on her own. Ever the polite girl, though, Susanna kept her thoughts to herself, but Violet knew her daughter like she knew herself. Susanna's "Mother, you've done a wonderful thing" had no warmth in it.

Susanna still seemed to be pulling away from Benjamin, too. What was wrong with the girl? Maybe it was too much sea air in Brighton. Or perhaps it was the near-death experience she'd had in London. Violet had had no plans to ask her about it, for she preferred to think that Susanna was merely settling awkwardly into her marriage, and that her troubled thoughts would resolve themselves once she returned to the States. At least, that was Violet's hope. She knew, though, that thoughts of Susanna would keep her up nights.

Perhaps, though, she owed it to both of them to say something before Susanna left. Tugging on Susanna's elbow, she pulled her daughter—and the ever-protesting Mrs. Softpaws—a short distance away from Sam and Benjamin, whose heads were bent over a copy of the train schedule.

"My dear, are you quite all right?" she asked over the whistles, screeching, and clacking of the station.

"Of course, why would you ask?" Susanna's fingers tightened around the handle of Mrs. Softpaws's cage as she turned her face, avoiding Violet's gaze.

"You've been out of sorts almost since you arrived in London. What troubles you? Does the London air not agree with you? Are you angry with me because you didn't have as much involvement in my investigative matter?"

Susanna shook her head absently. "No, Mother, I love London and I realize I don't have your talents."

Violet put a hand out to her daughter's cheek and gently pulled Susanna to face her. "Is there perhaps something of a more personal nature that bothers you?"

Susanna's eyes glistened, but no tears spilled. "Perhaps. I don't know. I'm just a little . . . disappointed, I suppose."

Violet felt a rush of embarrassment. "Were you not happy staying with us? Was that why Benjamin rushed you off to Brighton? My apologies if we—"

"No, no, that's not it. I was just hoping my life would be a bit more like yours . . ." Susanna's voice trailed off as she glanced over at Sam.

Now Violet understood completely. "Susanna, you cannot expect your husband to be like your father. Benjamin is a good man in his own right and adores you. I know you will be very happy."

Susanna swallowed and nodded. "I'm sure you're right. You'll come to Colorado soon, won't you?" she said, smiling with a brightness that didn't reach her eyes.

How could Violet possibly get away for a months-long journey to America? She and Sam would be in Nottinghamshire for weeks, there was the upcoming trip to Egypt, Harry was alone in the shop . . .

"Of course we will. Just as soon as we can. I can't possibly let too much time pass without seeing you again." Violet didn't know how they would manage it, but she and Sam would have to make a trip soon to see their daughter, to be sure all was still well with her. Maybe they would even look into the type-writing machine there.

This seemed to cheer Susanna up. "Everyone in town will be so glad to see you again," she said, her eyes now sharing the smile with her lips.

They rejoined Sam and Benjamin, who now had puzzled expressions on their faces. Susanna changed the subject before they could ask anything. "I can still hardly believe you are a coal mine owner, Father."

Mrs. Softpaws added her assent in the form of a particularly plaintive meow. Hopefully the cat would settle down once the Tompkinses were underway.

Sam couldn't help but puff his chest a bit. "Scaring up the financing was a bit of a struggle, wasn't it? Like finding hen's teeth. I suppose your mother's investigation ironically led to getting the loan."

"The investigation wasn't possible without your information about Mr. Hayes, Sam," Violet said.

"I certainly didn't sense his perfidy the way you did. Nevertheless, two well-deserving criminals will get justice, and I will get my coal mine. With your mother there to encourage me, it will surely be successful. Although I suppose I'm lucky to still have her, since the moment I left her alone for a mere twenty-four hours, she immediately got herself into a peck of trouble."

Violet smiled at Sam's affectionate look. She still wasn't sure about the wisdom of this coal mine, but was happy to accompany him to Nottinghamshire for the next couple of months while he oversaw the reopening of the colliery, especially since all was resolved in London.

Birdwell Trumpington had indeed collected an inheritance from a great-aunt. His undertaking shop was now open, and he had, unfortunately, played upon his employer's murder to secure his own clientele, advertising ostentatiously that he was equipped to manage *all* sorts of deaths, implying that he had cared for Mr.

Crugg's body and not that he had scurried away from the shop like a rat down the gangplank of a ship afire. How long he would be able to exploit Crugg's death, Violet wasn't sure.

Harry, who had just become the father of a baby boy who promised to be as brawny as his father, had graciously said he would manage the shop alone while Violet was gone. He had been amazed at all Violet had uncovered from what started as the innocent witnessing of a body emerging from a coffin six weeks ago. Fortunately, his disappointment over not being able to capitalize on the safety coffin idea was more than compensated for by the arrival of his new son. More worrisome was that Mary Cooke was on her own now, although Violet didn't think Hurst would press his suit in an inappropriate way while she was away. She hoped. She had also promised Mary that they would make that trip to Madame Tussauds when Violet returned to London.

Their train rumbled into the station. It would take Violet and Sam as far as Sheffield, where they would switch trains for Worksop, then take private transport for their final destination to what Violet hoped was a cozy hotel near the coalfield.

Violet was looking forward to the trip, if not necessarily the reason behind it. Who knew what delightful visits might lie ahead for her in Nottinghamshire, with its Sherwood Forest, limestone caves, and renowned lace factories? She had already reviewed a travel guide, which was safely tucked inside her reticule, and planned to visit every tourist site in the county while Sam proceeded with his business.

Perhaps she could set death aside for a while. Surely it wouldn't follow her that far north.

Author's Note

Victorians had a propensity for abusing credit, which was readily available through shops and banks. For most of the nineteenth century, credit was a fairly informal institution, largely based on personal trust and a moral assessment of the debtor. In other words, credit was based on social position rather than financial stability. Naturally, this led to the upper class incurring excessive debt, but the middle class was not immune to the temptation to buy on credit, especially given the exploding offerings of clothing and furnishings made possible by the industrial factories manufacturing goods at an unprecedented rate.

Although many Victorians successfully managed their debts, still more found themselves stuck in a quagmire of unpaid bills. In 1839, over four thousand men were arrested for debt in London alone, and of these, over four hundred men remained in prison the rest of their lives. Frequently, a desperate debtor would go for help to a "financier," giving him full control of his financial affairs in the trust that the financier would pull him out of debt. Many financiers, who lived in luxurious homes in upscale parts of London, had themselves been in bankruptcy court on more than one occasion—a fact that they often neglected to tell their clients. Usually, the financier took a hefty fee and the debtor's properties were eventually auctioned off at ruinous prices.

The **Debtors Act of 1869** consolidated the myriad of bankruptcy laws then in force in England. Most importantly, the new law abolished imprisonment for debt except in certain cases, such as when a debtor owed a debt to the Crown or a debtor had money but refused to pay a debt. It also reduced the penalty for obtaining credit under false pretenses or attempting to defraud creditors to a mere misdemeanor. The law was great for debtors but not so good for creditors, who no longer had prison as a threat to hold over a debtor's head in order to collect monies owed.

By the mid-nineteenth century the volume of London's dead was causing considerable public concern. In 1850, the idea of a great metropolitan cemetery, situated in the suburbs and large enough to contain all of London's dead for centuries to come, was promoted. An interested group formed the London Necropolis Company (LNC) in order to pursue this concept.

Surrey, with its proximity to London and regular rail service, was selected, and two thousand acres of the town of Woking's common land was purchased from the Earl of Onslow, who also provided the land for the original Royal Surrey County Hospital. Some five hundred acres were initially laid out for **Brookwood Cemetery** at the western end of this tract. The **London Necropolis Railway**, or LNR, was opened in November 1854 by the LNC—which hoped to gain a monopoly on London's burial industry—to carry cadavers and mourners the twenty-three miles between London and Brookwood.

The necropolis station at Waterloo was demolished by enemy bombing during World War II and officially closed in 1941, thus ending the railway service between London and Brookwood. However, large numbers of Allied service personnel were buried in the military section of Brookwood, and 3,600 bodies of U.S. servicemen were later exhumed and shipped to the United States for reburial.

The LNC's quest to gain control of the burial industry was not as successful as its promoters had hoped. While they had planned to carry between 10,000 and 50,000 bodies per year, in 1941, after eighty-seven years of operation, only slightly over 200,000 burials had been conducted in Brookwood Cemetery, equaling roughly 2,300 bodies per year.

In 1854, Brookwood was the largest cemetery in the world. Today, this is no longer true, but it remains the largest cemetery in the United Kingdom. The cemetery is still privately owned and operated, and is still open for burials. Approximately 235,000 people have been buried there.

Ironically, Dr. Robert Knox, one of the best customers of Burke and Hare—the infamous resurrectionist men of 1828—is buried at Brookwood.

The fear of being buried alive peaked during the cholera epidemics of the eighteenth and nineteenth centuries. Edgar Allan Poe was also interested in the topic, dealing with it in "Berenice" (1835), "The Fall of the House of Usher" (1839), and "The Cask of Amontillado" (1846), as well as addressing it very directly in "The Premature Burial," published in 1844.

This general fear of premature burial led to the invention of many devices that could be incorporated into so-called **safety coffins**. Most consisted of some type of device for communication to the outside world such as a cord attached to a bell that the interred person could ring should he revive after the burial. Some designs included ladders, escape hatches, and even feeding tubes, but many forgot a method for providing air. A coffin has one to two hours of air in it, making it highly unlikely that, even if someone "awoke" from the dead, he could be unburied before suffocating.

In 1798, P. G. Pessler, a German priest, suggested that all coffins have a tube inserted from which a cord would run to the church bells. If an individual had been buried alive, he could draw attention to himself by ringing the bells. This idea led to the first designs of safety coffins equipped with signaling systems. Pastor Beck, a colleague of Pessler's, suggested that coffins should have a small trumpet-like tube attached. Each day the local priest could check the state of putrefaction of the corpse by sniffing the progressively worsening odors emanating from the tube. If no odor was detected or the priest heard cries for help, the coffin could be dug up and the occupant rescued. Unfortunately, the problem with airless coffins was not addressed under his plan.

Dr. Adolf Gutsmuth of Germany was buried alive several times to demonstrate a safety coffin of his own design, and in 1822 he stayed underground for several hours and even ate a meal of soup, bratwurst, marzipan, sauerkraut, spaetzle, beer, and dessert, delivered to him through the coffin's feeding tube.

The early decades of the nineteenth century also saw the use of "portable death chambers" in Germany. A small chamber, equipped with a bell for signaling and a window for viewing the body, was constructed over an empty grave. Graveyard watchmen would check each day for signs of life or decomposition in each of the chambers. If the bell was rung, the body could be exhumed, but if the watchman observed signs of putrefaction in the corpse, a door in the floor of the chamber could be opened and the body would drop down into the grave. A panel could then be slid in to cover the grave and the upper chamber removed and reused. Who said reduce-reuse-recycle is a twenty-first-century concept?

In 1829, Dr. Johann Gottfried Taberger designed an improved bell system, described in his book *Der Scheintod,* meaning "suspended animation." This system had a housing around the bell aboveground that prevented it from ringing accidentally. The housing also prevented rainwater from running down the tube and a spread of netting prevented insects from entering the coffin. If the bell rang, the watchman needed to insert a second tube and pump air into the coffin with a bellows to allow the occupant to survive until the casket could be dug up.

Franz Vester's 1868 burial case was an elaborate variation on earlier bell-and-cord systems. One of the problems with systems using cords tied to the body was that the natural processes of decay often caused the body to swell or shift position, causing accidental tension on the cords and bell ringing by perfectly dead bodies. Vester overcame this problem by adding a tube through which the face of the corpse could be viewed. If the buried person should awake, he could either ascend the tube by means of a supplied ladder or, if not physically strong enough to do that, ring a bell to hail the watchmen, who could check to see if the person had genuinely returned to life or if a mere movement of the corpse had rung the bell. The viewing tube could be removed and reused once death was confirmed.

As recently as 1995, a safety coffin was patented by Fabrizio Caselli. His updated design included an emergency alarm, an intercom system, a flashlight, a breathing apparatus, and both a heart monitor and stimulator. Safety coffins have come a long way since the relatively simple bell coffins of the Victorian era. However, there are no documented cases of anybody actually being saved by a safety coffin.

On a side note, it is urban myth that the phrase "saved by the bell" comes from the use of safety coffins in the Victorian era. It is a boxing reference: A losing fighter being counted out would be "saved" by the ringing of the bell to end the round.

Laudanum was a favorite tonic of the Victorians. Ironically, the term comes from the Latin verb *"laudare,"* meaning to praise. Although the word "laudanum" generally refers to any combination of opium and alcohol, these formulas could become quite complex. Various preparations might contain ingredients such as crushed pearls, saffron, musk, nutmeg, amber, mercury, hashish, chloroform, belladonna, or cayenne pepper; used in combination with whiskey, wine, or brandy. Although extremely addictive, the concoction was effective at relieving coughing, diarrhea, and pain—important qualities in a time when cholera and dysentery regularly visited communities.

However, the drug was eventually used for any sort of ailment, from colds to cardiac diseases to menstrual cramps to vague aches to insomnia, and was administered to both adults and children. Because it was treated for legal purposes as a medication—although a doctor's prescription was not necessary to obtain it—and not taxed as an alcoholic beverage, laudanum was cheaper than a bottle of gin or wine, making it a great favorite among the working classes.

Suicide by laudanum was common in the mid-nineteenth century, as it was easy to obtain and easy to overdose on with just a few teaspoons. Accidental deaths were frequent, too.

Royal Surrey County Hospital, built in Farnham Road, Guildford, with advice from Florence Nightingale, was opened in 1866 near the University of Surrey and dedicated to the memory of Prince Albert. Today it is known as Farnham Road Hospital, and provides mental health services. The current Royal Surrey County Hospital is located on Egerton Road, about a mile away from its original Victorian location. The superintendent Nathan Blackwell and any descriptions of the hospital are all figments of my imagination. However, it was not uncommon for hospitals to exhume bodies from their own burial grounds for surgical practice. Excavations around Royal London Hospital appear to support old claims that the hospital's school was almost entirely supplied by cadavers who had once been the hospital's own patients.

As a small point of interest, Sarah Josepha Hale was the editor of **Godey's Lady's Book** (sometimes called *Godey's Magazine and Lady's Book*), the magazine from which Violet gets her hair tips, from 1837 through 1877. She was the author of "Mary Had a Little Lamb." *Godey's* became the most popular monthly journal of its day, despite its steep subscription price of three dollars per year. The magazine is best known for its hand-tinted fashion plates, which helped the publication become an arbiter of American taste. Hale held up Queen Victoria of Great Britain as a model of morality, intellect, and femininity, and the magazine regularly reported on royal activities in London. Hale used her editorial influence to popularize the putting up of Christmas trees, based on the royal family's tradition, as well as to advocate for the establishment of a national Thanksgiving holiday. Edgar Allan Poe had his earliest short stories printed in the publication.

SELECTED BIBLIOGRAPHY

Gray, Adrian. *Crime and Criminals of Victorian England*. Stroud: The History Press, 2011.

Pearson, Lynn F. *Mausoleums*. Princes Risborough: Shire Publications Ltd., 2002.

Rutherford, Sarah. *The Victorian Cemetery*. Oxford: Shire Publications Ltd., 2008.

Simmons, Jack. *The Victorian Railway*. New York: Thames and Hudson, 1991.

Warren, David J. *Old Medical and Dental Instruments*. Oxford: Shire Publications Ltd., 1994.

INTERNET REFERENCES

Brookwood Cemetery:
www.brookwoodcemetery.com

OObject
www.oobject.com/category/12-safety-coffins
An interesting look at twelve different safety coffins.

Victorian Web
www.victorianweb.org
A great source on all things Victorian.

Learn how Violet's story began. . . .

Turn the page for a special excerpt of Christine Trent's

LADY OF ASHES

Only a woman with an iron backbone could succeed as an undertaker in Victorian London, but Violet Morgan takes great pride in her trade. While her husband, Graham, is preoccupied with elevating their station in society, Violet is cultivating a sterling reputation for Morgan Undertaking. She is empathetic, well versed in funeral fashions, and comfortable with death's role in life—until its chilling rattle comes knocking on her own front door.

A Kensington trade paperback on sale now!

1

In the midst of life we are in death.

—The Book of Common Prayer (1662)

London
May 1861

Violet Morgan often wondered why she was so skilled at dressing a corpse, yet was embarrassingly incompetent in the simplest household task, such as selecting draperies or hiring housemaids.

If only they hadn't moved to fancier lodgings in a more elegant section of London, she wouldn't be burdened with having to learn a myriad of rules for keeping a proper home. Surely her domestic mismanagement was the source of her husband's current displeasure. How else could Graham have become so morose and embittered these past few months? Surely it wasn't the hot weather, which had never before made him so bilious.

Violet picked through her tray of mourning brooches, organizing them neatly for the next customer who wished to make a purchase. She slid the tray of pins into the display case and reached for the pile of papers Graham must have carelessly thrown on top of it. She sorted through the mix of invoices, newspapers, and advertising leaflets. A recent copy of *The Illustrated London News* caught her eye. Graham had circled headlines regarding events in the United States and scribbled in his own comments beside them. Her husband was avidly following current events transpiring across the Atlantic, hoping for destruction on both sides of the U.S. conflict.

One article opined on the expected duration of the conflict raging there. The Americans had recently engaged in hostilities, after years of Southern states bickering with those in the North. Since last month's first firing of shots at Fort Sumter, South Carolina, much taunting and posturing had occurred. How the citizens of the United States enjoyed fighting. Each side boasted the skirmish would last just a few months, and self-proclaimed experts declared that all the blood to be spilled in the contest could be contained in a single thimble, or wiped up by one handkerchief.

The newspaper agreed, but Violet felt that was foolish optimism. England's own civil war had gone on for almost a decade and nearly destroyed the country.

And to what end? The Roundheads eliminated the monarchy with the beheading of Charles I in 1649, and by 1660 the monarchy was back with his son, Charles II. Nothing changed, but thousands of lives lost and a king beheaded. Surely the Americans would end up with a fallen leader, too.

Another article, which Graham had not only circled, but drawn brackets around, focused on the South's hunger for recognition. During the past couple of months, the Southern states had pressed Britain to recognize their burgeoning nation. The poor fools thought they had Britain in a state of helplessness because they controlled much of the world's cotton, so necessary for England's cloth mills. They didn't realize that England had been storing cotton for some time and was flush with it. What the country did need was wheat.

Wheat was produced by the Northern states.

The crafty British politicians, though, were willing to host a confederate delegation in London and let it press its suit for diplomatic recognition, thus not publicly rejecting the South in case it should win the war.

Violet sighed as she separated the pile of papers into related stacks before removing another tray to straighten, this one full of glass-domed mourning brooches. Buyers could weave the hair of the deceased into a fanciful pattern and place it under the glass to create an everlasting keepsake to be pinned to one's breast.

To think of all those American soldiers who would die ignominious deaths, heaped into mass graves, without the distinction of a proper funeral and burial. How could her husband, a man whose profession was to bring dignity to death, wish for mass slaughter?

She replaced the second tray. The display case looked much better now that it was tidied up inside and out. She moved over to the linen closet, its door discreetly hidden in the wallpaper at the back of the room. Inside were shelves stacked with bolts of black crape for draping over windows, black Chantilly lace for mourning shawls, and fine cambric cotton for winding sheets. Except the cambric had all tumbled to the ground in a heap. How had that happened?

"Graham?" she called out. "Did you let our cambric fall to the floor?" Only when there were no customers at Morgan Undertaking would she dare raise her voice above the gentlest of tones.

"For what reason would I have done that? Maybe Will was the sloppy one going through it," he replied from the shop's reception area.

Perhaps, but Will was usually as careful as Violet.

Violet glanced at the mantel clock over the fireplace. Nearly ten o'clock in the morning, time to visit the Stanley family. She gathered up her cavernous undertaker's bag, filled with embalming fluids, tinted skin creams, cutting tools, syringes, fabric swatches, and her book of compiled drawings of coffins, mourning fashions, flowers, and memorial stones. Going to the display case, she pulled out a selection of mourning jewelry and added the pieces to her bag.

Violet lifted her undertaker's hat from its stand and tied the sash under her chin. The extra-long, flowing tails of black crape wrapped around the hat's crown were a symbol of her trade. Graham wore his own hat adorned with black crape when meeting with customers, as well. She peered into a mirror she kept next to the hat stand, pinched her cheeks to bring some color into them, and tucked an errant strand of hair under the brim of her hat before putting on black gloves. In his more jovial days, Graham used to tease her that one day he'd be rich because he'd cut off and sell her long hair, which he deemed the color of newly minted bronze ha'pennies and of even more value in its beauty.

With a quick farewell to her husband, she left the premises and boarded a horse-drawn green omnibus for Belgravia. Graham always insisted that they hire private cabs for transport to meetings with grieving families, contending it was more representative of the Morgans' socially elevated state, but Violet was still uncomfortable with their new entry into higher circles and usually ignored his demand. She wasn't quite sure their income supported the luxuries Graham contended were their due. The omnibus, London's horse-drawn public transport, cost a mere threepence to travel to most places through central London, and only sixpence to travel farther out.

She exited the omnibus a few blocks from the address she had been given, and walked the rest of the way.

The Stanleys lived in an up-and-coming neighborhood on the outer edges of Belgravia, an area known for its wealthy—and usually aristocratic—residents. The Stanleys' townhome wasn't quite as stately as the residences nearby, being situated in a long row of recently built units that reflected the current construction craze in London.

Nevertheless, this district was a few steps up from the London locale where she and Graham had settled after inheriting his father's undertaking shop. Graham's ambition was eventually to move to Mayfair, maybe even Park Lane, yet Violet was just as happy in their Grafton Terrace townhome in Kentish Town, a very respectable area north of Regent's Park.

Mostly respectable, anyway. They did have odd neighbors, Karl and Jenny Marx, who named all of their daughters after Jenny. Mr. Marx seemed to have no occupation other than writing letters and essays every day, sometimes under the name "A. Williams." There was also neighborhood gossip that Mr. Marx, or Williams, had fathered a child with his housekeeper, but Violet stayed out of such tittle-tattle. She lived in a pleasant area and had no desire to stir up anything ugly.

There was no black crape festooned under the windows and above the doors of the Stanley residence. Violet made a mental note of it as she pressed the "Visitors" bell. Some debate existed as to whether or not an undertaker should be using the "Servants" bell, but in Violet's opinion, anyone assisting the family with a proper departure from their earthly existence was certainly entitled the rank of Visitor.

A maid with swollen eyes and dressed in black opened the door. Immediately recognizing who Violet must be by her garb and large black bag, the young woman silently led Violet to the front parlor and closed the door before going to seek out her mistress.

The Stanleys were far wealthier than she and Graham were. A new grand piano, polished within an inch of its ivory-keyed life, stood prominently in one corner as a testament to fashion. The windows were draped in three separate layers of material, a sign that the Stanleys took current trends very seriously. Multiple linings were expensive, but kept out the dirt, heat, and noise from the street. The papered walls proudly displayed paintings and bric-a-brac, while the wood floors were covered with bright, intricately designed carpets. Violet's own attempts at interior decoration fell far short of the Stanleys' remarkable expressions of taste.

Here was a family that would demand a funeral of nearly aristocratic proportions.

The same maid opened the door to the room again, and a middle-aged woman, haggard beyond her years and dressed head-to-toe in black, entered. Violet nodded solemnly.

The other woman spoke first. "Mrs. Morgan? I'm Adelaide Stanley. Thank you for coming to attend to my Edward." The woman brought an extravagantly laced handkerchief to her eyes. "I can hardly believe he's gone. Such a good husband he was. I don't know how we'll manage." Mrs. Stanley twisted the soaked handkerchief in her hands.

"God finds a way to help us manage," Violet said, pulling a spare cloth from her sleeve and discreetly handing it to the woman, who accepted it with a fresh flow of tears. "Where is Mr. Stanley?"

"Upstairs in his bedroom. So calm and peaceful he was when he passed. Like an angel, despite the torture he endured from pneumonia. Do you wish to see him now?"

Violet considered. Mrs. Stanley was truly grieving, but was relatively composed, unlike some of the hysterical relatives Violet usually encountered, so it might be best to address practical matters first in case her customer should later collapse.

"Why don't we discuss Mr. Stanley's ceremony first?" she suggested.

"Of course, as you wish." Mrs. Stanley rang a bell and gave instructions for tea to another maid who appeared, dressed much like the first one. Violet and her customer sat in deeply plushed, heavily carved chairs and chatted innocuously until the maid returned. After steaming cups had been poured, the maid withdrew, and Violet pressed into the delicacy of arranging a proper funeral.

"I saw immediately upon approaching your elegant front door that Mr. Stanley was a man of some importance, is that not so?"

"Indeed. Edward made us quite comfortable through investment in the London and Birmingham rail line back in the forties. Once it merged with Grand Junction and the Manchester and Birmingham Railways, well, Edward had proven himself to be a very astute investor. He had many influential friends."

"Quite so. And this parlor tells me you are a woman of impeccable taste. Your extensive blue-and-white china collection is to be commended."

Mrs. Stanley was no longer crying. "You are kind to notice, Mrs. Morgan. Mr. Stanley and I strove to present the right sort of furnishings befitting our station. The china is all antique, you know, none of those newly manufactured pieces that have become so popular with the masses."

Violet shifted uncomfortably in her chair. Graham had ordered several new imported blue-and-white vases and jardinières to ornament their home.

"Of course," she replied, removing her gloves and opening her bag, which lay at her feet. "Mr. Stanley wasn't part of a burial club, was he?" Violet withdrew her undertaker's book.

"My, no. We never expected him to go so soon. We never had any thought of it."

"Actually, I applaud the fact that you never did this. Many burial clubs are operated by unscrupulous undertakers who tell grieving widows that they cannot pay out the money until the club's committee meets in three months' time. Naturally, since the burial must be completed quickly, she cannot wait, and the undertaker offers to loan her the money, and charges an exorbitant sum for the funeral.

"My husband and I would never engage in such a practice. I'm simply relieved that we don't have to try to wrest your money from such a club. You and Mr. Stanley were very wise not to have been deceived by one of these dishonest groups."

Violet reached over and patted Mrs. Stanley's hand, and received a grateful smile in return. She continued. "There is much you can do to ensure Mr. Stanley's status is properly recognized at his funeral. Let me show you." Laying the book open in her lap so that Mrs. Stanley could see it, Violet flipped through sections marked "Poor," "Working Class," and "Tradesman," stopping just short of "Titled" to the section marked "Society."

"Most people of your position opt for a hearse with two pairs of horses, two mourning coaches each with pairs, nineteen plumes of ostrich feathers as well as velvet coverings for the horses, eleven men as pages, coachmen with truncheons and wands, and an attendant wearing a silk hatband."

Mrs. Stanley's eyes grew wide. "Oh my. Is all of that necessary?"

Violet flipped backward in the book to the section marked "Tradesman." "Please be assured, we can assist you at a variety of levels. We could pare down to a hearse with a pair and just one mourning coach, and reduce the mourning company to just eight pages and coachmen."

"And that is the standard for what those in the trades do?"

"Yes, madam. For a tradesman such as a railway officer or a solicitor. The cost of such a funeral is around fourteen pounds sterling."

Mrs. Stanley frowned. "And for the other one? With all of the horses and mourners?"

"A bit more, at twenty-three pounds, ten shillings."

"I see. That is certainly well within our abilities. It wouldn't do for my husband to have a funeral that wasn't worthy of him."

"No, madam."

"Tell me, what sort of cof—resting place—would my husband have?"

"An exceptional one, made of inch-thick elm, covered in black and lined with fine, ruffled cambric; a wool bed mattress; and the finest brass and lead fittings on the coffin. Its quality would be nearly that of an aristocrat's. See here." Violet flipped to a page containing a line drawing representing the coffin she was suggesting.

Mrs. Stanley nodded. "A beautiful resting place for my Edward."

"Very elegant, I agree. Now, Mrs. Stanley, do the Stanleys have a plot or mausoleum?"

"His family is at Kensal Green."

"Perfect. A lovely garden cemetery." It truly was. It had attracted many prestigious families and even some royalty. Augustus Frederick, the Duke of Sussex, as well as Princess Sophia, uncle and aunt to Queen Victoria, were both buried there. The princess rested in a magnificent sarcophagus.

"But they're in the crypt under the chapel. We never thought about purchasing a mausoleum in a better section. We never imagined anything would happen to him," Mrs. Stanley said in explanation for why the newly wealthy Stanleys were not in a more exclusive part of the cemetery.

"Please don't fret over it, Mrs. Stanley. Take your time purchasing a location and we can move your husband later."

Violet steeled herself for the next question she must ask. "Mrs. Stanley, tell me, do you wish to have your husband embalmed?"

The look of horror that passed over Mrs. Stanley's face was a familiar sight. "Heavens me, no! What an un-Christian-like thing to suggest," the widow said, a hand across her heart.

"My apologies, I have no wish to offend. It's just that Mr. Stanley would be . . . available . . . longer if he was embalmed, and you could therefore have more visitors."

Violet hardly had the words out of her mouth before Mrs. Stanley was emphatically shaking her head. "Absolutely not. My husband will be buried naturally, as all respectable people are."

Embalming was a new concept in England. Although the practice had been around for centuries, with the ancient Egyptians routinely employing it as one of their many types of funeral practices, it had been mostly limited to royalty in Europe, and even then not frequently. The Americans whom Graham despised so much were already making use of it for their battlefield dead, and the French had written extensively on the merits of the practice, but, thus far, Morgan Undertaking had only performed it on a handful of corpses. Most people were still suspicious of doing something so unnatural to a body that would shortly be committed to the ground.

Violet, in particular, ran into difficulties with families who found it unseemly that a woman would be desecrating a newly deceased person by making cuts, draining blood, and injecting fluids to prolong the freshness of the corpse. Putrefaction typically started within twenty-four hours of death, requiring profusions of flowers and candles around the coffin during visitation, as well as a quick interment.

Violet jotted notes in a small ledger tucked at the rear of the book. "Very good, madam. We have a cooling table that we can place under the coffin to keep him comfortably set during visitation. I'll arrange for your husband's placement and will direct the procession to the cemetery personally. And may I make a few suggestions regarding other accoutrements that might aid you during this difficult time?"

For the next hour, the women discussed further purchases, including black crape for draping across the front of the house, photography of Mr. Stanley in repose, memorial cards, and mourning stationery.

Finally, Violet pulled out her tray of mourning jewelry, made mostly from jet, a popular material derived from driftwood that had been subjected to heat, pressure, and chemical action while resting on the ocean floor. "These pieces are made in one of the finest workshops in Whitby, Yorkshire, Mrs. Stanley. You'll find no better than what I have here."

The new widow picked out a glittering necklace and earrings for herself, both intricately carved, as well as simpler pieces for her two adult daughters, who would be arriving from Surrey in time for the funeral. Violet noted the purchases in her ledger.

Shutting the ledger and putting everything away, Violet addressed their final matter. "I would like to see Mr. Stanley now."

Fresh tears welled up in his wife's eyes. "Yes, of course, this way, please. Two of my maids have already washed him."

Family members or servants frequently handled the initial preparation of the deceased, and in poorer families they might handle all details regarding attendance on the body to save money.

Clutching her bag, Violet followed Mrs. Stanley up a wide staircase in the center hall of their townhome to the next floor of the four-story home. From the top of the landing they walked to the rear of the townhome to a shut door. Mrs. Stanley took a deep breath before opening it and entering, with Violet at her heels.

The room did not yet even have a musty odor to it, despite the heat. Given Mr. Stanley's large figure prone on the bed, she guessed he must have only been dead less than a day. The more corpulent the deceased, the quicker the decay. She glanced at a mantel clock in the room, which was stopped at four twenty-three, confirming that he had just died the previous afternoon. Clocks were traditionally stopped at the time of death to mark the deceased's departure from this current life and into the next. Tradition held that to permit time to continue was to invite the deceased's spirit to remain in the home instead of moving on.

Violet waited near a window while Mrs. Stanley went to her husband, who appeared to be sleeping quite peacefully under a coverlet, kissed his brow, and said, "My dear, the lady undertaker is here. I called for her because I thought she would be most tender with you. I hope you aren't angry with me for not hiring a gentleman undertaker."

She kissed her husband on the cheek this time and patted his chest, then nodded silently to Violet as she slipped out of the room, still teary-eyed, and let the door gently click shut behind her.

This was the part Violet both revered and dreaded, for her almost indescribably heavy responsibility toward both the deceased and his family.

She approached the body and set her bag down on a large table along the wall across from the bed. "Good afternoon, Mr. Stanley, it is a pleasure to make your acquaintance," she said, opening the bag once again and pulling out an array of bottles and a wooden box containing her tools. She arranged her bottles in the order they would be used.

Transferring the box of tools to the bed, she pressed the latch to open it. In what would have been seen as a bizarre gesture by the outside world, Graham had given her this set of Sheffield-made tools to celebrate their fifth wedding anniversary three years ago. Each time she opened the box now, she was reminded of how glorious their married life had initially been.

Graham and his brother, Fletcher, had been trained by their father, known as old Mr. Morgan, to take over the family undertaking business, which had been established by their grandfather in 1816. But Fletcher had a taste for the sea and eventually set himself up as a trader, taking tea to Jamaica, picking up sugar from that country, selling it in Boston to be made into rum, and returning with barrels of finished rum for sale to the Englishmen who craved it.

When old Mr. Morgan died, therefore, Fletcher was happy to let Graham buy out his share of the business. Soon after, Violet met Graham at a church social and was immediately fascinated by the work he did.

For his part, Graham seemed fascinated by a woman who was not repulsed by an undertaker.

Violet reached over and gently squeezed the deceased's hand. Rigor mortis, the chemical change in the muscles that caused the limbs to become temporarily stiff and immovable, had not yet set in, much to her relief, else she'd need to return the following day to finish her preparations, creating undue anxiety for his widow.

Her and Graham's relationship developed amid explanations of coffin ornaments, funeral hospitality, and the care of the dead. Within a year, twenty-year-old Violet Sinclair and twenty-three-year-old Graham Morgan were married, and took up residence with his mother, who remained in her own home after her son and daughter-in-law eventually moved to their more upscale lodgings. Together Graham and Violet rode in each day to their working premises on Queen's Road in Paddington, joyful in their death profession as only two young people in love could possibly be.

Violet sighed as she took out several jars of Kalon Cream. If only her life had remained so happy.

"Now, Mr. Stanley, this might look a bit frightening, but let me assure you that it won't hurt a bit. I promise to be gentle and to fix everything so that your wife will hardly notice that I have had to muddle about with you." Graham had taught her that talking to the deceased helped wash away the dread of working with a dead body. Many customers also talked to the deceased, and those who did, like Mrs. Stanley, seemed to adjust better to their losses.

She examined the contents of each jar, finally deciding that "light flesh" was the right shade. She scooped out some of the cosmetic, a dense covering cream that she rubbed into Mr. Stanley's face and hands. A corpse naturally paled as blood pooled downward, so cosmetic massage creams helped bring a more lifelike appearance back to the body.

After wiping her hands on a cloth, she used a paintbrush to apply a pale rouge to the man's cheeks and lips, thus further enhancing a living appearance. Once she was satisfied with his visage, she unrolled a length of narrow tan cloth and snipped off about a foot of it. She threaded a special needle, then sewed one end of the cloth to the skin behind one ear. Next, she pulled the cloth tightly under his chin, then sewed the other end behind his other ear.

The cloth would prevent Mr. Stanley's mouth from dropping open accidentally during his visitation and frightening dear Aunt Mollie or Grandma Jane as she was bent over whispering last words to him. Sometimes, instead of this method, she used a small prop under the chin, later covered by the deceased's burial clothes. Every undertaker had his own methods for preparing a body, and those methods were trade secrets.

"All finished, Mr. Stanley. I trust it wasn't too uncomfortable for you. We'll need to get you arranged in the parlor for visitation, then you'll have a journey of great fanfare to the cemetery. But first we must get you properly attired."

She'd forgotten to ask Mrs. Stanley to provide her with burial clothes. Well, there was no help for it, she couldn't possibly ask the woman back in here now, with her husband in such condition. Violet went to the enormous mahogany armoire that loomed in one corner of the room and searched until she found what she assumed was Mr. Stanley's finest set of clothes. She selected a shirt with the highest collar possible to cover the jaw cloth.

Dressing a dead body was exceedingly difficult to do alone, making Violet wish she had Will or Harry, the shop's muscular young assistants, with her. However, Graham had them busy on other assignments, so it couldn't be helped.

Trying not to grunt aloud, Violet pushed and pulled Mr. Stanley's limbs and torso as she struggled to undress him and place him in his finery. Once he was dressed and his hands positioned decorously on his chest, Violet packed up her bag and straightened out the bedclothes, ensuring no evidence of her work was left behind. That was something else Graham had taught her. An undertaker must be like a housemaid: all work performed invisibly and with as little inconvenience to the family as possible.

She returned to the parlor, where Mrs. Stanley was pacing back and forth, worrying the handkerchief Violet had given her between her fingers. "How is my Edward?"

"Resting quite comfortably, Mrs. Stanley. I think he would be quite pleased with how you've provided for him."

Violet assured Mrs. Stanley that she would accompany the coffin, along with a bier, for setup in the parlor the following day. "May I recommend that you perhaps go visit a close friend tomorrow and allow me to escort Mr. Stanley to the parlor privately with one of our assistants?"

"Yes, yes, of course. Whatever you say. You'll be careful with my husband, won't you?"

"Madam, I will treat him as if he were my own husband."

Perhaps she should quit using that turn of phrase, since lately Graham's behavior would have made her more than happy to see him trade places with Mr. Stanley.

Violet dropped her *carte-de-visite*, or calling card, which offered her compliments on one side and the Morgan Undertaking address on the other, on the silver salver in the hallway on her way out, pleased with how this customer visit had transpired and anxious over what mood Graham might be in when she returned.